RELENTLESS NIGHT

A NEW YORK KNIGHTS NOVEL

S.M. WEST

Relentless Night

ISBN: 978-1-989881-04-0

Cover Design: Najla Qamber Designs
Edited by: Leanne Rabesa
Photographer: Lindee Robinson
Models: Alyse Madej & David Turner

Your heart knows the way. Run in that direction. – Rumi

PROLOGUE

TOMMIE

Twelve Years Ago

If only I could rip my ears off. Block out the sound. It will drive me mad.

Drip. Drip. Drip.

Water leaks from somewhere and it's all I can hear, drowning out even the deafening silence. The splash of liquid hitting the floor is as loud and as maddening as a marching band performing on an endless loop. If only I could cover my ears… or get rid of them.

How long has it been since my hands were free?

My jaw clamps shut, and my teeth grind together, so hard I almost hope they explode into fine white dust. I'm looking for anything, any other kind of agony, to block out all the painful sensations zipping through my body.

A wild cackle escapes my dry, chapped lips and I snarl. I'm losing my mind. Chained like some animal and now I sound like one too.

I shiver.

It's freezing in here. Always cold. I'm so cold with nothing to cover me. Not even clothing for my body. And the blackness. I can't see a thing. The darkness is everywhere. Sound, smell and touch are the only senses of use to me.

"I can't see anything." It hurts to scream but a peculiar pang of optimism tugs at my gut at the sound of my own voice.

I am alive. For whatever that is worth.

My throat feels tight and raw, and I'm not sure if screaming will do me any good. I doubt anyone can hear me and even if they could, so what? They wouldn't care.

No one cares.

No one knows I'm here.

I might as well be dead.

Dead.

What would that be like? I might like it. I'd lose all my senses. No more cold. No more pain. No more hunger. No more sound.

Sound is the scariest. It's usually your first sign of trouble.

Or what if in death, I got all my senses back? I'd be able to see again. Would I want to see this place I'm in? I don't even know if it's a dungeon or a basement or… it doesn't matter. No matter how many times I blink, or how long I try to sleep, give my eyes the time to adjust, when I wake, it's still pitch black.

No, I rely on sound to tell me what's coming. My eyes never get used to the dark. Or maybe it's because there isn't even a speck of light in here. It's as if I'm hundreds of feet beneath the surface of the earth.

I might as well be dead.

Will I ever see the light of day again?

The sun. Will I ever see the sun again? I barely remember the sun. Bright. Warm. Vibrant. I'd like to see the sun again.

"Here comes the sun…" I try to sing, despite my aching throat, something upbeat. A song from my mother's favorite band.

It's been three days since I last had water. I think. It can't have been more. The body can't go more than three days without water, isn't that true? He has to come today. To give me water. Or maybe today is the day he doesn't come?

Maybe that would be better. I don't want to see him. It's always him. No one but him.

He hurts me. He hurts me. Hurts me.

A sob balls in my lungs, clogging my breath, and straining my chest and neck. The skin tears at the corners of my mouth as a low keening moan erupts from my parched throat.

I convulse, scaring myself. The sounds I make are wild and unnatural. Who am I? What am I?

I want to be dead.

My back is sore. So sore.

Shuffling my feet backward, only an inch or two at the most, my heels hit the wall and my body gingerly sinks into it. My back scrapes along the coarse, icy concrete and I hiss like a cobra. If only I had its fangs and venom.

My skin is raw.

I am cold.

Chattering, my shoulder blades burn and the sockets of my arm ache. Wrists bound and shackled high on the wall, just high enough to keep me hovering between flat footed and tip-toed. I wish my arms would snap from my body. Then the agony of limbs and hands suspended above my head would end.

The pain would be gone.

I don't know how long I've been like this. It feels like days but it could be months.

The jangling of keys breaks through the irritating drops of water and my heart twists and I still. So still, waiting for the familiar click that releases the lock and will be followed by the creak of a door. No light seeps into the room but his movement tells me he is here.

His footsteps are light. Measured and firm. I count them. Four, five, six... there's always thirty in total before he gets to me.

Once he's at the midway point, I bow, hanging my head low, and freeze. A dim light snaps on at his side. Expensive black Oxfords have the spotlight and just the hint of a hem to his dress pants shadows his shoes.

My breathing is so loud, so heavy in my head and I'm afraid he'll hurt me for how noisy I am. I wish I could stop my breath. He doesn't like to hear me unless it's his command.

Sixteen.

Seventeen.

Eighteen.

The heat of him is the first thing I feel, and I want to cry, beg him to wrap his body around me even though I want him dead. I dream of his death.

But getting warm is more important than anything else right now. I won't fight him. I long since stopped fighting. It's my fault I'm here. All of this is my fault. And I have nowhere to go, no one to save me. He reminds me of that all the time. I have no one to blame but myself.

Obedience is best. It's better to obey, even if he wants me to do vile, horrible things. Even if during every second, I pray for my death. His death. It's better to obey.

He's close. If I had the use of my hands, I could reach out and touch him. And he's so warm. I tremble at his heat as his strong fingers release my arms from the wall, and I fall into a heap at his feet.

A burn spreads through my arms like wildfire as the blood starts to flow in the reverse direction and he clears his throat. It's a deep rumble, similar to the prickles of his fingernails scoring my flesh, and I tense.

"Little One, kneel." He's a chilling voice in the near dark.

TOMMIE

"She's doing it again." Revulsion colors Anna's pretty features.

Glancing over my shoulder, I follow her gaze across the gym, curious as to what has my easy-going best friend riled up. The bubbly blonde from our Krav Maga class twists her ponytail around her fingers and hyena-laughs at something Kent, our instructor, says.

Gah, could she be any more of a Barbie doll?

She paws at him, fingers trailing the smooth expanse of his chiseled chest, her hands like magnets clinging to a fridge. While he's a decent teacher, his true talent is his stunning bod—a must-have to work at or frequent this trendy Brooklyn gym.

Normally, I'm against another's expectations of how one should look or act to be accepted, yet here I am, frequenting such a place. Truth be told, this gym has one of the best Krav Maga classes in the city, but maybe that's no longer a good enough reason to overlook the vacuous atmosphere?

Lips pursed, I'm suddenly bothered by the ever-present eye-candy. No wonder my teeth ache. Beauty and sex sell, and sadly, we're all for sale whether we know it or not.

Or maybe this ache has nothing to do with other people's vanity and judgmental attitude and everything to do with my guilt for succumbing to the hotness just like the next person? After all, I am sleeping with Kent.

It's just sex. Nothing more. Some might say we're fuck buddies but that would imply we're friends. We aren't. We have sex when the urge strikes. End of story.

"Tommie, aren't you going to break that up?" Anna, the little sprite that she is, crowds me like a mama bear ready to protect her baby cub, despite my five-foot-nine frame.

"Nope." I shrug and head for the exit, where I'm immediately hit with the oppressive humidity of the night air as I step outside.

"But what if they go on a date, or sleep together?"

Her repulsed expression suggests their potential sexual dalliance would be the worst thing to happen to humanity. Romantic relationships are serious business to my friend, whereas to me, they're too much work for little to no payoff. Just another façade we're made to believe is oh so important.

At twenty-six, neither of us has had an easy life, and while we were both held captive, our experiences have made us very different people. She's hopeful and I'm realistic and our differences don't end there. She's living with the only man she'll ever love, whereas I've been with far too many men to count.

I'm not holding out for love. I don't believe in Tennyson's saying, 'it's better to have loved and lost than to never have loved at all.'

I've already lost more than my fair share. I doubt I'd survive losing the love of my life.

We stare at each other over the hood of my car and I deliver a truth that won't surprise her even if she has a hard time swallowing it.

"It doesn't matter if he sleeps with her."

"Thomasina!" Kent jogs toward us and I cringe.

Despite the darkness of the night, the parking lot lights illuminate the bounce of his brown curls, the stretch of his tight shirt across his broad chest and the pumping of his bulging biceps. His boyish smile grows, practically kissing his ears, as he stops in front of me.

"Hi." Anna smiles politely when I'm not quick to offer a greeting.

"Hey." His glance at my friend is cursory, almost dismissive, but the dissatisfied arch of my brow causes him to make more of an effort. "Great job tonight, Anna. Keep it up."

"Thanks." She beams at his praise.

Our Krav Maga lessons are important to her. She may have lived a sheltered life and with her petite frame, one might think she's weak, but they couldn't be more wrong.

She's a fighter and has fought her entire life, in one way or another, to survive. Despite our differences, I understand wanting to be strong in body as well as mind.

"Yeah, she's badass." My smiling gaze conveys just how proud I am of her. "What's up, Kent?"

"Ah, I thought we could hang tonight?" Running a hand through his hair, he grins suggestively.

Ugh, it's time to call it quits. I'm no longer even remotely interested in him, only annoyed. And maybe a little guilty. He's a nice guy and will make some woman happy, but I'm not that woman.

"Can't." My tone is flat. "We have plans."

I give my best friend a meaningful glance. We don't have plans, but sex is the last thing I want tonight. I want my bed. Alone.

This is my choice and I vowed a long time ago to never let anyone make me do something I didn't want to do. Ever again.

"Oh." His grin falls into a frown and something uncomfortable tugs at me to think his feelings may be growing. That's definitely a sign to end things.

"See you next class." I open the car door and he grabs my shoulder.

"Ah, Thomasina." His tone is softer this time. "My sister's engagement party is next weekend and I want you to come."

My chest deflates with regret. Yup, he's becoming too invested in us and there isn't an *us*. I let this go on too long. I was trying to be nice, but bye-bye nice.

"No," I say bluntly.

His eyebrows rise to his hairline, surprised, and I bite back a frustrated reply. I was very clear from the outset what we were to each other and he agreed to no dates, no family and no friends.

Anna slides into the front passenger seat, likely uncomfortable, and she makes a point to slam the car door while he nods reluctantly.

"Night, Kent."

"Night." He encroaches on my personal space and I stiffen.

I'm not a fan of kissing and he knows this too. Somehow it feels more intimate than sex, and intimacy and feelings aren't things I welcome.

Romantic attachments are more trouble than they're worth, and kissing is right up there with love.

His lips graze my cheek, nowhere near my mouth, and I relax, grateful he is a good guy and respects my wishes.

I smile at him, warmer than my words but no more flirty or hopeful. I will let him down gently and soon, but not tonight. I slip into the car and shut the door. In the rear-view mirror, his shoulders slump and he hangs his head, trudging back to the gym.

I do feel bad. Not for standing my ground, but for rejecting him. I don't want to hurt his feelings. He wants more, but I've been nothing but honest about what I do, or more importantly don't, want or have to give.

"Awkward." Anna squirms beside me, and I'm not sure if it's at Kent's strikeout or my stoic resolve to shut him down.

We both watch in the car mirrors as the blonde runs toward him and immediately, his posture shifts—shoulders wide and head held high. She hugs him and relief washes away any regret. He isn't into *me*. He wants to be needed and the blonde does that for him.

During the drive to her home, Anna casts furtive glances my way and I sigh. "I can hear the wheels turning in your head over there. Spit it out."

"Don't know how you do it." Her brown curls bounce as she lifts a shoulder.

"Do what?"

"Be okay with Kent doing who knows what with that blonde, because you know they're going to go for coffee or something." She snorts and I nod. "If it were Coop, I'd want to gouge out the woman's eyes, and his."

Her face sours at the thought, as if the possibility of her boyfriend stepping out on her is real. It isn't. Coop is beyond devoted to her.

"I'm not serious about Kent. You know that."

"True. I suppose I just wish you wouldn't shut yourself off to the idea of a relationship. Maybe not with Kent. Actually, definitely not with Kent. He isn't your type."

She crinkles her nose and shakes her head, and we share a smile. She knows me well and we both know Kent was a distraction. A nice to look at distraction but nothing else.

"Seriously, you don't need a man to make you happy."

"Amen to that," I interject.

"But I just don't want you to shut out the possibility that some day, someone might come along that could be right for you. I'd hate for you to be so set on no relationships that you miss the *one*."

I snort and roll my eyes. "The one? Seriously, Anna, I don't believe in that shit and you know it, even if I can admit that you and Coop are perfect for each other. Ugh, and don't even start with how right Ry is for Tate, or Van for Carys."

A fake retching sound spills from my throat as my insides twist and I shove down any remote feelings that may resemble longing. Why do I suddenly feel like a tween again, unable to handle my emotions and wanting nothing more than to deflect?

She nibbles on her bottom lip. "You of all people have so much to give."

Her suddenly serious and genuine tone causes me to bite the inside of my cheek to keep from being swept away with all these unwanted feelings.

"Thank you." I quickly glance her way as I make a right onto a street a few blocks from her place. "I tell you what, I'll keep an open mind, okay? Maybe someday there will be someone for me."

She does a little lift in her seat and smiles. "That's all I can hope for."

"Fine. Okay, so can we move on from this mushy stuff? I've been holding off asking." Now it's my turn for my tone to sober. "I was giving you the time you asked for but I can't wait any longer. Have you made up your mind?"

My best friend is an aspiring artist, and wickedly talented. She spent three years completing her MFA in Visual Arts at Columbia University and now, not even a year on the art scene and she's already something of a sensation.

In fact, a world-famous Italian sculptor offered her an apprenticeship in Florence. Painting is her first love and her work is ridiculously brilliant, but she's been dabbling with a new medium—marble—and the few sculptures she's allowed Tate, our friend, to display in her gallery have gotten Anna noticed even more.

"I don't know." Uncertainty clouds her delicate features.

It's a big decision. If she accepts the offer, she could be off to Italy at any time with her boyfriend. Coop and I work together and it's no secret he's madly in love and would follow Anna to the ends of the earth.

"Whatever you decide, I support you." My chest tightens at the thought of her departure. "Besides, if you go, there won't be time for you to miss me. I'll visit every chance I get, and you know you won't be able to keep Van and Carys away, let alone Tate, Ry, Max and—"

"Stop, I get it. You better come see me, and we'll come home for visits."

My heart trips, conflicted because her once-in-a-lifetime opportunity means I'll be without one of my best friends. I'll miss her like crazy. But my feelings aside, if anyone deserves their dreams to come true, it's my girl Anna.

I park in front of her place and she hugs me. "Don't forget Tate's tomorrow."

Our friend has just had her second child, and Anna is gaga over the butterball. She can't get enough of him. Kids aren't my thing. I'm awkward, not knowing how to act and scared to death of being asked to hold the tiny beings. But I can't deny Tate's son is adorable, and deep down, I'm also excited for our visit.

She bounds from the car, waving when she reaches the front door of her building. From the cupholder, my phone chimes. As head of intelligence for Hart Corporation, a small global private security firm for hire by wealthy private citizens and select governments, I'm always monitoring someone or something. I get notifications all day and well into the night.

I press my thumb to unlock my phone and stare down at the alert. A chill runs along my spine and the hairs on the nape of my neck rise. He's back. I flick my gaze to where Anna was just standing, remembering how close she came to a fate similar to mine at his hands.

The day has come.

It was always inevitable and as much as I'd like to say it hasn't weighed heavily on my mind, it does. Sweat beads between my breasts and fear tastes vile in my mouth.

He is here.

He is in *my* city.

Older, but easily recognizable. Dark and menacing, and I battle to find my breath. To practice what years of therapy have taught me. I am in control.

His black eyes and wicked smirk taunt and torment me from the Page Six website. My stomach twists and sours in horror.

MAX

My eyes burn from the lack of sleep and the relentless pounding in my head reminds me just how long it's been since I've slept. Nearly forty-eight hours. The adrenaline high of leading a top-notch team of professionals in a successful cardiac transplant has long since worn off. But it was one hell of a rush — something I'm sure to never forget.

Although I'd never forget because of my patient. She's my youngest patient to date, and my age. That's why this one hit a little too close to home. A thirty-two-year old humanitarian is struck by a viral disease while in Africa, trying to better the lives of those less fortunate. The universe can be truly twisted and cruel. She literally paid with her heart.

Luckily, her dire situation, and general good health—save for her failing heart—moved her up the donor list and we got a match just in time. I should go home and get some sleep. She's doing well and is being monitored closely for any signs of rejection. If something were to happen, the staff have instructions to call me, no matter the time.

I quickly change and get out of the hospital before I cave and crash in a staff room or on a couch.

Slumping in the back of the Uber, I fish out my phone to text

Tommie. It's too late to call her but I can't wait to tell her about the surgery. She, of all people, would know how much tonight means to me. The corners of my mouth turn upward in a smile when I think about how I've bored her for years with my planned career path to becoming a cardiovascular surgeon.

Shit, I've got six texts from my sister, Tate. Years ago now, I chose to leave Cambridge, where I studied medicine, and move back to New York to protect my sister from our mother, Taya. I hadn't been there for Tate when she needed me the most and I'd decided I was no longer sitting on the sidelines while our mother threatened her family and future.

I was supposed to spend a few hours with her and my newborn nephew, James Evan Hart, but the post-op and wanting to stick around at the hospital forced me to cancel. I'd promised to make it for dinner, and if not, I'd call. I never did. I was too caught up with work at the hospital and lost track of time.

Without paying mind to the hour, my fingers hover over the dial pad, ready to call and apologize, when the twelve-thirty at the top of my screen registers. It's too late.

There is a good chance Tate's awake and feeding the baby, but there's also the possibility she's getting one of those rare and precious moments of sleep that moms everywhere covet and don't always take advantage of. I opt to text.

Me: Sorry, Bear. Leaving the hospital now. Will come over later today once I've got some sleep. Miss you and the little man.

Before I can slip the phone into my jacket pocket, it buzzes.

Tate: You're lucky I love you. We miss you too. Sleep, then come over. No excuses. Xoxo

My lips curve into a smile. I miss my twin, and her sweet baby boy, her second son. She's a natural at motherhood even if at times, she worried she'd be like our mother, cold and manipulative. Nothing could be further from the truth.

Immense joy washes over me at my sister living her dream, having a man who worships her and a family to love and nurture. I can't explain it in words, and I needn't with Tate. She gets it. That's the thing about being in the womb together for nine months, sucking each other's thumbs—we don't need words.

Once out of the Uber, I saunter into my Upper East Side apartment building and fire off a text to Tommie. She, too, has sent me a few over the past twenty-four hours wanting to know how everything went.

Me: You up?

Tommie: Cut to the chase. How'd the surgery go?

Me: Phenomenal. Patient is doing well.

Tommie: OMG, I wish I could hug you. So proud of you!

Me: A hug from you sounds perfect 😊 Are you at home or working?

Tommie: Working. Covering a shift. I want to hear every gory detail of the surgery! Breakfast?

I wince, not wanting to turn her down yet again, but having to. I need sleep before it's time to return to the hospital. With how crazy things have been the past few weeks, I haven't seen my best friend and it isn't for a lack of trying on her part.

Me: Sorry. Need sleep. Talk soon. Night.

Three little dots dance on my screen as I exit the elevator on my way to my apartment. The dots disappear and I wait, anxious for a response and hoping she's cool with it.

Nothing. The dots disappear.

A jagged breath sails past my lips in disappointment. After a few beats, they pop up again and I stand transfixed outside my door. It feels like forever before her text comes through.

Tommie: Kk. Night. xx

She isn't impressed and I can't say I blame her. I want to see her too, it's just been too hard these past few weeks with work and my mother.

Not bothering to turn on any lights, I nearly trip over my faithful companion. Gunnar's lying on the carpet only feet from the door. He jumps to his paws, attentive with ears pricked back and gaze alert.

"Hey, Gun, sorry I'm late. Did you have a good day?" Now on my haunches, my fingers sink into the thick swirl of black and caramel fur along my dog's neck. "My day was pretty fucking great. The surgery was a success. Feelin' awesome about that but beat. What about you?"

My dog leans into my strokes and I'm grateful to have him. He's the next best thing to Tommie. He's *our* dog and talking to him, when I'd rather be talking to her, helps. A bit. He was just a puppy when she asked me to take care of him. It was meant to be temporary while she was on assignment, but she didn't have the heart to take him back when she returned. I promised her Gunnar would be ours.

Sometimes I feel selfish having him when I spend so many hours at the hospital, but I can't imagine not having him and I do everything to make sure he's taken care of while I'm not here.

I spend a few minutes scratching behind his ears and nuzzling his wet snout before we meander further into the apartment. I've got plans for a hot shower and bed when my phone buzzes in my pocket.

Another text from Tommie.

Tommie: I'm so proud of you. If I don't see you soon, I'll hunt down your ass.

Laughing and smiling, I type out a reply as the tightening in my chest disappears.

Me: I'm going to hold you to it. Thanks, Tommie.

In my bedroom, I place the phone on the nightstand and glance to the open curtains with Central Park just beyond. The view causes me to stop. Every. Time. It's breathtaking, the lush canopy of trees drenched only in moonlight.

Of all the things I loathe about my family name, Conrad, and most of all, my mother, my place and this magnificent view is the only perk. Finding a place to live in Manhattan is a bitch, let alone scoring a prime location like this. Taya pulled some strings to get me this place and while I'd give it up in a heartbeat if it meant I'd be rid of her—free—the irony is, in between the endless hospital hours and spending my limited free time with my sister and our friends, I'm never here to fully enjoy it.

Maximillian Conrad may be getting a name as a well-respected cardiac surgeon in certain circles, but the Conrad name is very much synonymous with organized crime. And no matter what I do to shake that pall over my life, I can't quite seem to get out from under the darkness.

The Conrad business is small compared to the larger syndicates and crime lords who live and breed in this city, but it's no less deadly. And Mother has sunk her fangs into me, her venom incapacitating, and I'm trapped in her web.

I seek refuge from my dilemma with a shower, where the water washes away my somber thoughts, the stress of the past couple of days, and helps me to relax. Gunnar lies down on the floor by my bed and as soon as my head hits the pillow, I'm too exhausted to hold onto any of my worries.

The shrill ring of my phone wakes me and I blink, focusing on Gunnar. He snaps to attention, watching me as I reach for the phone, not bothering to check the screen. It must be the hospital.

"Conrad." My voice is groggy.

"Max, come now." I'm wide awake at my mother's icy tone and I'm in no mood to deal with her, even if it isn't smart.

"I can't. I'll come tomorrow."

Taya Conrad isn't accustomed to being told no, especially not by me. But I'm tired, and sick of being treated like one of her lackeys, always expected to be ready at her command.

"Max." Her voice is clipped. "This isn't your mother calling to talk. And I wasn't asking. Perhaps you need some incentive? I want to visit your sister, especially since the birth of my second grandchild. I've never even seen Adam and now she has another. What's his name? James?"

A bone-killing sensation slithers up my spine. My twin is my only weakness. The reason I am at my mother's mercy, and she uses her every chance she can. "Fucking leave her alone. Text me where and I'll be there."

I hit end, tossing the phone across the bed, and it slides off the side, landing with a thud on the carpet. Gunnar darts to the phone, standing over the small rectangular device, looking up at me as if I need help.

"Yeah, I do, buddy. I do," I mutter, scrubbing my hand roughly down my face.

Middle of the night, or in this case, pre-dawn calls from my mother aren't new. In fact, they are getting old, really old. She's been pulling my strings for years now and if I really think about it, all my life, but more so in the past five years, since we made our deal.

Back then, I agreed to come home because she was threatening to do to my sister what she had done once before, and there was no way I was going to let that happen again.

Tate was my parents' original pawn, exploited most of her teenage years and for nearly all her twenties. In exchange for a business partnership which gave them more power, my parents stole her freedom through an arranged marriage to an abusive psycho. They stopped at nothing, including killing her then-boyfriend, to get what they wanted, and for most of this, I was an ocean away and oblivious to the hell my sister was living.

After the murders of our father and Tate's husband, she was able to break free with the FBI's help, but my mother isn't one to accept defeat. She stepped right into my father's shoes as head of the criminal operation and was intent on getting Tate back. The woman is ruthless and would like nothing better than to trade Tate, again, to another sick mob boss for more power, if I don't toe the line.

Forget the devil, my mother makes that demon look like a puppy dog. In return for my full cooperation, she promised to never go near Tate again, and my sister's safety is paramount.

While she's now married to Rylan Wolfe, an ex-FBI agent, and he's more than capable of protecting her, if Taya isn't kept satisfied, she won't hesitate to get rid of Ry to get to Tate. It's been done before.

On the way to the bathroom, I retrieve my phone from the floor and see her new text with the address. I dress quickly and before grabbing an Uber, I take Gunnar for a short walk.

Mother has me watched and if someone is tailing me now, she'll be livid to learn I stopped to take the dog out before coming to her. But frankly, I don't give a damn. These are my small ways of asserting some power over my helpless situation.

She must have another medical situation and needs me. My predecessor was an older, wiry man, obviously blackmailed into caring for her men and as nervous as a cat. The first time we met, he wept at finally having reinforcements, as he put it. I haven't seen or heard mention of the doctor in years. Now *I'm* the on-call doctor.

The rising sun colors the morning sky a vibrant orange and pink, and somehow it feels all wrong, like jigsaw pieces that don't fit no matter which way you turn them. A brilliantly beautiful backdrop to my dire position.

The car pulls up in front of a decrepit warehouse, a new location for me but like so many other parts of the city or boroughs I've been summoned to over the years.

"Hey, Max," Tiny, an obese, sweaty gorilla and one of my mother's henchmen, greets me.

Like always, his labored breathing is louder than gale force winds and beads of sweat line his oily upper lip. I dip my chin in response, not wanting to talk to him any more than is necessary. I don't like the guy. He's dumber than a bag of hammers and never stops talking.

Mother has him around for his girth, not his brains. As he rambles on about how hot today is supposed to be, we pass a bunch of men, none of whom pay me any mind, and I force myself to focus on my breathing. Anything to stifle the mounting impulse to punch this oaf in the gut and leave.

Taya stands in the middle of the warehouse, flanked by greasy goons. If this wasn't real, I'd laugh at the cliché image. She's an attractive woman if you like the cold-hearted bitch type, and back in the day, she graced the runways of Paris and Milan. I can no longer appreciate her beauty—all I see is a monster.

Her biting glare chills every step I take in her direction. "Took you long enough. When I say now, I don't mean nearly an hour later." Her signature red manicured talons perch on her hips.

"What do you need?" I won't indulge her power trip.

One of her men steps aside and hunched in a chair is a man bleeding from his shoulder. Gunshot wound. I haven't met this guy before and come to think of it, it's the same for several of the men we passed on the way in. By now, I'm familiar with most, if not all, of the men within my mother's organization. If she's hired new men, why?

I get ready, scrub myself clean and tend to the thug as best as I can, fortunate my mother has narcotics and that there were no complications with the bullet removal. Performing procedures in dirty places like this is insane.

Infection is the biggest threat but insisting on a sterile location is futile. I learned that lesson the hard way and had bruises to show for trying to uphold my Hippocratic oath.

Tiny listens to my instructions for what to do over the coming days, as it's his job to carry out post-care duties, and I promise to check in on him in a day or two. Her injured men can't die in my care. Taya has made it very clear that if I fail to treat them to the best of my abilities, our deal is null and void, meaning Tate is fair game.

It's not to say I haven't lost a few of her men over the years, but in every case, I was sure to tell her up front that they weren't going to make it before I even started work on them. Sometimes I'm not there in time and there's nothing I can do. I've tried to impress upon her that I will always take care of someone in need, criminal or not.

I discard the paper gown, cap and gloves, scrubbing my hands clean before I go. Once done, I'm making my way to the exit when Taya steps in my path.

"Max, wait."

Exasperated, I grind my teeth to bite back my bitterness. "Yes?"

"I will need you more, on a regular basis, for the next several weeks."

"Why?" I'm not thrilled at the prospect of being in her company more than I already am, and it also means my hands will be even dirtier than they already are, if that's even possible.

"That's none of your business. Your job is to come when called. Not ask questions."

I don't have a response she'd deem acceptable and what I want to say would cause more harm. Instead, I nod and leave as quickly as possible. Although I can't possibly imagine what she needs me for.

Up until now, I've only ever had to deal with the aftermath of confrontations. There is usually someone to patch up. So why does she need me more often? Is she going to war? Or anticipating more injuries to her men? And if so, why?

During the ride back to my apartment, I mull this over and only get more frustrated as I'm no closer to a definitive answer. Before I drive myself crazy, I call to check on my patient, pleased to learn everything is good.

I need to get more sleep and then go back to the hospital, which means another raincheck and apology text to Tate. She's going to disown me.

With the text sent, I rest my head on the back of the seat, holding my hands out in front of me. They are clean, no trace of the blood that coated the gloves I wore not too long ago. But all I can see is blood.

I took an oath to do no harm, and while every person I've treated for my mother needed medical attention, I've no clue what damage was done on the other end. These people are enforcers and murderers.

How many innocent lives were lost at the hands of the men I have treated? As much as I'm ignorant to her business dealings, I'm still complicit, and the guilt is eating me alive. I have to find a way out without tossing my sister back into the fire.

TOMMIE

I find hot dogs obnoxiously pleasing. How a crudely shaped hodgepodge of unmentionable animal parts brings such comfort is beyond me but whenever I eat one, I can't help but smile.

Four hot dogs are tucked in the small insulated container at my side and I can't wait to sink my teeth into one. I'd been thinking about dinner with Max throughout my workout. It stung the other night when he turned down breakfast. It's been two weeks since we last saw each other when we typically see each other every couple of days. I miss him.

He's my best friend like Anna, and in some ways, easier to talk to. I think it's the guy thing. He's laid back, preferring not to over-analyze things.

After the gym, I grabbed our usual dinner choice at our favorite street vendor and I'm now camped at the hospital entrance he frequents. I made sure to check with Edith, his office administrator, to make sure he wasn't in surgery. If he was anyone else, I'd use my skills and tap into the hospital mainframe to see his schedule. But that's pointless since Max doesn't stick to his on-call hours. He lives at the hospital.

I've been waiting twenty minutes and I'm willing to wait as long as it takes so I can see him. I only hope he doesn't try to bail once we come face to face. We're close, but something is going on with him and I can't help but feel he's avoiding me. And I don't know why.

Instead of stewing over what's going on with Max, I've got plenty to occupy my time. Since the online alert, a few days ago, I've attempted to track *his* movements, which for almost any other target would be a cakewalk for me. Tracking people's moves, especially digitally, is my specialty and something I can practically do in my sleep. But this time, no surprise, it was near impossible. This is really a case of battling my mentor. All the underhanded and sneaky things I know how to do I learned from Zero, and he's the one protecting *him* from being detected or tracked by anyone, including me. No, especially me.

He has been in New York before, but never for more than two days and more likely a few hours' layover on his way to Europe, Asia or the Middle East. I'm only aware of a few because he's hard to track and if he doesn't stay long in the city, my alerts don't pick him up.

This time is different.

Starving for knowledge, I want to arm myself with as much information as possible, but the morsels I've unearthed barely keep me satiated. It's hard not to obsess over the man who took everything from me. A man who can't be found and in turn, can't be punished. In my frustration for more details, to determine if he's here to cause me bodily harm or harm to those I love, I haven't ruled out stalking him.

But truth be told, I don't dare get that close. My body may betray me despite my time in a mental health facility and years of therapy, all of which were to reteach both my body and brain new ways to react, to stay calm and remember that I am in control.

And I'm not only worried about what his presence means for me. My past coming to New York means danger for those I love. Van, my boss and savior, is about the only one who would fully understand what this means.

Evan Hart is founder and owner of Hart Corporation, and not only like a big brother to me, but a selfless guy who knows every gory detail of my life.

He's been out of town on a job this past week, and when he

returns, I'll have to tell him about the imminent danger. I groan, not looking forward to it. I've been a jittery mess these past few days, and my breathing techniques are taking longer than normal to bring me back to calm.

Van isn't the only one I have to talk to. There's Anna and Max. Anna knows all but not that Ash is back. I told her about my past when she came face to face with Ash years ago. After that incident, Ash had disappeared for more than two years. Interpol had sightings of him but nothing of use and never for too long.

And then there's Max. He knows some but not all about my past, and if *he's* here to cause trouble, I have to tell Max. In fact, everyone needs to know what we're dealing with.

Just then, Max exits the hospital. Tall and broad with his shimmering golden crown of hair and I'd know him anywhere. His steps are casual and self-assured. He's oblivious to my presence with his head down, forearms strong and defined at his sides, long fingers holding the phone that has all his attention.

I press my hand to stop the stomach flips, excited to see him. More and more I feel this way, though this time is more intense and only partially about the reality of having to share my entire despicable past.

We haven't seen each other in person in nearly two weeks, so I want tonight for us, to catch up and just be. And I need to tell Van first, he's due back tomorrow, and then I'll figure out when and how best to tell Max and Anna. With that thought, I push from the wall and step toward him.

"Hey!"

His head snaps up, missing me during his first quick scan of his surroundings. Almost not seeing anything. On the second time around, our eyes lock and I can't look away despite the tingles lighting my nerves on fire. A smoldering warmth, and something primal, tracks through his gaze like an electric current.

"Tommie." My name comes out husky and needy, unlike I've ever heard from him before.

This is different for us. Our reactions to each other. Yet I've felt something similar and fleeting before and each time, I've tried to push it aside. We're only friends after all. But being apart for days makes it difficult to dismiss how I'm feeling. I've missed him and I'm thrilled to think he feels the same.

With three long strides, he's in front of me and large, smooth hands clasp my face. A pulse of excitement skitters through my core. Lips crash onto mine like waves smashing against a craggy shore. Thrilling and violent. Earth-quaking.

It takes me a few beats to realize what's going on, or register that I should be pulling away, trying to stop this never-ending, life-affirming kiss. We're friends. Good friends

This is a good kiss. Shouldn't good friends have good kisses?

His tongue thrusts into my mouth and my brain is mush. Everything melts away, even the small voice trying to remind me that kissing is too intimate. Even if it is, it feels more than right. I'm kissing Max Conrad and it feels fucking fantastic.

No. We're best friends. Best friends don't kiss. Not like this. No matter how amazing it is. I finally manage to break away.

"Max." His name releases on a gulp of air and my hand presses flat against my stomach to steady the twists within.

"God I've missed you." His emerald green eyes twinkle and his lips spread into a shit-eating grin as he finally releases my face.

I instantly miss the warmth of his touch and my head spins. Barely stopping to breathe, he barrels ahead, as if our kiss never happened.

"The surgery was phenomenal. Everything I hoped it would be. I wanted to call so many times but there was still so much to do." His fingers rake roughly through his golden locks and he beams.

"Whoa, hang on a sec." I shake my head. "What just happened?"

He smiles sheepishly, threading strong fingers with mine like he's done a million times before, and it does ease some of my shock.

"I got carried away. I know you're not into kissing. Sorry. It's just that I've missed you so much."

My lips throb, swollen and thoroughly used, as the pulsing of my heartbeat drums in my ears. Sure, as a general rule, kissing isn't for me, and Max has, on occasion, planted a peck on my lips. Usually it's to annoy me or tease me for my no kissing rule, which he thinks is absurd, yet he also strangely likes my hard and fast rule. He's told me before that he likes that I don't kiss the men I go out with.

But this kiss was different. I'd willingly repeat that kiss, again and again. But I'm not sharing that with him, even if he is my best friend.

Best friends don't kiss like that. I have to keep reminding myself of this; talking about it would only change things between us. Maybe make things awkward. I don't want awkward. No more thinking about the kiss.

"Seeing you right now is bringing back the rush of the surgery and everything else." He pulls me along with him and some of the buzz from the kiss wanes.

Now the kiss from nowhere makes a bit more sense. He must be still riding the high from his greatest career dream coming true. He completed a heart transplant as the lead surgeon for crying out loud. That's a huge accomplishment even if it was several days ago. I'm exhilarated just thinking about it so I can hardly imagine what he must be feeling.

But the realization of why the kiss happened is a bit of a letdown. It wasn't really about me. What am I thinking? This is a good thing. It isn't about me. We're friends.

We walk for a bit more and then he releases my hand to hook his arm around my neck, tugging me in for a long side hug.

"Hey, you're a sight for sore eyes. Literally." Tiny lines of fatigue circle his eyes and mouth, and there's a weariness lurking in the depths of his eyes.

Shoving our kiss into a trunk in my mind, I slam it shut and lock it. "You too. Why haven't you had time to meet me? It's not like you've been preparing for heart surgery or anything."

I snake my arm around his trim waist and he scoffs, shaking his head. "Yeah, nothing like that."

"So I decided to do what I do best. Stalk you. That's why I'm here. I was staking out the joint, waiting for you. I've got dinner." I hold up my trusty blue and white polka dot lunch container and his easy smile doubles.

There's no chance he's eaten anything in hours. He's notorious for neglecting his own health despite his profession. Hot dog dinners are our thing and he'll expect at least three hot dogs just the way he likes them. Mustard. Nothing else.

"God, I love you." His lips brush my temple, and I squeeze my eyes shut, banishing the wetness pricking at the corners of my eyes.

What the hell is my problem?

I'm not usually emotional. Although I am sleep deprived and on edge. Max's protectiveness and nurturing ways aren't new. He has told me he loves me before and I have said the same to him.

If I'm being honest, he's one of very few who have gotten past most of my barriers. He doesn't expect or want anything from me. He's just that kind of guy. A tender-hearted soul. Easy to be with and easy to love.

"You better love me." I pat his hard stomach and laugh.

"Feed me, please." He drags me to the nearest bench, nowhere near "our" bench, which is across the street from his building, still many blocks away. He must be really hungry.

"How's your patient?"

"Good," he says between mouthfuls. "She had a fever yesterday, but the meds are working and it's under control." He stuffs half of the last hot dog into his mouth. "Oh man, you're an angel. Thank you."

"Don't talk with food in your mouth."

I bat at his arm and catch his hungry gaze on the dog in my hand. I've only had two bites, and I could eat the rest of it, easily. Given he couldn't even wait to eat, he likely hasn't had anything all day.

"You want this even with the ketchup and banana peppers?" I give him a lopsided grin, ready to relinquish the sausage to him.

"Are you sure?" His fingers are already on the wrapper, not really waiting to see if I protest.

I snort and roll my eyes dramatically. "Fine. I'll starve."

I am hungry but I'll survive. I'm happy to see him loving the food I brought. We'll most probably end up at his place and I'll grab something to eat then. I can wait.

"You're the best," he says just before sinking his teeth into the soft bun.

"Easy, remember to chew." I bump his shoulder and he slows his chewing. "So finish that and then tell me, how've you been?"

I barely blink and the hot dog is gone.

"Good. Tired, but good. And you?"

"Okay. Better now that I've seen your face."

He beams and nods. "How's Clark?"

We stand, and I roll my eyes. His joke was funny the first time he deliberately called Kent *Clark*, the mix-up on Superman's alter ego. But now he *always* does it. I no longer think it's cute or funny.

"Kent is fine, I suppose."

We walk to the line of taxis idling at the curb and he lassoes his arm around my waist, tucking me into his side. We are usually touchy and close but for some reason, he seems more so tonight. Or maybe it's me? Being with him right now is helping to calm the jitters I've had the past week.

"My place?" He opens the car door, rattling off his address before we settle into the back. "So, have things progressed with Kent?"

"It's over." I'm always ending things before they can even get started, and to spare his questions, I ask, "How's Barbara?"

My voice takes on an upper crust British accent, bringing a lively smile to his tired face. We don't usually talk about his girlfriend because she doesn't care for me and I'm indifferent to her.

Max also isn't one to share about her, claiming it's because there isn't much to say. From what I've gathered, I don't feel his heart is in it.

"I haven't spoken to her in weeks."

I'm not really surprised, since he hasn't had time for me either. "Okay. But things are cool?"

"They are over too."

"Seriously?" This kind of surprises me. His heart may not have been in it but I got the sense he was comfortable.

"Yep. She wanted more. She wasn't happy with the sporadic dates or my last-minute cancelations." He grimaces. "She wanted to move in with me. I didn't."

"Wow. So you called it quits?"

We pull up in front of his building and he nods, paying the driver. He steers me through the entrance to his building, where the doorman tips his hat.

"Good evening, Ms. Carrington and Mr. Conrad."

"Hi Gerald." Max dips his chin.

"Hey, G." I pat his lapel and smile. "Thank you."

The elderly gentleman smiles in return and his cheeks heat. "Lovely night for a walk with Gunnar, or are you in for the night?"

Max leaves us to grab his mail.

"We're staying in. I came by earlier, before your shift, to walk Gunnar. Although he may guilt-trip his daddy into another walk." I grin in Max's direction, who is busy going through a stack of envelopes by the elevator.

"Night, G." I wave and join Max as the doors slide open.

We enter his apartment and I turn on lights, a smile pushing at the corners of my mouth when Gunnar runs to greet me. "Hey, baby, I've missed you."

I bend, burying my face into the warmth of the dog's furry back and Max chuckles behind me. "I thought you said you came by earlier to walk him?"

"I did. So?" I continue to pet the dog while walking further into his place.

I found the German Shepherd when he was just a dirty, scrawny puppy. Beautiful but neglected. Despite a strict no pets allowed rule in my building, I took him home.

Before I could even contemplate looking for a new place to live, I had to go out of town on assignment and I didn't want to board my new pup, even with all his shots and a clean bill of health. Max offered to take him and he's been here ever since.

"Are you coming?" he asks from the living room.

My four-legged friend follows, lying at my feet as I snuggle into the sofa, flicking through our movie choices on the TV. Meanwhile Max walks back and forth from the kitchen with munchies and drinks. We've done this too many times to count.

"Oh, before I forget, I've got this fundraiser event for the hospital tomorrow night, will you go with me?"

He sits beside me with his arm resting on the sofa at my back.

"Tomorrow? Not a lot of time to find a dress."

Barbara used to be his plus one and for a split second, I wish they were still together. I hate these things, but I quickly dismiss the crazy thought. Barbara didn't like me, and if Max had been serious about her, I'm not sure what that would have meant for our friendship.

She likely would have made him choose, and I shudder, a quickening in my heart rate at the inconceivable. I'd like to think Max and I would always be friends, no matter what, but romantic relationships can change friendships.

"A dress? You have easily six dresses for the occasion." He smirks, all too familiar with my many evening gowns.

Clothes—designer clothes—are a weakness. And despite how small my apartment is, I have multiple portable clothing racks taking up at least half of my one-room place.

"Fine. I'll be your date." Nibbling on my lower lip, I falter on my choice of words.

For the first time in a while, we're both single. A strange heat coils around my insides at the thought of our kiss earlier tonight. Dynamite. I've never felt like that before and while exciting, it also scares me.

No, definitely not a date.

MAX

A constant buzzing causes my eyes to blink open. I'm in my living room. The phone is face down on the cushion beside me, vibrating, and my bicep is numb, with Tommie's head resting on my muscle. She's sleeping and Gunnar's head is perched on her thigh.

I don't want to move. She smells so good. Feminine and sexy. And I like having her in my arms, burrowed into me and comfortable. Soft and warm. We've fallen asleep together before, but never after kissing the daylights out of her.

I kissed her.

I wasn't thinking last night. All I saw was her. Waiting for me. Fucking beautiful and beaming. She was so happy to see me, and I felt the same way about her. Two weeks had seemed like an eternity to go without seeing her, and while we had texted during that time, it wasn't enough.

The phone rings again and I grumble under my breath. Gunnar lifts his head and I shift my gaze to the phone and its offensive sound. I pick up. *Witch,* my nickname for my mother, flashes across the screen.

Cradling Tommie's head, I get up and rest her head back on the cushion. She curls into a ball and her glossy dark hair cascades over the side, her long eyelashes fanning across her golden cheeks.

My breath stutters in my chest. I just want to curl up with her in my arms. She's so peaceful sleeping. Gone is the little crease between her eyebrows when she mulls over a problem. And her lips. They are so soft and plump and even though I shouldn't have kissed her, for many reasons—we're friends and she has a no kissing rule—I want to do it again. To feel her lips on me, an open-mouthed kiss, tasting and taking from her.

The phone buzzes again and I jog to my room, wanting not to wake Tommie. I'm surprised she hasn't even stirred. By the time I close the bedroom door, the buzzing has stopped, and a ping signals an incoming text. An address followed by nine-one-one. That's her code for urgent, to get there as soon as possible, no excuses. *Dammit.*

I dress and tiptoe out of the apartment with Gunnar to take him to relieve himself. Once I quietly deposit him in the apartment—Tommie hasn't budged—I grab a cab to the same warehouse as the other night.

During the ride, I text Tommie to let her know I had to leave, and in the same instant, a text from my mother comes in, frustrated I'm not there yet. She's always ticked at me and while I'm not thrilled to have left Tommie, maybe I'll find out why she wants me to be there more regularly. I'm curious, because anything that involves my mother is bad news.

Since last I was there, checking on the guy with the gunshot wound, she hasn't called, which surprises me but I'm not going to ask questions.

Tiny is once again waiting for me. Dread like a guillotine looms above my head. Mother isn't here and the warehouse is deserted this time. The hefty guy opens a door into darkness and it's only when he flicks on the flashlight that I make out the staircase descending into a pit of black.

I hesitate, unease tingling up my spine, and he pushes me forward. They've never taken me into the basement of any of the warehouses before. Makes me wonder what's down here and why now?

Once in the bowels of the building, he turns on a heavy switch, almost like a breaker, and the place is instantly flooded in a garish white beam. Like a maze, there are long concrete corridors branching off into dark hallways. But the stench is putrid and unmistakable. Urine, blood and disease.

Used to illness and not-so-great smells, I battle with myself to follow him. What the hell is going on down here? We walk down the main artery, past several junctures where haunting whimpers and pleas of help or mercy from faceless women bounce off the walls. *What the fuck?*

Women? While I don't like to be ignorant, I don't want to know about my mother's business. But from what I've overheard through the years, she's into guns, drugs, gambling, and I'm sure more. But I've never heard anything about women or prostitution. Is that what she's getting into? And if so, why does she have women down here?

An indescribable chill permeates my very core and my gaze sharpens on Tiny. His look is indifferent, nudging me onward with a harsh grunt to obey.

We stop outside a cell where a woman with long stringy dark hair, barely clothed, lies on a narrow cot, writhing in pain and clutching her abdomen. Her hands are coated in blood, as is her abdomen and the bed.

The tinny smell, one I know so well, is overpowering, and despite the familiarity, my last meal roils in my gut. Weak in the knees, I fight past the nausea and disgust. I've only ever tended to thugs and goons. Who is this woman? Why is she in a cell? Are all the other women I heard in cells as well? How many are we talking and why are they down here?

And what the fuck do I do about it? How can I get them out of here?

The medical bag my mother keeps for me is on the floor, open and waiting for me to use its contents. I remove a pair of nitrile gloves and iodine, forcing my breaths to slow and even out. My hands are moist and I'm not sure if any kind of treatment is going to make a difference as it looks like she's already lost a lot of blood.

I need to focus. I'll be no good to her if I lose my shit. With one more steady breath, my doctor mentality is in check and I perch beside the woman.

"No. Not her." Tiny yanks my arm. "The cunt dies."

Sloughing off his hold, I press several gauzes against her gaping wound, trying to stem the bleeding.

"I said no." He pulls me to standing and spins me to face a man I hadn't noticed until now. "Him."

Franz, one of the more sadistic men among my mother's ranks, is hunched over in a corner, also holding his stomach. I'd been too shocked and concerned when I laid eyes on the woman, I didn't realize someone else was hurt. And suddenly this makes sense.

The woman and Franz got into an altercation. I indulge Tiny and examine Franz's wound. Knife injury. He's not bleeding nearly as much as the woman and the cut is relatively small and shallow. He needs tending to but I'm triaging, and the woman is priority one.

"I'm taking care of her first." Not waiting for Tiny to allow it—*screw him*—I'm at her side again.

It's a gunshot and it doesn't look good. With my hand on her back, I search for an exit wound. She moans in agony. There isn't one. Fuck, this is a mess. The bullet is still inside her.

Tiny growls, towering over me, and his hand digs into my shoulder.

"Back up and I'll be quick." I'm insistent on helping her despite knowing, deep within me, that it's futile.

I don't have the proper instruments or drugs or a surgical team, and she's lost a lot of blood. Even if I could get out the bullet and stave off infection, she needs a transfusion.

This time Tiny is rough, pushing me from the bed onto my knees. The muzzle of a gun presses into the back of my head.

"Fuck her. The bitch stuck Franz. She got what she deserves." His fingers burrow deeper into my shoulder and it feels like he could snap the bone in two.

Punching him in the throat or worse, stooping so low as to belt his balls, is tempting. But he's got the gun and if I'm shot, I'm no use to anyone. And I can say goodbye to any chance of saving this woman. She'll surely bleed out.

I work on Franz as quickly as possible and once he's stitched up, I order Tiny to get him someplace dry to rest. It's way too damp down here. The big guy wraps his meaty hand around his buddy's waist and hoists him into his arms. Franz is pale and clammy, but he'll make it. Thank Christ for small mercies.

"Let's go, doc." Tiny motions with the gun for me to follow.

Appearing to agree, we walk toward the exit but I veer to the side at the last minute and come to a crouch by the dying woman. My hand rests on her burning forehead. Her breathing is labored and she's moaning in agony. She's ashen and limp; this doesn't look good.

"No. Leave her." Tiny's bulky shadow looms above me and if I had the time, I might reconsider my disobedience.

"No."

Ignoring his intimidating presence, I rifle through my medical bag for painkillers. It may be the only way I can help her now. To make her last hours somewhat bearable.

Tiny grabs my collar, hauling me into the air and slamming my chest into the wall. *Oof.* My ribs rattle, feeling as if cracked, and I wrestle to break free. But his large meaty hand cups the side of my face, grinding it into the concrete.

Ragged and abrasive, the wall scrapes my face like a grater on cheese. *Ouch.* His knee jams into my back, constricting my torso, and it's suddenly hard to breathe.

Air rushes into my lungs as he whips me around to face him. My fists are out and swinging but I'm not fast enough to block his right hook to my jaw.

Thud.

My head bounces back against the wall and my teeth come together in a cringeworthy crunch. *Ah, fuck.* I duck the next punch, roll along the wall and break from his grasp just as his knuckles slam into the unyielding wall, right where my head should have been. Tiny wails, now clutching his sure to be swelling hand.

"I'm gonna fucking kill…" He lunges at me and I weave away, still bracing for a potential hit.

"Enough." Taya's shrill command stops her man from coming at me.

Relief should override anything else but rage bumps through my veins. I want to get a few hits of my own in, if only to blow off some of my anger.

"You'll do no such thing. Take Franz. Go." She points in the direction we came, and without a word, Tiny obeys.

"What the hell is going on?" I point a finger, which is vibrating with fury, at the dying woman. She looks worse than before my fight with Tiny and I leap toward her.

"She's paying for her mistake. Let's go." Mother wraps her hand around my bicep.

"With her life?" I wrench myself free. "I can't leave her like this. Let me at least give her something for the pain."

I don't wait for a response, grabbing the morphine-filled syringe from my bag. She curls her fingers around my wrist, nails cutting into my flesh.

"No. You're not to waste another moment on her."

I jerk from her hold. Whimpering, the pallid woman opens her eyes, dark like night, and our gazes clash. At first, her stare is glassy and wild, but in a beat or two, a clarity that wasn't there before seeps into her orbs.

"Please…" Her voice is reed thin and the little color she has left drains from her face. Just talking to me is taking a toll.

"What?" I lean in closer to hear when I should be telling her not to speak.

To save her energy. But for what?

There is no hope.

Taya's hand is back on my shoulder but not pulling me away. She leans in closer, also wanting to hear what the woman has to say.

"Freedom..." Her eyes close and just when I think she is lost, they flash open again. "Comes at a price."

TOMMIE

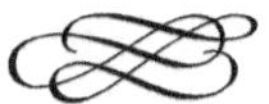

Arms above my head, I lean to the left and yawn. A crack from my back ripples through my body. *Ahhh, much better.* But that's not all. A sharp pain sits along the side of my neck and my fingers work to loosen the knot that took up residence while I slept on the couch.

Gunnar thumps his tail on the floor and my hand runs through the thick fur on his head as I push up to stand. "Hey, Gun. Mommy needs coffee and some stretches to feel human again."

Despite the aches and pains from being curled up on a couch for nearly ten hours, it's the first time since the alert that I've had a full night's sleep. Most have been restless with worry as I try to anticipate his move and decide what I'm going to do.

But last night, I fell asleep on Max's shoulder and slept right through the night—so much so, I didn't even hear him get up. Before going to look for him, I grab my phone and there's a text from Max from about three hours ago. He had to leave.

I'm disappointed that he isn't here but I shouldn't be surprised. He has a patient recuperating from heart transplant surgery for crying out loud, of course he's at the hospital.

Yet melancholy seeps into my bones, weighing on my still sleepy form. We had last night to catch up, but it wasn't nearly long enough. I still have so much to say to him.

I traipse into the kitchen, making a beeline for the pre-programmed waiting-for-me-to-push-the-start-button coffee machine. *Thank you, Max.* While it brews, I have a quick shower and throw on last night's clothes, all the while and so not like me, going over last night in painstaking detail.

Last night. Wow, it was just all around bizarre and not necessarily in a bad way. Thrilling and pleasing and confusing… more confusing than anything else.

We slept together, which isn't new. I've crashed here before when I'm too tired to go home, and sometimes we've even slept in the same bed. But never tangled up in each other's arms like we're a couple, and never after he's kissed me.

Max kissed me. The heat of his hands on my face and the soft, strong press of his lips upon mine still linger, the sensation so strong it's as if he's kissing me right now. And it wasn't a peck on the lips, and it wasn't to tease or annoy me. No way. That was a full-on tongue-and-teeth kiss.

A seesaw of emotions confuses my mind. Pleasure and elation, and anxiety and regret, and each one competes for the top spot.

He's my best friend and an awesome catch. Not only smart, funny and caring, but also hot as hell. And I'd have to be dead not to have thought about what it would be like to be with him.

But I won't risk our friendship for… for what? Amazing chemistry? A night of hot sex? A romantic relationship? I snort and twirl my hair around my finger. No, not a relationship, and that's at the crux of all my concern. We can't have a relationship. I'd mess it up, for sure. All I know is pain and loss.

And then what? Max is good for me. An awesome friend. I feel whole and safe with him and I can't wreck that. Or worse, lose our friendship. Lose him. He's good for me in so many ways. Take last night as an example. I've been unable to sleep for days, yet only hours with him and I'm snuggled in his arms. Safe and secure, sleeping like a baby.

No... My phone buzzes on the counter and Van's name flashes on the screen. No, I can't lose Max.

"Hey, you. Are you back?" The steaming coffee cup presses against my lips as I take a careful but much needed sip.

"Yeah, late last night." His voice is throaty, almost as if he just got up too.

"You sound tired. Did the job go as planned?"

"Yup. All is good and I'm beat but glad to be home. When are you coming in, thought we could have lunch? You up for it, Tommie girl?"

"Yes to lunch." I beam, warmth spreading through me, dampening the persistent dread of what I have to tell him. "I should be at the office in about an hour. I just wanted to take Gun for a walk."

At the word *walk*, the dog trots over to my side as if to say he's ready to go. I can't help but smile. Even though Max's text says he already took Gunnar out, and the dog walker will come later this afternoon, I could use the exercise and time to clear my head.

"Okay. Are you going over there now?"

"I'm already here. I stayed the night." I no sooner say the words than I inwardly groan.

"Really, so you and Max, huh?" I can definitely hear the cocky grin in his voice.

"It isn't like that and you know it, so don't go implying something that isn't there."

We've been having this conversation for months now. Van insists Max and I are going to be a *thing*, and while teasing is totally in character for the man I think of as my older brother, relationships or, more specifically, *my* relationships, aren't his favorite subject. In fact, he's been known to talk about anything, even nail polish or fashion, to avoid discussing who I'm seeing.

"I know your friends. But... I don't know, there was something in your voice."

If we were talking about anything else, I'd push him to finish his train of thought, but this isn't something I want to pursue.

"Can we move on?"

"Have you given any more thought to something more with Max?"

His question hits a little too close to my own thoughts this morning and I nearly spit out my coffee, coughing.

"No." This isn't an out and out lie. My inner thoughts of what ifs aren't something I want to share with Van or anyone.

"You have chemistry."

All taste for coffee or breakfast evaporates and I grab the leash to get Gunnar ready to go outside. "Chemistry or not, Max is just a friend."

"You sound a little flustered there, Tommie." His teasing tone is back, and I wish he was in front of me so I could hit him. Playfully. Of course.

"Van." I cringe at the whiny sister-like tone to my voice.

"Fine, I'll drop it but not before I say this." He pauses and I tense, uncertain as to what will come next.

"Seriously?" Now I do sound like an exasperated little sister.

"Hear me out. You can't keep going on like this." His words are warm, his tone protective.

"Like what?" Despite being happy he's back and looking forward to lunch, I'd rather skip the life lesson.

"All the guys you date. They're useless, nameless asshats and you deserve so much better. You deliberately avoid any kind of intimacy or connection."

"I'm getting into the elevator. I might lose you." It's juvenile to hope our conversation will be cut short by metal and wood, and in the same breath, it's useless. Max's building recently had signal boosters installed so there's very little chance of severing our connection.

"Nice try, Carrington." His wry tone is followed by a sigh. "Just hear me out for a few more minutes."

I snort, twisting my lips. "Who are you and what did you do with Van? You're giving relationship advice now? I hope you don't charge by the minute."

Ignoring my quip, he's matter-of-fact as he says, "Sex is a big fuck you for you, and no pun intended."

I let out a short bark of laughter, and he barrels on without judgement or criticism to his tone. "Sex is power for you. You're taking back what *he* and others took from you."

Exiting the elevator in a daze, I rest against a wood paneled wall in the foyer, letting Van's words wash over me. It's as if Van already knows *he* is in the city.

The day doorman catches my eye, smiling and tipping his hat in greeting. I force a tight smile and push myself forward and out of the building.

"But that's not all it can be. Sex is also intimacy and pleasure. A bond. And that scares the shit out of you." Van lowers his voice until it's softer and caring, and his concern pricks at my chest even as I lash out.

"Don't shrink me."

With long, quick strides, I push past the unease and bubbling irritation. He isn't saying anything I don't already know. Heck, I jumped to the idea of sex with Max and as glorious as I hope it would be, shit I *know* it would be, it's the intimacy and connection that scare the shit out of me. I already have too much to lose.

"Hey, I didn't say that to tick you off," he says apologetically, and now I feel like more of a jerk than moments ago.

"You didn't." I try to reassure him that I'm okay.

"As for relationships in general, you've got a lot to share with the right person." His words echo Anna's from just the other day and my insides clench. "And if the time ever comes when you find the one, you'll need to be open and honest if you're ever going to have a meaningful and trusting relationship. You need to trust more than just me."

"Van, while I don't like talking about this, I get it. Message received." I try to keep any irritation out of my voice.

He's well-meaning like Anna, and they both want me to make peace with my demons. Not that a relationship or a man will make me whole or happy, that's not what he's saying, but rather that I stop resisting any kind of emotional investment. And he's right. My automatic response to anything too deep or with too much risk is to run.

Van, by virtue of finding me, became the only one I fully let in. In some ways, I had no choice. I was just a teenager and truly alone. I'd lost everyone and everything and while trusting someone was as dangerous and scary to me as drinking battery acid, I needed someone.

He'd rescued me and had been nothing but protective and kind. He wasn't pushy or nosy despite having every right to ask me a million questions. Again, trusting him was as easy and risk-free as bungee jumping—if you catch my drift—and I was scared shitless of letting him in because what if I lost him?

I'd already lost everything, I couldn't bear to make new connections, find new people to love, only to have it taken away again. Ten years later and I've got a small family of friends, some who are in my inner circle and most that I keep at arm's length. But even then, they are closer than most people.

"You still there?" His gruff voice cuts through my tumultuous thoughts.

"Yep. Sorry." I stop along the path in Central Park, across the street from Max's apartment building, and Gunnar lifts his leg by a tree.

"Hey, I don't usually force this kind of conversation but sometimes you need to hear something more than once for it to stick."

A chime, signaling an incoming text, causes me to pull the phone from my ear.

Max: Hey, sleeping beauty, you up? Will you be at HC in an hour or so? I need to talk to the guys and would like you to be there.

I wrinkle my forehead, wondering what this is all about.

Me: I'm heading to HC in a few. Will be there. Everything okay?

Max: It will be. Talk soon.

"Van, I have to go. Max is coming into HC."

"Yeah, I just got a text from him too."

"Do you know what it's about?"

"All he said was Taya Conrad."

"Shit. That…" I purse my lips, capturing the nasty words I like to use when describing Max's mother.

"Yeah, my thoughts exactly. This can't be good. Guess we'll find out more shortly."

"Yes. And Van?"

"Yeah?"

"Thank you for caring enough to put us both through that relationship torture talk."

I detect a smile in his voice. "I'll always care enough to torture you."

And isn't that what big brothers are for?

TOMMIE

Van, Ry and Coop are in a conference room when I arrive at HC, heads together and deep in conversation. They pause, each turning in their respective chairs to look my way.

A warm brotherly smile spreads across Van's dark stubbled face, while the corners of Ry's mouth tip upward ever so slightly and he gives me a quick nod.

"Tommie, where did you get those skyscrapers?" Coop dips his chin to my nude Valentino rock-studded patent leather stilettos that I lucked out and found in the back of Max's front hall closet. I can't remember when I last wore them or how they wound up there. "You're looking very *Atomic Blonde*."

He's referring to the Cold War spy Charlize Theron plays in the movie he just named, and I can't contain my smile. Coop knows better than to comment on my legs or about how they make me stick out even more among the Avenger types roaming these halls.

I'm not the only woman to work at HC, we have several talented, badass operatives in the field that are of the female persuasion. Van is very much an equal-opportunity employer. But I am the only woman among management and contrary to what some might think, most of these guys don't subscribe to stereotypes. I'm treated with respect, have a voice at the table and have had led many a tactical exercise from the intelligence perspective.

"Hmmm. I always thought of myself more as a Captain Marvel of the keyboard." One eyebrow arches and I twitch my lips in an attempt to mimic the action hero from said movie.

"Damn, I'd have to agree with that." Coop snickers. "Now all I'm seeing is glowing eyes and killer explosives."

Amusement sparkles in Van's hazel eyes as he pulls a chair out for me beside him. I hesitate, wanting to tell him what I didn't on the phone, and for that we need privacy.

"Can we talk before Max arrives?" I hook my thumb over my shoulder in the direction of the other offices.

"Sure."

His hand rests on my back, guiding me from the room. I snicker, ignoring Coop's humorous remarks about how it's rude to keep secrets as we walk down the hall.

"What's up?" He shuts my office door and strides in front of where I'm perched on the edge of my desk. "Is this the tongue-lashing for our convo earlier?"

Fun still dances in his gaze, but his features are more serious. I shake my head and walk around to sit, resting my elbows on the desk.

"Ash is in New York."

Without uttering a word, his stoic, unwavering expression gives away that he already knows. "I found out yesterday once the case wrapped. The notification was waiting on my phone. When did you?"

"A week ago. Page Six?" I ask, referring to the *New York Post*'s celebrity gossip site, and he nods.

"Before you ask, I was going to call but also hoped it would be like the times before and he'd be gone without incident. Besides, you were under and couldn't have done anything anyway."

"We've talked about this. On a case or not, if you need me, you know how to get a hold of me. I would have pulled out if…" He sits across from me, elbows now on the desk as he takes my clasped hands in his. "You know, forget about that. I want to focus on something you said. Without incident? Did something happen?"

Shaking vehemently, I rush to assure him, cursing my careless words. "No. Nothing has happened. But the longer he stays in New York…"

I can't bring myself to finish the sentence and his grave expression suggests that I don't need to. We both know that as long as Ash Naire is in this city, it isn't a question of if he'll do something but rather when.

"You can't stay at your place. Come stay with us. You're alone and it's too easy to get in there." His jaw is taut as he's quick to brainstorm solutions.

I can just imagine the words he's biting back. He never wanted me to move into the building where I live. The security is flimsy at best, if not non-existent. Although, given my past, Fort Knox wouldn't satisfy Van's protective gene.

If he had things his way, I'd be living with him and his wife, Carys, who is also Ry's younger sister, and their kids. But like I said when I signed my bachelor studio lease and still believe now, I can't live my life in constant fear.

From the day Van freed me from my prison, we both knew Ash would come for me. Although I imagined his strike would be swift and stealthy, not this, so far, discreet taunt.

"Already ahead of you. I plan on telling Max everything and I'll ask if I can stay with him." He raises a brow and once over his initial surprise, he relaxes into the idea. "His building has better security than most and he's never there so there's little risk of putting him in danger."

Van frowns, leaning back into his chair and crossing his arms. "Don't underestimate him. We're all at risk until he's behind bars."

The unsettling truth grows along my spine like a thorny vine and tightens around my throat. Yes, Ash coming for me was inevitable. We have unfinished business—the sick asshole never got what he deserves.

A six-by-eight-foot cell would do the trick, or preferably a rusted shank to the gut, but if Interpol and Scotland Yard can't get anything concrete on him, the chances of incarceration are slim.

Van hadn't rescued me from Ash's lair. I'd been carted off to another place as punishment and it was purely coincidence, or maybe fate, that Van was there looking for someone else when he found me.

Once safely away from Ash and somewhat able to speak coherently, I tried to remember something to help Van nail him. But where I'd been held captive was unknown to me. I was literally and figuratively in the dark.

All I had was his first name and that of his hacker sidekick, Zero. It took some digging and plenty of time, since all we had were the few details from Van's assignment and those two names, to find him.

When I came across his picture online, Ash was standing beside a British government official. That said it all. He was living in London —still does, and was a well-respected businessman—still is.

Van shared the little we had on him with local and international law enforcement, but they said it wasn't enough to make anything stick. So like us, they are watching and waiting for the chance to nail the bastard.

"Hey, sorry to interrupt." Ry sticks his head into my office, taking in our serious faces and straightening to his full height. "You guys okay?"

"Yeah." Van turns to face his best friend, and co-owner of HC. "We gotta talk later."

He looks back at me with the unspoken question—am I good with Ry, and likely the rest of the crew, knowing every sordid detail of my past? What can I say? Not really but yes. I nod and he offers a tight-lipped smile.

"All right. We'll talk. Max is here and in the conference room. We're waiting on you two."

"Thanks. Give us a sec." Van's gaze doesn't veer from mine and I stand, coming from behind the desk as Ry leaves us alone.

"Let's go." Leading the way out of the office, Max comes to mind and my curiosity is even more piqued, wondering what he has to say to us.

"Hey, Tommie girl." Van taps me on the shoulder. "I'm proud of you for wanting to tell Max. It's a big step."

I swallow past the apprehension building in my throat. Sharing won't be easy but it's long overdue. Max is aware of my past in general terms, and the death of my parents. He doesn't know all the sordid details but enough to know I was held captive.

"Thanks, and yeah, but it's time."

The conference room is full, most of the chairs around the large, wooden table taken. Ry's hands rest on the back of a chair and when he sees me, he wheels it out in a gesture for me to sit.

Smiling, I step toward Ry, nerves bubbling in my stomach, more confused as to why Max is here. He's standing at the front of the room, he hasn't seen me yet, and there's a bruise on his face. What happened?

I want to go to him, demand answers. Who did he get into a fight with? Does it have something to do with Tate, his sister?

A rush of excitement floods my body, drowning any anxiety, when a smile dawns in his eyes at the sight of me. The corners of his mouth tip up, lighting his handsome face, and I can't help but think of his lips upon mine. And at how happy I am to see him.

Resisting the urge to go to him, I swipe my hand across my cheek in the spot where his is bruised in a question. His head moves from side to side as if shaking off my concern and then he mouths that he'll explain later.

Later. Now would be better, but I have the sense whatever he's about to say may answer all questions.

MAX

A woman died last night, and I did nothing to help her. I tried but it wasn't enough, and what about all those other women I heard in that basement? My head's pounding and my insides are raw.

After leaving the warehouse, I went to the hospital to check on my patient even though I was utterly useless. Unfocused, angry and lost.

Technically, I have the day off with plans to slay the paperwork on my desk, but after last night, I have to do something.

My mother is responsible for an impressive list of crimes, some of which I can't even imagine. And while I don't know for sure what she's up to, I can't shake the sinking feeling it's some despicable shit.

Tate's safety is still my concern, and even more so now that she has children. There are many reasons to toe the line and keep my mouth shut, but I can't let whatever-this-is happen. It's clear lives are at stake. My next move is either the cops or Ry and HC.

The police are the logical choice given HC is a private firm, known to work outside the confines of the law, yet going through the proper channels means there's only one chance. Well, one chance for Tate and me, that is.

My mother must have at least one person, if not more, in the police department on her payroll. All it would take is one conversation with the wrong cop, or something entered in their systems, triggering an alarm, and everything would blow up in my face. My mother would be on to me.

HC is the better bet. They may operate in the gray areas, but have been known to work with, or share what they find with, the law. And while a visit to HC may cause Taya to question my motives, it isn't like I haven't been there before.

At this point, it's a risk I'm willing to take. Besides, once Ry and the others know everything, they'll take additional measures to keep Tate and their boys safe.

The conference room is full when I arrive but no sign of Tommie. It's important she is here for this. I'd have preferred to tell her about my involvement with my mother in private, but waiting isn't an option, and she'll understand that. Based on what I saw last night, time is of the essence.

"Max, is Tate in any immediate danger?" Ry's expression is tight, and I'm comforted by his unwavering commitment to my sister. She is his number one priority, always.

"Max." Tripp dips his chin as he sidles up beside us and takes a sip of his coffee.

"Not that I'm aware of. But that may change after this."

My brother-in-law growls, curling his hands into fists. "You're killing me here, man. Let me go get Van and Tommie."

Before I can say anything else, he's gone and Tripp's stare pins me to the spot. He's clearly still mulling over what I just said.

"Come on." He leads me to the front of the room.

From across the room, Coop tracks my moves and his dark eyes shine with interest. He's the only one who looks even remotely laid back about this spontaneous meeting. The guy exudes a carefree attitude despite being just as vigilant as the rest of them.

I get the intensity. My mother has wreaked havoc on most of their lives and try as they might, she's still an ever-present threat to our small but mighty self-made family. She's vile and destructive and there's an eager, electric vibe in the air.

Any of them would jump on any proverbial bandwagon to get rid of her once and for all. Well, I'm about to kick off said mission with me leading the charge.

The large oval table sits in the middle of the room and most of the ten chairs are occupied save for two, which I'm guessing are for Tommie and Van, or maybe Ry. Men and women stand along the walls, mostly faces I vaguely recognize from past HC family barbecues or when I've visited the office. All told, there's about twenty of us in the room.

Ry returns, a flash of fire in his eyes; I can almost feel his impatience and right now, it's directed at me. He grabs the top of a vacant chair and when Tommie enters, followed by Van, he turns the chair, motioning for her to sit.

Long midnight locks, wild and free, frame her face, and her dark almond-shaped eyes sparkle. She's in last night's dress, one of those designer numbers, what does she call it? Ready-to-wear? It fits her curves as if made for her.

Her face is pensive, searching, almost immediately finding mine. As I trace the graceful sweep of high cheekbones to the fullness of plum-colored lips, the desire to kiss her sneaks up on me like a rogue wave.

Now isn't the time or the place to be having these thoughts, and while I've got a lot of other pressing things on my mind, Tommie is the light in it all. I'm not surprised by the thought or that I seek her out in the middle of all this crap. We're friends and I want more. What happens if I act on my feelings? How does she feel?

She smiles, frowning at the sight of my bruise thanks to my run in with Tiny. I brush off her concern. Once she hears me out, it will all make sense. She sits and Van takes the empty chair next to her.

Ry stalks to the front of the room. "Thanks everyone for gathering so quickly. I'm not going to waste time with any preamble. Max, over to you."

I try not to read anything into his curt tone and bare bones introduction, if I can even call it that. While I'm no stranger to most, a warmer hand-off would have been nice, but I get that he just wants to understand what, if any, new threat exists.

"Thanks, Ry. Hi everyone." I swallow past any misgivings I might have in doing this to a group rather than just Ry and Tommie and jump right in.

"Since coming back to the United States, I've been working for my mother, Taya Conrad. She thinks of it as a mutually beneficial arrangement but it's extortion. In exchange for being her very own on-call doctor, she leaves Tate alone."

I don't bother to explain who my mother is and judging from the spines straightening, raised eyebrows, and a few gasps, I needn't. Many eyes go to Ry, who is leaning against the wall closest to me.

Ry's jaw is hard like marble and a scowl forms. "Why am I learning about this just now? You've been back for nearly five years."

While ticked, he isn't shocked, and he's likely already guessed that I had some kind of deal going on with my mother. The man isn't stupid, and he knows her all too well. I hate my mother, especially for what she did to Tate, and yet I'm still giving her the time of day.

Even still, I don't care for his tone or the fact that he has no qualms about acting this way in front of his staff. Although he likely feels the same way with me divulging this to more than just him.

Perhaps in my haste to do something, I didn't think this through. I rang an alarm bell, calling for them to circle the troops, when I could have been more strategic about my approach.

"Protecting my sister is important to me and I didn't see any other choice."

"If you'd come to us, we would have figured out another way," Tripp says from the other side of the room, and I'm taken aback by his understanding tone.

He's usually the last one to speak and when he does, it's to the point and unapologetic.

"Together." Van's voice is neutral, adding to the no-blame sentiment as he tips his chair back to see both Ry and me.

Tommie watches silently. Her look is familiar, reserved for when she's immersed in a case and determined to get to the bottom of whatever puzzle she's trying to solve. Is she upset with me? That I sprang this on her in a room full of her colleagues? Or does she see my turmoil? I'm guessing the latter, given the softening of her gaze the longer we stare at each other.

"I'm protecting your sister and was trying to protect you too. Can't do my job if I don't have all the details," Ry says through gritted teeth and my hackles rise as I break the connection with Tommie.

"I'm not your job, nor do I need protecting." My arms fold to lock down the gathering annoyance.

"Hey, let's move on," Coop cuts in, casually resting his dark muscled arms on the table and clasping his fingers together. "Max, what happened? Why are you here, telling us this now?"

Uncrossing my arms, I rub my hands together to dispel my pent-up frustration and suddenly nervous energy. I save lives, transplant hearts for a living. Why the hell am I nervous? Maybe nervous isn't the right word, on edge is more like it. Not feeling the need to apologize for protecting my sister.

"I've wanted out for a while but been unable to find a way…" I pace to the window, refocusing the direction of my thoughts, and the heat of all eyes burns into my back. "This morning, she called me to a warehouse I'd been to before to tend to a stab wound. That isn't unusual. Those are the kinds of calls I get. But today, we went into the basement of the building. That was new and…"

I turn around to face the team, now shoulder to shoulder with Ry who isn't looking at me but rather straight ahead. I sense some of his ire toward me has dissipated, with his shoulder not as taut and his breathing more even.

"There were women down there. I heard cries and maybe even someone calling for help. It was dark, so dark I couldn't see anything, but the basement was like a labyrinth of corridors—"

"Fuck," Ry bites out, now turning to face me, and we share a silent, weighted look as if he already knows what I'm talking about.

"Were there cells?" Coop asks.

My head snaps in his direction and I nod, suddenly fighting back the bile creeping up my throat. "How did you know?"

"Women?" Van asks, now standing and then Tommie too.

"Yes. I couldn't see anything or anyone, but they were crying. And then I was taken to a cell where a woman was dying of a gunshot wound. It looked like she somehow got into an altercation with one of the men. She stabbed him and he shot her."

"Taya's working Cavallo?" Tripp scrubs a hand down his face, rubbing at his blond day-old growth.

"What?" I cock my head to the side, not sure what he means, although I recognize the name as well as recalling a connection to what happened to Anna years ago.

"Cavallo is a major mafia crime family, and when Anna was kidnapped, we discovered a warehouse much like what you just described, with women in cells." Worry etches Tommie's features and there's an uneasiness in her tone. She's walking toward me and this can't be easy for anyone to hear, let alone a woman who herself had been a captive.

"At the time, the family was believed to be either in or getting into human trafficking," Van says as if he's coming to her rescue, and it gives me pause.

I glance back and she has stopped her approach, somehow stranded between the chair and me. Van stands at her side, placing a hand on her shoulder, and an unwanted and unexpected surge of jealousy zings through me. I want to be the one to comfort her.

"I'll talk with NYPD Organized Crime Control Bureau and get the latest on what the family is up to. Taya has been known to do business with them."

I shake away the confusing thoughts, totally in knots about Tommie, and obviously this ugliness with my mother is clouding my judgment.

"There's more and it could be relevant to Cavallo. She told me a few days ago that she's going to need me to come more often. I pushed for more details, but she wouldn't tell me why."

The room is silent while we mull over that piece of information and what it could mean. I don't want to speculate if my mother might be selling women, and with me being a doctor, I quiver to think. The possibilities don't sit well with me.

Tommie wears an empathetic expression as she sits back in her chair and crosses her legs.

"We'll need you to get more. That's not enough. Has she called you in yet? Do you know what she wants you to do?" Van moves to lean on the wall next to Ry.

He thrusts his hands in his pockets and it's an aggressive gesture, as if trying to stop himself from doing some damage.

"I can do that. This morning was the first call since then and unfortunately, in line with what I've done before. Well, except for the woman that she wouldn't let me treat, although she wouldn't have made it anyway." I scowl at the memory of the horrific events that took place only this morning.

"Okay, team, we need to start a docket. You know the drill—not all of you will work directly on this but be prepared to jump in when needed." Ry pushes off the wall, striding to stand beside me. "Tripp, you take point. Coop, I know you're about to leave but I need you working on intel with Tommie until that point. We're in the digging phase and need info fast."

There's a lot of murmurs and head bobbing as people shuffle out of the room. A few come up to Ry with questions and he steps away from me.

It's strange, because nothing is any more solid than it was a few hours ago, but at least I feel better, more hopeful. Ry and the rest of HC are invested in this and action will be taken.

"You okay?" She nears and my heart squeezes at the concern swimming in her warm gaze. Why does she affect me like this?

"Yeah. Are you with what you just learned?"

"I don't like it. Now I dislike your mother even more. But it certainly explains a heck of a lot where she's concerned. I always wondered why you'd go to lunch with her and do stuff when it was obvious you don't like her."

I nod with a rueful smile. Tommie even asked me as much once or twice over the years and I always felt like shit dodging her questions.

She tugs on my sleeve and inches closer. "You could have told me, you know."

"It wasn't that I didn't trust you," I'm quick to say, feeling every bit the shit I hope she doesn't think I am.

"I know." She rubs at my arm and my heartbeat races. "What I mean is I hate the thought of you going through that for so many years, alone."

"Yeah." Ry steps right into our space, interrupting and not giving a damn. "Max, you're not alone. Why did you think you had to play vigilante?"

His expression is hard despite guessing it comes from a good place and it only intensifies my defenses.

"It wasn't like that. You and Tate were happy. Of course, I knew you'd protect her, but I couldn't live with myself if Taya hurt my sister again. Or if…" I trail off, unable to finish the thought.

We both know what Taya is capable of and his countenance softens as does his tone. "And what if something happened to you? I promised your sister I'd take care of you, and how the hell would I be able to explain that to her?"

I shove my hands into my pockets, willing my balled fists to relax. "I wasn't thinking of my safety."

"I get it. You wanted to make it up to Tate for all those years you were in England and as much as it eats you up, she wanted it like that. You were safe thousands of miles away and she could breathe easy. I don't agree with it. I would feel like you, man, if the roles were reversed and we were talking about Carys. I get it. But putting yourself in the fucking lion's lair with that bitch is crazy and it's going to blow your sister's mind."

I groan and rake a hand through my hair. Tate is going to kill me when she finds out what I've been keeping from her. I could tell her we're even for all she kept from me when she was married to Bobby, but something tells me she won't find it even remotely funny.

"Listen, just keep doing what you're doing for now. I know you want to help those women and we'll do what we can. I'll bring in law enforcement, feed them what we can so we can make this legit. And most of all, make it stick." Ry pats my shoulder and my phone buzzes.

I pull it out to find a text from the hospital. My patient has a fever. "Damn, I have to go."

Tommie sighs, tugging once more on my sleeve, which she's been holding all this time. "I wanted to talk."

"Me too. Are you still good for the fundraiser tonight?"

"Yes." She mock gags. "Pick me up at my place?"

"Yup." I lean in to kiss her cheek. "Ry, let's talk about how to tell Tate, I want to be there."

He nods and as I turn to leave, Tommie grips my forearm to stop me, wrapping her arms around my neck. All the tension seeps out of my body. She pushes herself into me as if wanting to crawl inside and I almost lose my mind. If we were alone, I'd let her.

"And see you later." She kisses the edge of my mouth and pulls away.

MAX

After monitoring my patient and her fever, which is still there but steady, I go home to get ready for the hospital fundraiser and then instruct the driver to bring the limo to the front of the building. We're going in the opposite direction to pick up Tommie and we need to get a move on. As I step into the elevator, a text comes in.

Tommie: Are you still good for tonight? Patient okay?

Me: Yes, all good. Coming to pick you up now.

Tommie: I'm still at the office. Can you pick me up here?

Me: Sure. What about your dress? Or are you slumming it tonight? 😉

Tommie: Cute. I picked it up from home during lunch.

Me: OK. On my way.

Tommie: See you soon.

Traffic is a nightmare and Tommie hustles through the front doors of the HC building. She has a black garment bag in one hand and a small overnight bag in the other. The driver hops out to open her door.

"Hey, thanks for coming to get me." She slides along the seat, stopping to bump against me. "I lost track of time. Sorry."

"You're doing me a favor."

"Where to, Dr. Conrad?" the driver asks, locking eyes with me in the rear-view mirror.

Quirking a brow, I take in her pantsuit, which resembles a sailor uniform but way sexier and is not appropriate for tonight's dinner. At some point today, she made it a point to change out of yesterday's dress.

Her gaze holds a question of her own. "What? We're already late. We should get going to the dinner."

"But where will you change?"

"In the car." Unzipping her navy pants, she shimmies the fabric down her long golden legs without a care for the driver or me.

A stirring starts low in my belly and I hit the privacy button to raise the partition between the front and back of the car. What the hell is she doing?

Unintentional or not, this is a striptease, without the music—none needed—and I have to force myself to look away from her striking, and soon to be bare, body.

"Head to the fundraiser," I say to the driver through the intercom and make the mistake of letting my eyes stray in her direction.

She is now topless. Her bronze skin shimmers against the rich purple fabric of her bra, cradling her firm, round breasts. Sweet agony pulls at my balls, desire licking at the base of my spine, and I shift uncomfortably beside her.

The urge to reach out and trace my fingers along the edges of her bra, riding the swell of her chest, rushes through me. I flex my fingers, curling one hand around the armrest to stop myself.

"Someone could see you." I compel my eyes down her torso toward her slim waist, round hips and the perfect V between her thighs.

Sweet Moses, I have gone to heaven without leaving earth. The matching silk panties, covering her mound, are mesmerizing. Wrenching my head to look out the tinted window, I realize it's unlikely anyone can see a thing inside the car but that thought doesn't make this any easier.

A zipper ticks and fabric rustles. "It's just skin and bones. You're a doctor, you should understand. It's no different than the clothes I wear."

I turn to face her once more as she lifts her fine ass off the leather seat to hike the dress up her body. I'm not uncomfortable with naked bodies. In my profession, I see more than my fair share and a breast is no different than an elbow to me. Well, in a clinical sense. But this is Tommie. She isn't a patient. And she's gorgeous, inside and outside. And right now this is a lot of glorious skin.

If I'm being honest with myself, I'm having a hard time remembering we're just friends. She's my best friend.

I want her. And it's more than desire and arousal. I care about her deeply, and now, seeing her like this, puts my emotions in a tailspin. I haven't been able to stop thinking about our kiss. The impulse to touch and taste was too great.

"What do you think, if a man sees my tits, he knows me? That he can see into my soul?" An innocent desire simmers in her coffee bean gaze and it's easily recognizable because I feel it too.

"It means nothing," she whispers. "No one sees my soul. Understands my heart. No one. Unless I let them in."

My fingers sink into the warm satiny flesh just above her knee and I battle for the control to stop there. I will not venture any farther. It's hard when touching her calms some of my inner turmoil.

"Yes. That's true." I'm all too familiar with only knowing some of Tommie.

We *are* close but there is a part of her, some of her past that she keeps locked away. It isn't a secret that I only know some of her backstory. I want more with her and if she does too, she will have to let me in, tell me all.

Her feet slip into the opening of the gown and I reluctantly remove my hand from her knee. The sheer bodice glides up her slender body and settles into place. With the flick of a wrist and some fancy hand movements, she pulls her bra from beneath the dress. My throat is immediately dry.

Lavender, silver and gold gossamer fabric, like iridescent butterflies, rests on her now braless chest. Tantalizing. *Help me.*

"Fuck," I release a pained groan. "If I'd known you were putting on a show, I'd have..."

"You'd have what?" Her voice is low and husky.

She leans toward me and heat flares, spreading like the burn of alcohol coursing through my body. My attraction isn't going away; I need to talk to her but now isn't the time, or more importantly the place, not in the car, not like this.

I have to make an appearance at this thing, and we won't make it out of the car if her feelings are mutual. And I can't forget about my mother. Tonight's an opportunity to get more information out of her since she'll be there. So I do the only thing I can think of to derail this slippery slope of desire—I make a joke.

"I'd have stopped the car and got out." My voice is pained, and she laughs, fastening the side zipper before facing me.

"You like?" She looks like she's stepped from the pages of Vogue even without a drop of makeup on her face.

"A lot," is all I manage to say, adjusting my pants that are somehow shrinking by the second in the crotch.

I'm exhausted fighting the urge to touch and taste, or worse, blow my load. My best friend is an enigma. With looks a wannabe model would kill for and a mind geniuses would envy, she's one of a kind, all the way.

I want her, but am I willing to take the risk to have her? What if she runs once we talk and I lose her?

For the rest of the drive, I busy myself with my phone, trying to stop the swirling sensations of desire and confusion. Finally we arrive and she's nothing short of magnificent. Dark glossy wisps of hair dance around her beautifully exotic face.

"You're amazing." I take her hand and lead us from the car.

"You mean my dress?"

"You in that dress *are* stunning, but I mean *you* are amazing."

A lilting melodic laugh springs from her elegant throat. "You're good for my ego." She pats the lapel of my tux. "I'll keep you."

"You better." My arm snakes around her trim waist, bringing her flush against me.

"Does this hurt?" Her fingers lightly glide along my bruised cheek.

"Nah. It's fine." We still and she releases a breathy sigh as my eyes dip to her slightly parted lips.

"Listen, we can't get into this now because I've got to get in there but…" Kissing her is all I want to do. It would be so easy to take what I crave. My tongue delving into her sweet, warm mouth. Her heaving breasts against my chest and hands on me.

Fuck, we can't.

Or can we?

"You're my best friend and I want more." My hand tightens on her hip as we press together. "And I think you feel the same way."

"What do you mean, more?" Her hand, resting on my shoulder, digs into my jacket.

"You and me like this." We're hip to hip now, facing each other, and I take a quick look around.

We're outside and any of my colleagues could walk by at any moment. I've got to control myself.

My lips crash onto hers, one hand stealing into her hair, and she leans in, grabbing the back of my neck.

Yes, she wants more too.

Before we get too carried away, she pulls away first, a smile tugging at her now-swollen lips, and I feel it in my groin.

"Yeah, I want more too." She brushes her lips once more over mine.

"Oh I so wish I didn't need to go in there." I tear myself away from her warm, sexy body.

"Me too." She loops her arm with mine once more. "So let's just get this over with."

"Okay. Shall we?" I clear my throat, turning toward the entrance of the museum, and she nods, cheeks pink, as her arm rests snugly in the crook of mine.

The event is teeming with our Board of Directors, senior hospital administration and staff, as well as wealthy donors and supporters. Barbara, my ex, stands five feet away from us with her date, Dr. Keith Branson.

He's an endocrinologist and ten years my senior. Decent guy, excellent physician, and my lack of reaction—I feel nothing at seeing her or her date—only confirms our break-up was long overdue.

She flinches and doesn't recover quickly enough for me to miss her response to my date. Astonishment shifts to disappointment, then hurt. Tommie was never her cup of tea, as she would put it. She considered my best friend a threat even though nothing happened, but I suppose Barbara saw what we weren't ready to accept at the time.

Tommie and I belong together.

My ex approaches in a simple navy gown, functional and attractive, and her blonde hair is pulled back into her standard, no-nonsense bun.

"Oh boy." Tommie removes her arm from my elbow, interlacing our fingers as Barbara nears, her gaze stuck on where we're joined.

"Max." She air kisses both my cheeks. I've fallen into the 'acquaintance' camp. Those fake kisses and her tight, forced smiles say so much about her.

"Barbara, it's lovely to see you." I dip my chin in greeting and she pays me no mind, giving Tommie her own set of empty kisses. "I'm surprised to see you here."

"Well, I hadn't planned on it, but Keith heard…" she pauses, perhaps waiting for some kind of reaction from me to her date. She doesn't get any. "Well, that we're no longer together, and he invited me."

"That's great." I smile, unfazed. "I know how much you love these things. Well, please excuse us, we're going to get drinks. Enjoy the evening."

Her eyes dim and she slips on her perfunctory smile. Dr. Branson stands back, watching the exchange. I nod, giving him my unspoken approval although it isn't necessary, but somehow, I get the sense he's waiting for it.

"That wasn't awkward at all." Tommie's sarcastic.

"Yeah, sorry about that. I didn't think that one through. I knew she'd be here but..."

"Hey, it's okay. Was this the first time you've seen each other since splitting?"

"Yup." I sidle up to the bar, suddenly feeling lighter and not sure if it's for having faced Barbara or because I'm here with Tommie.

I've never liked these things and even with Barbara on my arm, I dreaded them. What we had was nice, a way to pass the time, but really no substance. I glance to Tommie. My relationship with Barbara was nothing compared to what I feel for the woman at my side.

"What'll you have?" I tap my fingers on the bar.

"Champagne, please."

I place our order and take in the room, grunting when I spot my mother not too far from us. "The ice queen is here."

She follows my eye line and groans. "I know you have to talk to her, but do I have to go with you?" She wrinkles her nose like something smells bad.

"Thanks for having my back."

"I'll go with you. It's just that we don't like each other."

"Really? Because there is so much to like about her." My sardonic grin brings out one of her own. "I won't subject you to that."

"I knew there was a reason why I love you so."

Her words aren't something new but on the heels of that car ride and then our kiss and our desire for more… her words carry more meaning, so much more than before.

We share a silent longing. I wish we were anywhere but here. When we get home, we are moving our relationship forward. And I'm not talking sex, although I'd certainly be down with that.

Tommie breaks our connection and pecks my cheek. I want to keep her at my side, hold her close, but don't.

"You go get that over with. I see Edith and her husband over there. I'm going to say hello. Come join us when you can."

I nod with a groan, wishing I could follow her. I much prefer a lighthearted chat with my administrative assistant any day of the week. But I can't let this opportunity go to waste.

"Max." Regal in her long white gown, my mother smiles and kisses my cheek while squeezing my bicep affectionately.

I'm sick just thinking about the woman from this morning. Taya basically ordered her death.

"Mother."

"Where's Barbara? I thought I saw her with you?"

"She's here but with someone else."

"What? Oh no." Frowning, her chemically-filled face barely moves and her lips twist. "You broke up? What happened?"

She doesn't care for Barbara any more or less than she would any other woman I'm seeing. She only cares about the Stafford name. They are well respected in the medical community and in my mother's twisted mind, my association with Barbara gives her legitimacy.

"We're over. The decision was mutual."

"That's such a shame. What happened? Barbara's such a lovely—"

"I don't want to talk about it."

"Fine." Her lips press into a thin line and she inhales deeply, pushing down her frustration. "Did you come with anyone?"

"Tommie."

She flinches, narrowing her eyes. "That's unfortunate."

"Don't start."

"Speaking of being difficult." She drops her voice to a whisper. "About this morning. You need to be more cooperative. More and more, it's a challenge to get you to come when I call. This operation needs to run smoothly, and you need to play your part."

Her tone is hard as is her expression and while I'm pleased she brought this up, I'm both surprised and disturbed that she's mentioning her work and my involvement here. She hasn't done so before. In fact, she's been more than discreet.

"Fine. Tell me why you'll need me more." I step closer, making sure she is the only one to hear our conversation. "Are you planning a war? And what about those women?"

She stiffens, tightening her lips together, and it's unlikely I'll get anything out of her. From the corner of my eye, a tall dark-haired man, well dressed, pushing his mid-forties, approaches.

Instantly, Taya melts. Her cheeks flush, steely blue eyes liquefy, and she smiles. And I don't mean her usual cold-hearted smile as if she's seen how you die and can't wait for that occasion. This is a genuine, full-faced brightening smile.

"There you are." Mother angles toward the mysterious man whose eyes, for a brief second, are trained elsewhere, beyond us.

"I'm Ash Naire." His tar black eyes flick to me, sharp and penetrating like the tip of a knife piercing flesh. "You must be Max. I've heard so much about you."

His voice is deep with a slight accent that I can't quite place. He extends his hand. The handshake is strong and steady, much like his unnerving gaze.

"Hello. I wish I could say the same, but this is the first I'm hearing of you."

I don't hide my ignorance and annoyance and my mother makes a *tsk*ing sound low in her throat, signaling her disapproval. The corners of his full mouth twitch up but that is all. No smile.

While I haven't met many of my mother's associates over the years, this one is a hardass. His expression morphs back to impassive. On the surface, he's as calm and uninteresting as the surface of a lake, but my insides convulse at the aura of inhumanity surrounding him.

I sense a darkness unlike any I've come across before, and I've had many a chance with those in my mother's company. At first blush, he and Taya are a lot alike and that makes me more than a little wary of the guy.

"Max, Ash and I are…" she pauses, looking up at him like someone who needs his permission to speak freely.

What the hell is going on? I've never seen my mother like this. Not even with my father, whom she adored.

"Acquaintances," Ash says, and the shine in her gaze dims somewhat.

"Well, I wouldn't quite say that." She rests a hand on his forearm and there's a sharpness of her own to her words.

I've never seen the woman so blatantly rejected before, no one dared, and what's more interesting is how quickly she recovers.

He's unperturbed and distracted, once again glancing over my shoulder as something indescribable flits through his wicked black eyes.

"Excuse me." Without another look at us, he leaves in the direction he came.

Mother flicks her white blonde hair over her shoulder, painstakingly forcing a synthetic smile in an attempt to hide her wounded pride.

Ash saunters over to the corner once more and casually rests his back against the wall. He excused himself for no other reason than to be alone.

Sophisticated, controlled and impenitent of his rudeness, he's transfixed on something or someone else. Whatever it is, it has his complete and utter attention.

But I'm not fooled. His interests may be preoccupied, but this man is very aware of everything going on around him.

His dark face is taut, hard like the impenetrable rock of a mountainside, and my body vibrates when for a split second his lips tighten and lift to form a snarl. He bares his stark white teeth like a wolf ready to sink its fangs into its next kill.

TOMMIE

Edith is a sweet woman, motherly and a bit of a spitfire at the same time. She's a fool for Max with his calm demeanor and good looks. She'll do just about anything for him.

"I know I'm repeating myself but you're the most beautiful woman here." She beams, her short, doughy arm still attached to mine. "Isn't she, Roger?"

She taps her husband on the arm and he smiles dutifully, nodding his head. Roger is maybe an inch, perhaps two, taller than his wife, but where she is round, he is reed thin. He's also the exact opposite to her gregarious nature, quiet and easily going unnoticed.

"She sure did." His blush reddens the longer he forces himself to hold eye contact.

"Stop it, you're going to give a girl a huge ego." I rapidly bat my eyelashes, deliberately exaggerating the move. Edith tilts her head back to laugh, delighted.

"Poor Max is stuck with the dragon lady." She frowns in their direction and pulls me closer. "It's really a shame she won't leave him alone. Yes, she's his mother, and I don't want to take that away from anyone, but that woman is the furthest thing from a mother." She purses her lips in pure disdain.

Nodding, I glance over my shoulder, commiserating with her on Max's predicament, when everything stops.

The chatter and music fades and a creepy silence blankets any sound within my mind. The room shrinks and darkens, and even the people and things around me vanish or freeze like inanimate objects, uninteresting and inconsequential.

Everything narrows to one point, or more precisely, one person standing in a darkened corner of the room. His gaze isn't on me, thank God, but I'm sure he knows I'm here.

My teeth begin to chatter as if my blood is literally turning to ice. I need to get Max and get out of here. Maybe if I leave for a few, I can text Max and he will meet me outside.

FLUSTERED, I interrupt Edith as she rambles on about something else, something I completely missed. "I'm so sorry but excuse me. I'm not feeling so hot. I need to go to the washroom."

"Oh dear, I'll go with you." Her soft wrinkled hand wraps around my wrist and I flinch at the contact.

She stiffens and I regret my instinctual reaction to retreat. None of this has anything to do with her but she doesn't know that. It's not her. It's me. And more specifically, it's *him*.

"No, that's okay. Thank you."

"But you look suddenly very pale." She frets, her brown eyes filling with concern, and her husband finds the courage to look at me.

"Edith's right, are you sure you're okay?"

"I'll be fine. I just need to splash some water on my face. I think it's all the people. It's hot in here."

I step back from them, positioning myself in a way that I can see him while I exit the room. Concern etches their faces and I try to smile, a real one so it will calm their nerves.

"I'll be fine. I'll be right back."

Fortunately, the ladies' room is empty. After sending a text to Max to let him know where I am and that I don't feel well, I collapse against the wall, squeezing my eyes shut to stop the black spots from swimming in my vision. My focus is on deepening and lengthening my breath. I can't have a panic attack. Not now of all times. I've had one too many in my lifetime and they're debilitating, not to mention how vulnerable and exposed I'd be.

A few minutes pass and finally, my breathing is under control and my mind clearer. But I'm not out of the woods yet. My hands tremble when I turn on the faucet and as the water runs, I let it flow for a few seconds to get colder.

The deafening thrumming of my heartbeat fills my ears as the organ batters against my ribcage. Coming face to face with him was inevitable, but I never imagined tonight could be a possibility.

Still shaking, I cup my hands together, filling them with cold water, so cold it chills my bones. I splash my face several times, grateful for waterproof mascara, and blot my cheeks dry with a scratchy paper towel.

The bathroom door creaks. Someone enters the bathroom and while I'm no longer alone, I don't bother to look. I'm not ready to plaster on a fake smile. Then the click of the lock banning entry causes me to pause and try to quickly get over my terror. And then I realize my mistake. I left the safety of numbers in the ballroom, so intent was I on getting away, and now it's too late. Terror is here.

"Thomasina." A low, gravelly voice, the one of my nightmares, is a shot to my heart.

I twirl in his direction, but don't have a chance to fully take him in. He pounces like a starving beast. His body presses into mine, pushing my back into the wall, and his long fingers wrap around my throat, tightening and releasing his grip intermittently like a pulse.

My dark, depraved past comes flooding back and I struggle to breathe. Unable to swallow, saliva gathers in my mouth and I wonder if I could drown on my own body fluid. At the very least, it would be an escape from this man.

"Let me go." My demand is forced as I thrust my body against his, repulsed at our proximity.

The longer he holds me, the more I become his captive. I tug at his hand around my neck with both of mine as my fingernails scrape at his flesh and the cuff of his jacket. A disturbing smile crawls along his mouth, souring my insides, and his obsidian eyes are molten, singing my flesh.

"Halt."

It's only a word.

One little word.

Four letters.

Yet it wields so much power, hurtling me back a decade. My hands fall to my sides and I still. The word locks my mind, body and soul, physically and emotionally. But it's different than before.

Not meaningless, but his command no longer holds the power it once did. It isn't as intense or incapacitating. I'm not on my knees, powerless and folding in on myself like a turtle.

But my muscles remember. Every fiber is taut, every joint is tense, and it's like I'm standing on the edge of an abyss. My body is on the brink of his order, just waiting for my mind to pull the trigger.

To succumb.

"I've missed you." The tip of his forefinger skates down my cheek, wiping at my tears. Tears I didn't even know had fallen. "You're as beautiful as ever."

"Please let me go."

My wobbly voice sickens me, as does my politeness. I hate how easily he reduces me to a scared little girl, so eager to follow his instruction and please. So eager to make him stop.

"You've been a bad girl, Thomasina. A very bad girl. I should skin you alive for what you've cost me."

His grip intensifies around my neck and air stops flowing. As each second passes and his hold tightens, his smile grows.

Everything burns.

Hurts.

My eyes bulge. Saliva rises like a tide up my throat and mucus builds in my sinuses. It's as if every part of me is working with him to stop any oxygen from filling my lungs. I beg with my eyes for him to release me. But there is no hope; I'm staring into the darkest depths of hell.

"And Evan Hart. I've a special plan for him. He deserves to die slowly and painfully." He loosens his hold but doesn't let go.

His hatred toward Van, the man who saved me, is evident in his hostile eyes. I won't let him hurt Van. I'd die first and will if that's what it takes.

"Nooo." My fevered wail is foreign to my own ears.

The tears are uncontrollable now. Torrents rushing down my cheeks. Hot and wet.

There's a knock on the door and my first thought is Max, and I'm overcome by relief and more fear, if that's even possible. He would kill Max.

But then a dainty voice says through the thick wood, "Hello? Please open up. Are you okay in there?"

I want to scream for the woman to get help, but that would draw his attention to her. There is no telling what he'd do. He could just as easily ignore her as kill her. He doesn't fear consequence and pays the interruption no mind.

He hasn't a care about anyone finding him in the women's washroom, abusing someone, no less. Nothing ever fazes him. We are all on this earth to entertain him. Humans are his to do with as he wishes. His greatest pleasure is bringing pain, destroying lives.

"Leave Evan alone, please." Remembering how much he likes my pleas, especially the most mild and polite ones, I willingly slide into old patterns. Manners are important to him.

He chuckles, loving my distress and clearly knowing he's struck a chord. There's no point in me denying it. While I've tracked him this past decade, he too has been tracking me. I no longer have any doubt.

He likely knew where I was all along. I'd foolishly pushed that thought out of my mind all these years. Even knowing he had the best hacker I've ever met, Zero, doing his bidding, I refused to face the simple fact he could take me whenever he wanted. It was only a matter of time.

"And you now go by Tommie. What a travesty. You're not a man."

Large fingers grope my breast and because I'm not wearing a bra, he easily finds my nipple, pinching hard.

"You're a woman."

The pain shoots through me and every one of my organs spasms and shrinks as something cold and poisonous seeps into my bones. My blood toxic. My heart stone.

It doesn't matter that it's been ten years since Van rescued me from his clutches.

It's as if no time has passed.

I'm still at the mercy of this man.

He was slowly killing me all those years ago and it feels the same way right now.

The mess of my mind clears. The wild thrumming of my heart, hard in my chest, steadies to a firm rhythm and my breath slows. He didn't kill me then and he won't get to do it now.

My terror is violently shoved aside, rage taking its place. How dare he lay a hand on me? I won't accept the past as my future. I am not his and never was.

I knock his hand from my breast and writhe to get free. The fingers of his one hand still dig into the flesh of my throat and he clamps down harder than before.

"We're not done, Thomasina. We'll never be done. It will do you good to remember that." He leans into me—his hot breath, acrid with the bitter smell of smoke, washes over my face. "I could have come for you at any moment, so don't go running to Evan. Or Max. Or anyone at Hart Corporation. If so, I will deal with them in my own special way." His voice drips with intimidation and I won't deny, panic skitters through me and he must see it. "Something tells me you won't."

His fingers flex, pushing me into the wall, and my larynx burns, the crushing sensation overwhelming. My head is going to explode, until just as suddenly, he releases me.

Bending forward, I cough and gulp, inhaling copious amounts of air, so intent on breathing I don't see him leave. The next thing I know, I hear the voices of women outside the bathroom.

One says chidingly, "This is the women's washroom, what were you doing in there?"

"Did you see that man? How rude of him, and he locked himself in—"

When the ladies round the corner into the bathroom, silence descends like a heavy, dark curtain.

Their gazes fall on me, hunched over, my face red and tear-stained.

"Oh my God, are you all right?" an older woman asks as the ginger-haired one rushes to my side.

A middle-aged brunette turns back toward the door, saying she's getting security. I rush past the three women, out into the corridor, hoping to find Max. We need to get out of here.

I crash into his solid frame and his scent hits me like a solid, comforting blanket. I wrap my arms around his waist, burying my face into his chest, not wanting him to see the state I'm in but also needing his warmth and strength.

"Sorry I took so long." His strong comforting arms hold me. "What's wrong?" He brushes the hair from my face and thrusts me backward to get a better look at me. "What the hell happened?"

"I wasn't feeling well." I use the excuse I gave Edith, unable to look him in the eye.

I will tell him, but not now. We need to leave.

"Were you sick?" His strong jaw is set hard and concern rolls off him in waves.

Max Conrad has both the sexy, protective streak many women flock to, and a tender, caring side others crave.

"Can we just go? I know you have to be here but I'm—"

"Of course." His wrists rest on either side of my neck and his eyes dip to where his warm, reassuring hands cup my face. "What happened?" Fingers trace what I'm guessing are now marks along my neck.

He freezes, furrowing his brow and stabbing me with a concerned glare. "What the fuck happened? You've got bruising as if someone choked you."

He's too observant and a damn good doctor. "Can we just leave, and I promise I will tell you everything."

His strong fingers softly cradle my cheeks. "You're scaring the shit out of me. Do we need to call the cops?"

I glance down the long hallway over Max's shoulder in a way to avert his gaze, but I'm hit with another blow.

He is there.

Ash.

He's standing forty, no, more like fifty feet away, resting his shoulder against the wall with his legs casually crossed at the ankles. The pose is odd for him. It's almost a lazy, carefree look and I've never seen him anything less than alert and challenging, ready to strike.

His black as night eyes bore into my skull even at this distance, and an overwhelming sense of falling swamps me.

We must get out of here. The police won't help. He'll be gone by the time they arrive.

"No. Please let's leave."

MAX

We burst through the large door into the dark summer night, her long sable hair flying behind her. Holding my hand tightly, she races down the stairs like Satan is on our heels.

I had called the driver on our way out and fortunately the car idles at the curb. Shoulders tense and stomach in knots, I'm sick with worry. Her neck... someone tried to choke her, and leaving without making sure whoever did this is dealt with doesn't sit right with me.

The driver stands with the back door open and before Tommie slides in, she peers over her shoulder, casting a hard glare back at the entrance we just exited. Ominous expectation, ready for someone to walk out of those doors. But who? By her expression — the devil himself.

What the hell happened? My heart bashes around in my chest and I feel my blood pressure climbing. Was it my mother? She's controlling in every aspect of the word and wouldn't be above threatening Tommie to stay away from me. But with force in a public place? That doesn't make sense.

Taya is more discreet than that; she has a reputation to uphold, although she's no less violent behind closed doors.

I'm not even buckled in when Tommie's body presses against mine and she rests her head on my shoulder, her forehead nestling into my neck.

"Talk to me," I murmur into the crown of her dark head.

"I will, but can we just sit for a bit? And talk when we get home?" Her warm breath coasts over my neck, sending tingles through me.

I'm briefly soothed with the knowledge that I'll know more soon and for now, all she needs is to be with me. My arms tighten around her body. We sit in silence for the entire drive to my place and remain so as we take the elevator up.

Once in my place, she kneels to pet a happy Gunnar, who's wagging his tail and leaning into her as she strokes behind his silky ear.

I walk further in, turning on lights, and while I want answers now, I don't push. "What can I get you?"

"I'm good, thanks." Still shaky, she walks down the hallway toward the bedrooms.

Both dog and I follow like shadows as she passes both guest bedrooms and enters my room, stopping at the end of the bed. She's in my room and I don't know what to make of it.

"I need a shower," she whispers, her back to me as she trudges to the bathroom. "Then we'll talk."

"Are you okay?" I flick on the light behind her and she nods, not sparing me a glance.

Revulsion mars her features as she stares at her reflection in the mirror. I don't like what I see, or more specifically, how she's reacting to what she sees. Her expression is laden with shame or blame. But for what?

If only I knew what the hell was going on, then I might be able to help. I'm struggling to stop myself from conjuring what could have happened to make this night take such a drastic turn.

Patience. I need patience. Anything else won't help the situation. Time is what she clearly needs. I will give her that and then we will figure it out together.

I turn the door and minutes pass with no sound from the bathroom as I undress, anxious to get out of the proverbial dark. After several long minutes, the shower still hasn't started. Tapping on the door, I peer in to find her in the same spot I left her.

"Tommie." Now standing in front of her, my hands grasp her shoulders. "Look at me."

I'm close enough to see how her dark chocolate eyes teem with unrest. It's deep and persistent. The kind that spreads through your muscles, blood and bones. My knees lock, fighting the urge to buckle under the weight of comprehension. Whatever this is, it's huge.

"I need help with my dress." She lifts an arm, revealing the side zipper, and relief courses through me.

Maybe I'm overreacting and her fixed state is a simple access problem. She's stuck in her dress. But the longer I think about it, the more uneasy I become. She was more than resourceful when she put her dress on in the car. She didn't need my help.

The zipper ticks down her curves and I slide the dress from one shoulder, far enough that she can do the rest herself.

Earlier tonight, overcome with attraction and arousal, this would have felt like an invitation, but now all I have is an overpowering desire to protect.

"You good now?" I clasp her shoulder and she nods. "Call me if you need anything."

"Okay."

Eventually, the water turns on and I gather a shirt and the smallest boxers I have, leaving them on the bathroom counter while she showers. Coming to the end of the bed, I sit, trying not to jump to conclusions or speculate any further about the night's events.

Every possibility ends with her being assaulted. And if that's the case… fuck, I can't go there unless I have to. The waiting and not knowing is driving me more insane.

With my head in my hands, elbows propped on my thighs, I wait. I'm not sure how long it is until her legs pass my vision, on her way to the far side of the bed.

She slips under the covers, pausing when our gazes collide. "Is it okay if I sleep here? In your bed?"

Never has she looked so young and so vulnerable. Her face is bare, hair knotted in a large messy bun on the top of her head and my t-shirt hangs off one shoulder.

"Sure, but let's talk." My heart lurches in anticipation.

"Yes." She pats the empty side of the bed and I make my way next to her. "I've been thinking about telling you this for some time now."

"This? What do you mean?"

"About my past. I was going to tell you today, and then when you told us about Taya, I figured it could wait." She hangs her head, staring at the sheets.

"None of that has anything to do with you. With us. If you're worried it's too much. Never. I'm always here for you."

Deep guilt, or dare I even think, shame shimmers in her gaze and I don't fully understand, but I hope she lets me in, so I finally get the full picture. So I can help her. So I can be there for her how she needs me.

Nodding, she smiles through a sheen of tears. "Just a week ago, my past popped up online, and since then I've been lost, trying to figure out what to do and also hoping it would go away."

"Did you tell Van?" The thought of her dealing with this alone is my first concern.

He's a pillar of strength for her, and while at times I wish she would turn to me, I'm grateful for him. Grateful that she has someone to go to.

"Yes." Her fingers lightly graze my stubbled cheek. "I know it's time to face the past. Even with years of therapy, none of what happened is fully behind me. No justice was served even though we tried. And tonight has made it abundantly clear that now's the time to end this, once and for all. He isn't going away."

"He?" My spine stiffens.

Someone is responsible for what happened to her, that isn't a surprise, but I always figured from what I know of Van, he would have taken care of it. He would have made sure those who hurt her paid. It doesn't sound like that's the case.

Her lower lip trembles and her head turns away from me to look straight ahead, pulling back her shoulders as if strengthening not only her posture but also her resolve.

"This isn't easy for me. I never told you everything because... well, let's just say if I hadn't had to tell Van, I wouldn't have. It's ugly and unbearable and I'm to blame."

A raw, bottomless pain saturates not only her voice but her entire being, and my chest threatens to explode. My heart breaks. She hasn't even begun to tell her story. I'm blind to what she faced and yet I ache to shield her from those memories.

I care so deeply for her, love her, and I'm so helpless against the pain and suffering she has already endured and which I'm sensing is threatening to hurt her again. God, if only I could erase it all, I would.

TOMMIE

"He knew my father." My teeth clack together, hard, and my nostrils flare. I don't want to do this but have to, for me.

Tonight was horrible, and the longer I keep my past to myself, the longer Ash has power over me. He threatened those I love and wants me to keep my mouth shut. But if I do as he says, he keeps all the power. Not going to happen.

"I was ten when my parents died in a fire."

Max already knows this, but he doesn't know the story behind it. Why there was a fire in the first place and who started it. All I've been able to tell him is how I was an orphan in a horrible situation where I was abused until Van rescued me.

"One day, after school, I came home to find my father arguing with a man in his office. I'd never seen him before, and they didn't know I was there. The stranger was berating Papa."

I pause and it's as if I'm standing in the hallway shadows of my home listening to this stranger's sharp, demanding voice, spewing hurtful, offensive things at my father.

"If you knew Papa, you'd know that was unheard of. He was a proud man, no one ever treated him with anything but respect. Yet this man was not only insulting but threatening my father and family. And worst of all, my father stood there, silent, taking everything this man threw at him. Not once did he fight back."

"What did you do?" He slides closer, resting his hand on mine in my lap and I intertwine our fingers, comforted by his presence even if I'm afraid to share this with him.

"My father owed him money. A lot of money. I was really bothered by what I saw but I was also cocky. Very computer savvy, a budding hacker." The thought pulls a humorless laugh from deep in my chest.

If I could go back and talk to the younger me, before everything fell apart, oh what I would say. My arrogance led to my downfall.

"I was so mad at this man. I'd never seen my father so dejected and I was sure I could help. I used the only power I had and went online to find anything I could about him. He was a businessman, wealthy, and little did I know, for all my digging, I was leaving the equivalent of my fingerprints everywhere."

A deep sigh drains the tension mounting in my shoulders, but it's short-lived. My anxiety isn't going anywhere.

"I hacked his bank accounts. It was a stupid idea and at the time, the biggest fucking thrill. I thought because he had so much money, he'd never miss a few hundred thousand."

I shake my head, fingers curling, and angrily thump a fist against the top of my thigh.

Max releases my other hand to stop my self-harm. "No, don't." His tone is firm as he wraps his warm hand around mine. "Don't beat yourself up. Please. I don't blame you for whatever happened."

"Well you should, and you might change your mind once you hear it all."

I swallow against a sudden agonizing rigidity in my throat and blink away the sting at the back of my eyes. So much for therapy. I thought I'd overcome the excruciating shame and guilt but it's all here.

"Are you okay to go on?" His hand cups the nape of my neck.

"Yes. I need to. I moved his money. My plan was to give it to my father and he'd use it to pay the man back. Isn't that genius? Pay the bastard with his own money. It didn't take me long, only hours, to realize how flawed my idea was and I quickly undid everything. Again, I foolishly thought no one would be the wiser and I'd figure out another way to help my father."

We share a weak, pathetic smile. Both lamenting the naivety of a silly girl.

"Papa didn't know what I'd done, and I thought I had time. I was wrong. This horrible man had his own brilliant hacker and they knew everything. I'd messed up. It was too late. The next day, I came home to men in my house. My parents were held at gunpoint and that despicable man promised them death, and as if that wasn't enough punishment, he told them he would spare me a similar fate. I would live but I would be his."

An uncontrolled moan leaps from my throat and tears fall fast and free down my cheeks.

I've been deliberately not saying his name. Not tonight, not after seeing him and having his hands on me again. It's all too much right now.

"Fuck." His forehead rests against mine and as I begin to cry, he wraps me in his arms.

There's still so much more to say but my shame chokes me, crushing my lungs. Endless guilt rips me in two like the crude, gut-wrenching cut of a serrated blade.

I push away, needing to finish this. "I was his captive for five years. At first, I was locked in a room. Alone. Fed and schooled. He only introduced me to his tech guy. For the longest time, those two were the only people I saw.

"He messed with my head. Tried to reframe my memories, show me how I was to blame for the death of my parents and my own captivity. He wore me down through isolation. Then coercion and violence."

Max's eyes widen, horrified and enraged, and I look away, unable to maintain eye contact if I'm to tell him the worst of it.

"I thought I was in hell, but I was so wrong. Hell was still to come. It started when I was thirteen, I think. Time didn't have meaning."

"What started?"

"The... sex." I mash my hands over my cheeks, wanting to hide... hide my shame.

He makes an indecipherable mumble at my side and uncontrolled rage vibrates off him. Hanging my head, I fight the urge to vomit or run, and instead I refuse to cower despite the shame and draw on strength and courage. He won't get away with what he's done.

Wiping at my wet face, I straighten and look at Max. His expression holds nothing but love and concern.

"At first, it was only him..." I hiccup, my breath catching on disgrace, which I stomp out with my rage.

"Fuuuck." His hands fly to his hair, gripping the sides of his head as his teeth gnash together.

My shame and guilt are constant struggles. While the past few years have been more days of victory than anything else, thanks to my therapy, I'm still unable to spill all the sordid details. I'm not ready, maybe I never will be, to share everything.

"He kept me in a cell."

"A cell?" He freezes but his gaze is alert and I almost see when the similarities of what I'm saying and what he witnessed in the warehouse basement hit him. "Do you think they are connected?"

I shake my head. "It isn't likely. Sex slavery is rampant all over the world. I was in England, I think, but I can't be sure. That's where Van found me."

"Tell me whoever did this to you is dead." His warm green eyes are fiery, and his body strung so tight that he might snap.

Air pushes through my tightened lungs and I say, "He's alive and in New York. I saw him tonight at the dinner."

Max grabs both my arms, squaring my body to look straight at him. "What? He lives in New York? Why didn't you tell me?"

"No, he lives in Europe. We think. His address of record is in Madrid, but we've had teams on the ground a few times and we've come up empty. We've never found him there."

"Why is he in New York? What happened tonight?" Worry emanates from his every word.

I tell him how my captor has come to New York before but never for more than a day or two. Then I explain what happened tonight—a confrontation and veiled threats—but I don't share all the gory details.

Withholding the more heart-stopping moments of the night is for my benefit more than his. Max wants to know everything. I just can't go through it again so soon. I'm already scared enough as it is.

Throughout it all, I'm deliberately not mentioning Ash by name. It's almost like Harry Potter and He Who Must Not Be Named. I worry if I utter the name, I'll conjure him into being. Right now, he's a nameless, faceless villain, and at times, it's like what I'm sharing could have happened to someone else.

"He did this?" Max's fingers delicately trace my neck where I'm sure I've got full-on bruising by now.

I nod, sinking my teeth into my bottom lip to quell the awful memory of Ash strangling me.

"I'm calling the police. They should arrest him." He springs to his feet and I scurry after him.

The dog leaps to my side—I wasn't even aware he was in the room —and I lunge to grab Max's arm. "No. Please don't."

He stops, peering at me over his shoulder, shocked. "Why the hell not?"

"He's slipped through our fingers every time we've tried to get him. This will be the same."

The women outside the ladies' washroom come to mind. They did see Ash, and I suppose we could try to track them down. But it would take time, and while we do that, who knows what Ash will do.

I shake the thought from my mind. "And even if we could press charges, they won't stick. It'll only provoke him and then who knows what. We need to think this through. Van is telling Ry and the rest of them. We'll fill them in on tonight and figure out what our next move is. We've got to be smart about this."

His shoulders finally deflate as if relenting and he nods. "Fine, but you're in danger. You're staying here and I'll get increased security."

My first impulse is to decline his offer and the added security, but I won't be safe on my own. Even after all these years and all my training with Van and HC, Ash is my weakness.

It's sad to admit but fear and my basest of instincts to survive override everything else when Ash is in front of me. All my training and skills take a back seat, or hell, leave the building, when I'm in his presence.

But still, staying with Max puts him in danger. For tonight, I will stay here.

"I wish I'd known…" He comes to stand in front of me. "Not just about tonight but all of it."

"Earlier, I just needed to get out of there."

He pulls me to him, and we cling to each other. It feels like he needs me as much as I need him. His strong arms are comforting, and I bury my face in the crook of his neck, stealing greedy breaths of his spicy, masculine scent. His scent calms me and makes me feel safe.

He kisses the crown of my head before resting his chin in the same spot. "I'm here for you. I won't let him hurt you again. We have to make him pay."

MAX

The delicious smell of bacon and eggs hits my senses and my stomach growls. I haven't eaten since last night, and even at that, I think I had two shrimps before I went looking for Tommie.

As I enter the kitchen, she stands at the stove flipping pancakes in my Audio Slave t-shirt. It's huge on her, and Gunnar sits dutifully at her feet, hoping for scraps. Man, I could get used to this. I'd like to wake up to her every day. In my bed. In my life.

"Hey, that looks good on you." I motion to my shirt, one silky shoulder exposed as the excess fabric around the neck hangs off her.

It's a struggle not to kiss her. Last night was tough for her, emotional for both of us, and I'm not sure if being intimate is what she needs right now. The horror of her past couldn't have been easy to recount; I had a hard time and it didn't even happen to me. But all of that changes nothing for me. My feelings for her are as strong as ever.

"I hope you're hungry. I went a bit overboard." With a mitt on, she removes a plate stacked with pancakes from the oven and my mouth waters.

"I'm starving." A plate of bacon and another with eggs are already on the table.

Tommie sits and I grasp the nape of her neck to kiss her softly. I'm not able to keep my hands and my mouth to myself. She leans into the kiss, one arm curling around my waist.

"Now that's a good morning," I murmur against her warm, soft lips.

"Good morning." She peers at me through her dark lashes as a flush works its way up her elegant neck.

She is so delectable. So strong, and I'm in awe of her. I want to tell her all this but also sense she's feeling me out based on everything from last night. We talked about taking our relationship beyond friends, then I learned about her past and she was assaulted. Not to mention she's gun-shy about relationships in general.

"Did you sleep okay?" I pull out the chair beside her.

"Sort of." She shrugs. "How are you doing?"

"Me?"

Why is she asking about me? I'm not the one who went through an unspeakable ordeal.

"Yeah. What I told you last night wasn't exactly easy to hear." Do I detect a hint of worry in her tone?

She loads several pancakes onto her plate, and even with my gaze on her, she doesn't look at me, busying herself with her food.

"No, it wasn't, but my concern is for you. How are you feeling?"

"I suppose I feel better for telling you. I've been meaning to for a while now." She's matter-of-fact as she grabs the butter and slathers her pancakes.

A wad of butter smears the tip of her thumb and her hand goes toward her mouth, but I intercept the movement. My hand wraps around her wrist, bringing her thumb toward my mouth.

"Tommie, look at me."

Her warm eyes connect with mine and everything feels much better.

"Last night. Your past. None of that changes anything for me. Like I said yesterday, I want you. I want more. And if anything, sharing everything with me only makes me want you even more."

My hot tongue sucks on her thumb and she gasps, eyes widening and cheeks heating.

"Max." My name is a breathy moan.

"Yeah?"

"I feel the same. As crazy as it may be, whatever this is between us, I want it too. But it scares me. There's so much going on right now. Your mom. My past. It's a lot to overcome."

"Yes. But none of that will change us. We'll face this together."

She nods, her smile growing, and I'm hopeful that I've put any of her reservations to rest.

"Let's eat and then head over to HC. Talk to Ry and Van. This looks awesome. I can't wait to dig in." I kiss the tip of her glistening thumb and release her wrist.

Shaking her head, she laughs and leans in for a quick kiss. "You're my best friend and I don't want to lose that. You're right, let's start with talking to Van and the guys."

We eat breakfast in silence until she pauses, placing her knife and fork on her plate. "Do you have to go into the hospital today?"

"Yes, just for a bit. How about dinner and a movie back here tonight? You could stay over again."

"Maybe." She pushes from the table with her dirty dishes in hand.

"What do you mean maybe?" I shove the last forkful in my mouth and turn to face her.

"I mean, let's talk to the guys first and see what they say."

Bounding from the chair, I march to her side and lean in, kissing her soft and sweet. Maple syrup lingers on her lips. She whimpers into my mouth and wraps her arms tightly around my neck. For long, hazy moments, we're lost. The world is no more.

We kiss until our lips are swollen and my body is strung tight with need. My hand drifts down her back to cup her perfect ass and she releases a hungry moan in the back of her throat.

She's the first to pull away, breaking our kiss as she rests her forehead on mine. "Max, what if this goes all wrong?"

Her coffee-colored eyes pin me, and I instantly regret how selfish I'm being. There is a strong let's-take-this-slow vibe coming from her.

"What are we talking about? Us? Or the stuff with my mother? Your past?"

"All of it, I guess. But more us. What if we mess this up? We're best friends. I can't lose you."

"Okay. First, you'll never lose me. Never." I grasp her backside and she squirms but doesn't move. I take that as a good sign. "And finally, what if nothing is messed up? What if we only get better? Stronger?"

"I don't want to mess up our friendship. I need you in my life." My chest aches with the vulnerability in her voice.

"We're not going to mess anything up. I need you too." I'm filled with conviction. I believe in us. "I've never felt like this about any other woman."

She examines my features and whatever she sees eases some of her uncertainty as her brows relax and she stops nibbling on her bottom lip.

"Let's come to an understanding." My hands slide up her sides, resting on her hips with a gentle, reassuring squeeze.

"Go on."

"No matter what happens." Releasing her, my hands move to her face. "We won't let it ruin our friendship." I cup her cheeks. "We'll always be friends."

"Really?" Her eyes close briefly, almost as if in relief at my words. "I don't have a lot of people in my life. In my inner circle. There aren't many people I *need*. But you're someone I need."

The raw truth of her words burrows in my heart. I've always felt our deep connection, even when neither of us dared face that we've always been more than just friends.

My mouth captures hers, needing to feel and taste the significance of us in her words.

"I need you too." My body against hers, hands on her, matches and fuels my determination to have more with this woman. "We'll be better together. Trust me."

Heat spreads through my chest as she burrows into my arms as if at home.

MAX

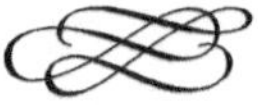

"You should have called last night." Ry sits in a chair facing Van's desk at HC.

After a not-so-great night of sleep, or more like not much sleep at all, Tommie and I agreed that filling in Van, Ry and the others was the first thing we needed to do.

We've been here close to half an hour and she's just finished retelling the events of the hospital fundraiser. This time, she is way more detailed than she was with me and I try not to take offense. These are her colleagues and she's being professional and smart about it.

Besides, if I'm being honest, I'd have lost it at the dinner if I'd learned someone, whoever the fuck he is, tried to strangle her.

Tommie sighs, nodding once. "I was shaken but I wasn't alone. I had Max."

"Yeah, and what if he'd come after the both of you?" Ry dares one of us to challenge his logic.

"My building has security."

I'm quick to defend our decision, or at least instill confidence in the guys that I can take care of her. I may not have combat training, but I'd never let anything happen to Tommie.

"Security," Van scoffs, nailing me with a stern glare. "A breeze for the likes of him."

It's clear he's taking the opportunity to school me on just how real and dangerous this situation is. And despite my rising hackles and my many questions, it isn't hard to see the picture is grim.

"If he wants to get to me, chances are, he will." Tommie pins Van with her own hard look. "We both know he will."

My insides chill. "Who is this psycho?"

All heads turn to me. Tripp and Coop are silent and brooding with their backs against a wall. Ry and Tommie are sitting across from Van. I'm too restless to sit still and since our arrival, I've been pacing at the back of the room.

Not once last night did she mention this guy's name. It didn't go unnoticed and I chose not to press her. Things were already intense, and it wasn't like I could go after him in that moment. I wasn't about to leave her.

Van shares a pointed look with Tommie before glancing at me. "Ash Naire."

My heart races and adrenaline surges through my body; fuck, I'm hit with the realization that I could have done something had I known.

"I met him." Tight and flat, I don't recognize the voice as my own. "Last night."

Tommie leaps to her feet. "What? How?"

"He was at the hospital fundraiser. Taya introduced us. I got the sense it's business."

She pales, coming to me and I take her hand in mine, not able to fully grasp how or what she must be feeling. I'm having a hard time processing that I shook hands with the very monster who did horrible, unspeakable things to her. And worse yet, when she was just a child.

"Tell us everything." Ry's dark expression mimics his voice.

"That's it. It wasn't even five minutes and then he left."

"We knew he was in New York but haven't been able to keep a tail on him. Since I met Tommie, we searched for the bastard, and once we located him, we've tried to keep an eye on him. That is easier said than done." Van leans back in his chair, anything but relaxed.

"We keep in touch with international law enforcement agencies. He goes by Ash Naire but we don't even know if that's the name he was born with. He surfaced on Interpol's radar about twenty-five years ago in Amsterdam."

He balls his hands into fists on the top of his desk and tension rolls off him like a tsunami.

"He's popped up all over the world, most recently in Europe, and has been linked to human trafficking in many forms. Sex slavery is believed to be his number one trade."

Judging from his tone, there isn't any guesswork to be done. Sex slavery *is* his business. I swallow back the bile burning my throat. The more I learn about this man, the more incensed I am with my mother. Those women in that basement are slaves being sold for sex. Is she in business with this vile excuse for a human?

Outrage wildly clutches my heart. And Tommie… They must be stopped. As if following the same train of thought where my mother is concerned, Van continues.

"My contact at NYPD says Taya isn't involved with Cavallo's skin trade. They do business, gambling and there's evidence of guns, but so far nothing to suggest anything else. But you saw her with Ash." He dips his chin in my direction, stepping from behind his desk, and I nod.

"We know Naire had ties to Cavallo when Anna was kidnapped," Tripp says.

That was four years ago and this is news to me. "What?"

Tommie twists her fingers in mine, squeezing. "Ash was here back then. We didn't know at the time—we've gotten better at tracking him but even then, it's not foolproof. Remember, Anna was found in a basement-like prison. There were women in cells and Ash had been there. From what Anna said, he seemed to be in charge. But by the time we made the connection that the man she was talking about was the same man I knew, he'd gone to ground."

"But he never really left, now did he?' Tripp's voice is rough. "And from the looks of things, Taya may not be in bed with Cavallo but with Ash."

"Why? I mean, if Ash is already doing business with Cavallo, why would he need my mother?"

As much as I hate to admit it, I can see why Taya would want to branch out. She's always looking for ways to build her business and gain power. Unfortunately, human trafficking is a booming business. But why would a man like that want to deal with a lesser outfit? Someone other than a kingpin?

"Taya's operation is smaller, less conspicuous, and from the little we have on Naire, the guy doesn't like the spotlight. He wants power and money, but he doesn't need to be at the forefront. Cavallo is big. Hard to miss," Coop says. "And something tells me Cavallo would be in charge. No one else."

"Good point. Maybe Naire and Cavallo split? Went their separate ways? Or maybe Naire has his fingers in both pots?" Tripp rubs his scruffy chin, contemplating his theories as he pushes from the wall. "She has a solid organization and infrastructure. A ready-made network for him to infiltrate. Playing both organizations would be risky, but he'd want at least one partner. Someone to take the heat, someone for law enforcement to go after should he need to escape. That's his MO after all."

"Yeah, he'd want a partner. He's done it before. That's how I found Tommie. Years ago, the target I went after, when I found Tommie, turned out to be his partner. At the time, I didn't know Ash existed," Van says. "It was Tommie who told us about him and then with more intel, we were able to get a handle on him. And even at that... he keeps slipping through our fingers."

My mind swims with all this information. I tried to distance myself from Taya's world and I wonder, had I not chosen to turn a blind eye, could I have stopped her from even looking at selling humans?

"This is a global problem where humans are being bought and sold for sex, forced labor or human organs. Nearly half are children and of those, almost eighty percent are women, working and living in vulnerable situations, which make them easy pickings, whereas others are often coerced or deceived." Tommie's tone is solemn.

It disgusts me to think there are more slaves in the world today than any other time in history. And Tommie. She was subjected to that.

"For Ash, Taya would be easier to control than Cavallo, who's bigger, more powerful." Ry now stands and walks to the window.

"So now what's next?" I'm anxious to get started, to put an end to this.

"We merge the Taya case with Ash. I'll find out more from NYPD, FBI and Interpol." Van bends, typing on his keyboard. "And Tommie, you're staying with me."

"No." At least three of us say it at the same time. Tripp continues, "Carys and the kids."

"He's right." Ry peers over his shoulder. "Whoever she stays with will be in danger."

"I'll stay here," Tommie says.

"What?" My tone is borderline pissed. "We'd agreed you'd stay with me."

"No, we didn't. I agreed to last night." She lets go of my hand with a rueful smile. "I can't stay with you long-term. You'll be in danger. I'm already putting all of you in danger by working here, being your friend."

She glances around the room, taking us all in, and our expressions say it all. None of us want to hear this; her safety is paramount. Coop and Ry start to speak over each other, telling her she's talking nonsense, she's family and danger comes with the territory.

"Guys, it's already decided. We have rooms here, designed for this very reason. I'm staying here." Just then her phone pings, glancing at it. "I have to take care of this."

Waving her phone, she walks toward the door and then looks back at me. "Max, I'll talk to you later."

I don't want her staying at HC, even if the place has top-notch security and she's making sense. Once she shuts the door, the guys continue to talk about who'll do what.

"Max, we need you to find out more about Ash from Taya." Van turns to me. "But tread carefully. Don't push too hard or do anything out of the ordinary. Now that we know what to look for, we need to start digging."

"Yeah, and see if you can find out more about their plans. She said you need to be more available. Let's see if it's connected and if so, how." Tripp places his hand on the doorknob with Coop right behind him. "Talk later."

As they leave, Ry nears my side. "We have to tell Tate. Can you come tonight?"

"Yes. I've got rounds at the hospital. I'll bring dinner and we'll tell her together." I check my phone, making sure I haven't missed a call from the hospital or worse, my mother.

"Sounds good. Van, talk to you later." Ry closes the door behind him and I'm left with Van.

He perches on the edge of his desk and his eyes flick to mine. "How you holding up with all this? With what Tommie told you?"

"I want to kill Ash Naire." A knot of tension swells in my gut.

He nods solemnly. "I've been trying to catch that sick bastard for over a decade. This feels like our best shot. He's here and in our backyard. He won't get away this time."

TOMMIE

Max pops his head into the surveillance room to say goodbye. He tries one more time to get me to stay with him.

"After the hospital, I'm going to Tate's. You could hang out with Gunnar and I'll tell the front desk not to let anyone up."

I press his hand, appreciating the thought and not having the heart to tell him that Ash isn't going to announce his arrival. I won't know I'm in danger until it's too late.

"You and I both know staying here is the safest place."

Van has three floors dedicated to HC. We're on the floor with offices and it looks like any other in this building. Another has storage, holding cells, and several rooms that could pass for any state-of-the-art hospital in the country, complete with operating rooms and recovery bays.

And the final floor has virtual reality training simulators, some tactical rooms and several bedrooms with their own bathrooms. Those are used for our overseas staff or when we need a safe place to keep someone for a day or two.

"Gun and I will have to stay here with you because I'm not going to sleep without seeing you with my own eyes." His fierce green gaze is intense, protective even, and my insides heat.

"It isn't like we won't see each other. I'll visit but we'll have to be careful. Ash is watching me and likely everyone else around me too."

His large hands slide around my waist, propelling my body against his, and my insides tighten. This feels different between us. It isn't simply a hug. We're way past the friendship line and as loud as the warning bells are in my mind, I can't seem to pull away.

"I won't let anything happen to you. I care about you. A lot. And in case you're thinking your past changes anything between us, it doesn't," he says, and it's all the things I never knew I needed to hear.

Holding my chin between his thumb and forefinger, he leans in and a shiver ripples through me. His lips are soft against mine and I get lost in his kisses. His mouth relentlessly showers me with emotions that best friends shouldn't have for one another.

The hollers and whistles of my crew, standing around us, finally snap me out of my daze. "Max, you devil," one guy says while another teases, "Get a room."

With his hand in mine, we leave the surveillance room toward the reception area. My cheeks burn and my mind is too scattered to form a coherent thought.

I'm too confused and wired with my arousal and deep feelings for Max. Emotions I haven't dared let out into the light, and now he seems to feel the same way. This, in itself, is dangerous.

I have a lot to lose by giving into my feelings for my best friend. If a relationship with Max doesn't work, and there are so many ways in which it couldn't, some so much worse than others... I can't bring myself to think about it. I can't lose him.

And on top of all that, my past and future are coming at me, all at once.

"Sorry about that." He stops just before the exit, turning me to face him. "I'm not sorry about kissing you. I want to kiss you again, but we need to talk first. Fuck, I want to talk now." He pulls me to him, resting his forehead against mine. "But…"

"I know, you've got to go. Listen, after work, I'm heading home to grab some things. I'll stay here tonight. How about breakfast tomorrow? I'll come to your place?"

I lick my lips, the taste of him still on me, and his eyes dip to my mouth and darken.

"You're killing me." A smile tugs at his lips. "Can we make it early? I'll come here?"

"Sure. I was thinking your place so I could see Gunnar too. But that's fine, I'll drop by later in the day."

"I'll bring breakfast burritos." Just the thought of one of my favorite foods causes me to lick my lips and a big smile spreads across his face.

"From Charlie's?"

"You bet." His lips lightly press into mine. "Stay safe and I'll text later."

"You too. Bye."

The remainder of the afternoon flies by and I'm consumed with thoughts of Max but also Ash and Taya. I can hardly believe how my world has collided with Max's. It looks like his mother and Ash are working together.

In some ways, it seems destined that we will finally get them both now. And that thought brings me both hope and trepidation.

Once done for the day, I drop the little I have in one of the rooms at HC and then head to my apartment to get some clothes. On the way, I pop into a family-run coffee shop, just a stone's throw from my home and I also use it as a drop location.

I've enlisted the help of some of my CIs to find more on Ash and I'm here to leave details of the job. I use QR codes, an optical label that looks like a matrix barcode. The information is readable by a smartphone.

The unisex washroom, or more specifically the underside of the trash can, is where I leave the barcode for pick up.

When leaving, I decide to grab a coffee despite how insanely long the line is tonight. Or maybe it's the cashier who is insanely slow. I've never seen her before. She's a petite, bubbly thing with cute giggles and megawatt smiles that could light the Christmas tree in Rockefeller Center.

She must be new and is definitely loving the job. Each customer gets the full welcome treatment and while I'm all for someone enjoying what they do, Chatty Cathy is causing a backup of customers out the door.

Fifteen excruciating minutes pass while I wait my turn. If the coffee wasn't so good I'd forget about this. During the wait, I get a text.

Van: Where the hell are you?

I don't even need to see him to tell he's not too happy with me.

Me: On my way home to grab some clothes. I'm going back to HC. Relax.

Van: You should have told me. I would have come. I'm on my way.

Me: I'm fine. Seriously, chill. I'll text you when I'm back at HC.

Van: Don't do this again. You know better.

Sighing, I feel like shit for just leaving. After this morning's meeting, and knowing the guys were on this, I started to feel better. Safer. But Van is right. As much as I don't want to be a burden to my friends, Ash is a threat.

Coffee, home and then back to HC. The sooner I report to Van that I am safe and sound, the better. I don't want him stressing about me.

"Next!" the blonde pixie says, beaming so brightly that I squint. "What'll it be?"

"Black coffee, please." I pull up my mobile wallet.

"I love your dress. Is that the Prada gabardine?" She cocks her head to the side, twirling the end of her ponytail.

"Yeah, thanks. Could you just get my coffee, please?" I don't want to be rude, but I feel the sharp stab of every impatient glare from those behind me in line.

Unfortunately, she doesn't take the hint and remains in front of me with no signs of getting my order or taking my money.

"It's gorgeous on you. I love Diane von Furstenburg's latest line of wrap dresses. Have you seen them? With your height and hair, oh my God, you'd be stunning."

I quirk a brow, impressed. Normally, I'd give her props for knowing fashion, and yes, I have one of the DVF dresses she's talking about, but I want to get going.

"I'm kind of in a hurry." She shrinks a bit and I'm a bitch, so I throw her a bone. "If you like those, you should see the latest Versace ready-to-wear collection."

Perking up, she tells me she's studying fashion design and then fires three more fashion-related questions at me. I balance being friendly with my mounting frustration—I need to get back to HC before Van calls a search party. Eventually, she gets my coffee.

"Here you go." She hands me a paper cup. "Have a great evening and when you have time, I'd love to chat some more."

She beams at me, hopeful, and I return the smile. The comforting heat of the coffee seeps from the cup into the palm of my hand.

On the way to the door, someone bumps into my side, and it isn't a little tap, more like a full-on tackle.

Knocked back, I fall into a small crowd waiting for their lattes and cappuccinos, and my java tumbles from my grip, spilling down my dress before landing on the tiled floor. Hot liquid hits my fingers and I hiss as the heat burns my flesh.

A large hand grabs hold of my arm and I whip to face the oaf. "Why don't you look where you're going?"

"I'm so sorry." An older man with a protruding belly and rotund jowls flusters about in front of me, dabbing at my wet arm.

"Don't touch me," I snap, pulling away from him.

He stands remorseful, slicking back his longish white hair from his forehead. "I don't know what happened. Let me buy you another coffee."

"No." Coffee was a bad idea.

"Please. What were you having? Black coffee? Milk and sugar?"

Regret swims in his green eyes behind the large spectacles perched on the bridge of his nose. His cheeks redden as the seconds tick by without my response.

"Fine. Just a black coffee." I step to the side, casting my eyes to where my dress is now soaked. At least it's black so even if it stains, I should be able to wear this again.

Then it dawns on me. How's he going to get me a *quick* cup of coffee? It took me over twenty-five minutes to get the first one. I should just walk out but I'll do the right thing and tell him to forget it.

Casting my gaze in the direction of the order counter, I blink, convinced I'm seeing things. The stranger already has another steaming cup of coffee and is headed my way. What the? How did he get it so fast?

The girl behind the counter sends me a sympathetic smile. She must have seen what happened and let him jump the line. I gift her a grateful one in return and make a mental note to thank her next time.

"My deepest apologies. Let me pay for your dry cleaning." He points to my dress and I shake my head.

"That isn't necessary. Thanks for the coffee." Raising the warm cup at him in salute, I take a long-awaited sip.

Before he can say another word or something more bizarre or disastrous happens, I leave the coffee shop and hustle toward my place.

Outside my apartment, a text comes in from Max. He's on his way to see Tate and I send words of encouragement because he's anxious about his sister's reaction to his news—that he has been working with his mother all these years.

I take another gulp of coffee and open my door. Relieved to finally be home, I slump against the wall of my one-room apartment and scan my surroundings, looking for any signs of entry. I've got a few boobytraps rigged throughout the place as well as a camera or two.

I pull up the app on my phone and check the security feed, fast-forwarding through the past twenty-four hours or so. Nothing. I sigh, happy that Ash hasn't been here. Yet. I won't fool myself into thinking he won't come to my home. He will, but I won't be here.

Finishing the last drop of my coffee, I toss the cup into the garbage bin and head over to my clothing racks to find something comfortable to wear before I pack.

But the room tilts and things start to spin. My vision blurs as the light in the room fades in and out. Everything is spinning and blackness eclipses everything.

MAX

On my way to Tate's to tell her about our mother, I text Tommie to check in. She's just arrived at her place to pick up some clothes, and then she's going back to HC.

She calms my nerves about telling Tate, and I only hope she's right that my sister will understand and get over it.

The Uber Eats driver pulls up with our dinner, pho, a Vietnamese soup and Tate's favorite, at the same time I do. Yes, I'm buttering up my sister since she won't be happy with me when she learns about everything I've been doing behind her back for years.

My phone beeps on my way into the elevator and with my hands full, it's tricky to check. A text from Taya. She wants me now.

I should stall. The elevator arrives at their floor and on the way to their front door, I think of an excuse to delay my mother. I text that I'm headed into surgery and won't be able to come until much later. Then I power off the phone, not sure if it was the best move but I've got to tell Tate in person and the longer I wait, the worse it'll get.

"Hey, come in," Ry whispers at the door before I even have a chance to knock.

His son James is sleeping peacefully in his arms, swaddled in a light blue blanket. My smile is hard to contain at the sight of the proud papa.

Even though James is their second child, I still marvel at the tough ex-FBI agent and security expert when he's with his children. He's a big, soft teddy bear.

"Lookin' good," I say and his cheeks redden as his lips press together.

"Thanks. Listen, I'm going to put him down."

"Okay and where's Adam?" The little tyke is usually running around and making lots of noise but the place is quiet.

"He's with Ma tonight."

"Ah, that's too bad."

"I'll be right back. Leave the food on the table, and Tate's in the kitchen washing some baby things."

"All right." I'm tightly wound, anxious to see my sister.

One look at me and she'll know something is up, and at first, she'll be pissed. I can't blame her, and I'd rather skip over that part.

I enter the kitchen and she turns to face me. Her blonde ponytail flicks to one side like a horse's tail.

"Hey, Bear, how are you?" I shove my hands into my pockets, hoping to hide any sign of my nerves.

"Max." She dries her hands on a kitchen towel and then hugs me.

We stand like that for a few beats, both of us finding our center. Being one half of a whole, which is what we've felt like our entire lives, our connection runs deep. I'm most balanced and feeling like myself when we're physically close.

"I feel like pinching myself. I can hardly believe you're here. Is this a dream?" Her sarcasm isn't hard to miss as she pulls away. "Better yet, I should pinch you."

She nips at my side and I wriggle, backing away. "Very funny. Smartass."

"I can't believe you're actually here. What is this, like the second time in as many weeks? That's unbelievable."

"Okay, if you cut the ribbing, I'll stay. If you can't, because I know how much you can't resist the chance, I've brought dinner for you, but I'm leaving."

Laughing, she takes me in from head to toe. "Okay, I'll stop even though this is fun." Her eyes twinkle like she's got a few more tricks up her sleeve. "Seriously, I was shocked when you called and said you'd bring dinner. What's going on?"

I open my mouth to speak and she holds up a finger. "And before you feed me some line, Ry told me you have some news and that he's going to leave us alone for a bit. So don't bother avoiding the truth."

"After dinner." Partly relieved and partly annoyed that Ry told her there was news, I delay our conversation. "Where are the bowls?"

"We only need spoons and forks. We can eat out of the container." She points to a top drawer. "Thanks for coming, Maxie. I've missed you."

"I've missed you too." The sharp edge to my tone doesn't hide my dislike for the moniker I can't seem to shake.

Dinner is relaxing, despite my nerves at our impending conversation, and something I didn't realize I needed. My sister regales me with cute, funny and stinky stories of her days spent with her beautiful baby boy and rambunctious toddler.

And she's glowing like a proud and loving mother, and Ry is also more relaxed than usual, never taking his eyes off his wife. The man worships my sister, but with the addition of their sons, he looks at her as if she set every single star in the sky.

"I only got a glimpse of the little guy, but he's growing fast," I say when Ry stands to leave, signaling time to get serious. "I had wanted to see Adam too."

"I wish some days I could just stop it all. They are both growing so fast," Tate says wistfully.

He leans over and kisses her forehead. "I'll be back in an hour."

"An hour?" She casts him a doubting look. "You've never gone to the office and been back in an hour."

"Fine, I'll be back in two." This time, his hand grips the back of her neck and he plants a long, slow kiss on her lips.

I look away, my mind suddenly going to Tommie and all that's happened in the past few days, adding new layers to our friendship. My heart pounds at the thought of my beautiful best friend.

It's dangerous to want more, to consider more, yet I've flirted with the idea. And earlier today, when we kissed at HC, I saw a healthy dose of lust or longing or something similar in her eyes. There's so much going on right now and I wonder if it's the right time to ask for more. On the other hand, all this stuff with my mother and Ash only shows how precious life and time is. So why not now?

"See you later, Max." Ry dips his chin.

"Sure. See you."

"Okay, spill."

"It's Taya." I cut to the chase, knowing Tate doesn't need a preamble.

"Oh God, now what?" She drums her fingertips on the table, setting her mouth into a thin cross line.

"I've been working with her ever since I came back to the US."

"What? Working with her? What does that mean?" She latches onto my forearm, gripping my muscle tightly.

"After Bobby and our father died, and you were with Ry, she threatened you. She told me she had plans for you, much like what she did with Bobby. Another marriage to another monster for the benefit of the organization. And I couldn't have that."

"There's no way she would have gotten away with it." She's vehement.

We both know that isn't true and ruling out Taya as a threat would have been a big mistake. She's not above marrying Tate off, even if that meant kidnapping my sister, or worse.

"Really? I wasn't going to let her hurt you again after everything you went through with Bobby."

"So you let her put a bullseye on your back?" My sister slaps her hand on the table; the baby monitor crackles and I worry she'll wake James.

"Look, I know you're upset but I was in a position to stop her. In exchange for coming home and being her doctor, she agreed to leave you alone. And she's done that."

"Be her doctor?"

"I clean up her bloody messes. I take care of gunshot wounds, stabbings, the guys who are beaten up, the drug overdoses, you name it. I'm pretty much on call."

Tate covers her face with her hands and lets out a sad sigh before looking to me. "And you've been doing this since you came back?"

"Yes. I didn't really think it through at first. I had to figure out how I'd get supplies and drugs and I couldn't use my normal, legal channels. The hospital wasn't an option."

"No way. Max, you're a well-respected cardiac surgeon." She rests her hand over her heart, the glow from earlier long gone. "If you got caught stealing stuff from the hospital your career would be over. What are you doing?"

"The black market. She set it up."

"Max, she's taken more than enough from us." She slams her hand once more on the table and pushes to stand, now pacing the length of the dining table.

"Your safety is my biggest concern, Bear." She stops in her tracks, our eyes locking, and images of all the times I couldn't help her flash in my mind, only serving to fuel my conviction. I did what I had to and even though I've hated every minute of it, I'd do it again.

"I'll do anything to keep you safe. To keep Adam and James safe."

Nodding, she presses her trembling lips together and grips the back of the chair, staring across the table at me. "You've got to stop. She can't keep taking from us."

"I am stopping."

What is Tate going to think when she learns about how I've been helping Taya? How I let a woman die the other night? I can barely stand the thought.

"You might want to sit down for this." I motion to the chair, not sure if I'm suggesting this out of concern for her or delaying the inevitable—telling her just how horrific our mother really is.

"Just tell me, dammit." Tate leans into the chair, her nostrils flaring, and her palpable anxiety hits me in the chest.

"It looks like she's involved in human trafficking."

She sucks in a breath, her hand flying to her mouth as she closes her eyes. When she opens them again, water pools in her eyes and she blinks back the tears.

"Human trafficking?"

I nod solemnly and tell her about the woman with the gunshot wound at the warehouse. She listens, growing paler by the second.

"I wanted to go to the police but we both know how that could have turned out. That's why I went to Ry and Van. I won't be party to that. It was bad enough with the drugs and guns but snatching people off the street, selling them into sex and slavery of other kinds. I can't and won't abide by that."

"Oh my God. I can't even… this is horrible. I'm glad you went to Ry. You must feel… I can't imagine how you feel." She comes around to my side of the table and we embrace.

"I'm helping them and sharing everything."

Tate nods, knowing all too well what it means to work with HC. Once upon a time, she was an FBI informant on her own husband. "You need to be careful. If she finds out…" Her voice cracks and she mashes her lips together.

"I will." My voice is strong and reassuring. "Ry and Van are working with the NYPD and others. We have to stop her once and for all."

I give her the run down about Ash and Tommie, knowing Ry will fill her in more and also sick to think of what will happen if we don't put an end to this. Thoughts of the dying woman, Tate many years ago when she was at the mercy of my parents and Tommie rush at me.

Failure isn't an option. I won't allow Taya or Ash to ruin the lives of so many women and I can't work for her any longer. If I keep this up, I'm afraid I might lose my sanity or worse, my humanity.

There's a knock at the door and we both look to the front entrance.

"Who is that? Are you expecting someone?"

"No." She chuckles, shaking her head. "It might be our neighbor, Mrs. Marzel. She adores Adam and now with the baby, she finds any excuse to drop by and see him. Earlier today she claimed to be out of sugar."

Smiling, she ambles toward the door. "Why don't you grab the wine bottle and our glasses and take them into the living room."

"Tate, wait." On edge from what we've just discussed, I quicken my pace to her side. "Let me get it."

I gently shift her behind me and her features are a mixture of worry and disbelief as if I might be overreacting. "Okay, but I'm sure it's fine."

She's been at a distance from my mother for some time now, but I know all too well what is possible. And I did dismiss Taya's summons earlier tonight.

I open the door and my mother pushes past me to stand in the hallway with her hands on her hips. Platinum blonde hair is brushed tightly back into a bun, making her angular features appear even more severe. Suddenly, I'm regretting my stupid decision to lie to her.

And for a brief, insane moment, I wonder if Taya knows what I just shared with Tate. Is she on to me? Does she know I'm double-crossing her?

"Did you think you could lie to me and I wouldn't find out?" She grabs hold of Tate's bicep, bringing her close, and my focus is on where her bony fingers dig into my sister's flesh.

Tate's eyes widen like saucers and a whimper escapes her mouth; that's when I notice my mother is holding a gun.

Fuck. This is my fault. I jump to separate them in some way, but Taya shoots me a deadly glare, pressing the weapon into her daughter's temple. "I'd hoped to finally meet Adam, but one grandchild is better than none. I have a man with James as we speak."

As if hit square in the gut, a guttural sound slips from my taut lips. Almost like an echo, my sister cries out, battling to be free of our mother's hold. I've got to get to the baby.

"I will take the child and you'll never see him again. Max, you seem to have forgotten that I am dead serious about our arrangement. You break your end of the deal and I'll break mine."

My mind races, trying to figure out if she's bluffing about a man having James or not. At the end of the hallway to the bedrooms, there is an outdoor terrace.

We're six floors up but there are fire escapes. Metal stairs on the exterior of the building that anyone, if they really wanted to, could climb.

She means business. My mother is determined if nothing else to always prove her point. Get her way. Why the hell didn't I think of that before lying to her?

"Do not do this. Let Tate go and call off your dog. I'll leave with you now."

My hands are shaking, unable to contain my fury, and she laughs. My sister trembles, body tight, incensed, and like any mother—well except ours—she'll kill before she lets any harm come to her son.

I won't let it get to that. I'd rather kill my mother with my bare hands before I let that happen.

"Leave us alone." Tate's tone is dark and vibrating, despite the weapon, which is now pressed into her side.

Movement causes me to look toward the hall. A hulking shadow lumbers from the bedrooms and as the large man steps into the light, we can see baby James in his arms.

If the situation wasn't fraught with danger, the scene would make me smile. It's Thanos holding a baby. Fortunately, the baby's still sleeping. I'm grateful for that small mercy.

Tate now tries even harder to pull away, but she's wrenched around to face our mother, their noses almost touching with the gun wedged between them. The vision gives me pause.

Two blonde women, so similar in their striking bone structure and alluring figures that it's clear they are related. One light like the bright sun and the other as dark as the pits of hell. How is it possible for someone so vile and heartless to bear a child as loving and kind as my sister?

"I will take him," Mother says and Tate stills.

"Fuck. No." I step forward. "I'll do whatever you want." Even if I live to regret it, I will do anything to prevent her from hurting the baby or my sister.

"Bring him to me." Taya ignores me and her man moves with purpose, careful so as not to misstep and upset or harm the baby.

"I'll leave now if you put him down." I dip my chin toward the bassinet and the man stops, casting a glance at his boss, maybe hopeful to give the baby up.

Taya nods and his chest deflates, relieved to put the baby down. He places the child in the bassinet as he would a China doll. Then he passes me, watching warily, to stand beside Taya.

"Max, go to the door. Now."

I obey and she releases Tate, who runs to her son, clutching him in her arms. "Get out." Her face reddens. "Max, don't go with her."

"I have to." I offer a dim smile. "I'll call you later, Bear. It's going to be okay."

MAX

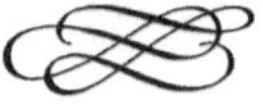

Mother ignores me as we leave the building, staring straight ahead. Her thug keeps a tight hold on me and throws me into the back of the idling car, squeezing in after me.

Her driver, the same guy she's had since I returned from England, pins me with his steely blue eyes. I pause and his usually blank expression is somber, as if he knows what's in store for me.

"Drive, Riff," Taya says to him before turning to me. "Don't you ever lie to me again."

She's out for blood and my major misstep tonight only proves she knows my whereabouts most of the time, if not all the time. I can't screw this up further and risk tipping my hand. If she doesn't already suspect me of something, tonight's fiasco is sure to give her pause.

Dammit.

"Understood. It was stupid. I hadn't seen Tate in a while and when your call came in…" I trail off, angry with myself for sounding like a kid begging his mother's forgiveness and for getting myself into this situation. But this is how I must play this.

"Listen to me and listen good because I won't repeat myself. Next time I will show you." She grabs my face, holding my gaze. "You lie to me again or disobey and I will make you wish you were dead. And just in case you misconstrue that to mean your own death, no my dear son, I will get rid of someone you love."

Cold paralyzing fear pierces my spine. Tommie, Tate, my nephews, those at HC or the hospital—anyone could be in danger. She has no limits and murder means nothing to her.

She violently releases her hold, pushing my head back into the seat rest and picking up her phone again. With that gesture, I realize I need to text Ry and tell him to get to my sister. Tate likely has already called him but just in case.

I fish my phone out of my pocket and the goon beside me clamps his fingers around my wrist, wrenching the phone out of my grasp.

"Let me just text Ry." There's no point lying. I've got to be on my best behavior with my mother if I'm to gain back any bit of her trust.

She nods. "One text."

I turn on the phone and notice nothing from Ry, Tate or Tommie. I send a quick text to Ry and it's only when I put the phone away that I realize Tommie was supposed to text me when she got back to HC. I suppose she could still be at her place and I make a mental note to check my phone again, as soon as is possible.

We arrive at a different warehouse and I keep my mouth shut, doing as I'm told. There are five women in the basement of the building, all young, easily under twenty-two, with varying backgrounds and looks. All are under the influence of something.

Their gazes are vacant, glassy, and their movements slow and uncoordinated. For the most part, they are clean, although a few faces are tear-stained. My job is to make sure they are healthy.

I'm a riot of fury as I go through the motions, conducting a physical exam and charting their weight, measurements, heart rate, blood pressure, and finally, blood tests. All this proves our theory. I'm cataloguing these women like cattle for the slaughter.

And when my mother's cold, flat voice hits me, I want to grab these women and run. "They need birth control."

My chest squeezes and I shift my gaze from the sterile instruments lining the makeshift tray to my heartless mother.

"And how do you propose I get that?" I'm unable to keep my sarcasm and hostility out of my tone.

Stone-faced, she snaps her fingers in the direction of Tiny. He lumbers over with boxes of the birth control shot. Of course she has them at the ready.

Biting my tongue, I administer the injections, and when done, I peel off my gloves and turn to face her with a stabbing glare. "That takes care of pregnancy, but it won't prevent STDs."

"We're done here." She pivots on her heel, briskly striding away.

Tiny grabs my bicep, hauling me after her, and the men standing guard take action and start to round up the women. As we head one way, they take the women down another dark corridor of the underground. Fuck. Why can't I stop this right now?

Tonight is a bust even if it confirms what we suspected. All the police will have is my word and a really good lawyer could easily refute anything I have to say.

Those women are like lambs to the slaughter. A gun peeks out of the waistband of Tiny's pants and it's tempting to grab it. But then what? I don't know how to use the fucking thing.

Battling with myself every step up the stairs, I pull from his grasp once we're in the warehouse. My mother motions for me to follow her into the only room on the floor, her office.

"Max, I need you to keep your mouth shut and do your job."

It takes everything in me to respond civilly. "Understood."

"Like I said before, I will be contacting you more frequently. Be available."

I nod, grinding my teeth to keep from losing it on her. She flicks her hand as if to dismiss me, but I'm not done. The evening can't be a total write-off. I want more information and see an opportunity.

Pretending to leave, I turn my back to her and then pause, peering over my shoulder as if it's an afterthought. "What's your deal with that guy, Ash Naire?"

She is shrewd; I've no doubt she's questioning my motives and she confirms my thoughts when her eyes narrow into thin slits. "Why are you asking?"

"I've just never seen you that way with another man. Well, not since Father."

It's subtle and fleeting but she recoils slightly at the mention of Warren Conrad, our dear old dad. Say what she wants about him and all his shortcomings when he ran the business, which she arrogantly does whenever she gets the chance, she can't deny she loved him.

"What way?"

"You came alive at the hospital fundraiser when he joined us." A shadow shifts across her features but she remains silent at my observation. "I was curious to know more about the man."

"You know, Tate, Adam and James aren't the only ones you need to worry about." Now she's on her feet, rounding the desk to stand in front of me.

Her angular features, the very ones that gifted her a modeling career, are harsh and treacherous like the sharp edges of a hunting knife.

"Tommie." She twists her mouth into a victorious snarl.

I grind my teeth and something claws at my insides. Again, another reminder of how I'm constantly watched. Not only does Tommie have to worry about Ash but now my mother has her sights set on her too. Screw that.

"Did you know Ash noticed your date at the dinner?" Her tone is mockingly sweet, and tension pinches at my spine.

She doesn't know that I'm aware of their history. That Ash is a vile, fucking monster who kidnapped and raped the woman I love.

"What's your point?"

"Be careful, my dear son. When you go fishing, you'd better be prepared to deal with whatever you catch." She purses her lips and sits at the desk.

"What the fuck are you getting at?" My pulse quickens at her second threat in as many minutes.

I stride back toward her desk, leaning over to get in her face. Why I didn't do something about her long before this is beyond me. I was too focused on protecting Tate, not thinking about how to bring down our mother. Hopefully she is none the wiser, but her days are numbered.

"That's enough." Her icy gaze flares with an unknown emotion and there's a creak followed by footsteps behind me.

Looking in the direction of the door, I straighten and turn to face the devil himself. Dark features, strong defined jaw and a light dusting of grey at his temples. He has an ultra-domineering presence about him. He's easily forty if not pushing fifty. He a sick, sick man and I can't wait for him to get what he deserves.

"Maximillian." Ash extends his hand and I want to cut it off. "What do you want to know about me?"

Was he here all this time? Watching and listening? Suspiciously, I shake his hand and blistering hatred coats my throat. I don't want to pretend with this madman. Not since Bobby, my sister's dead husband, have I wanted to kill someone with my bare hands. I pull from his grip and force my fingers to not curl into a fist.

"What are you doing with my mother?" I don't care if I come off sounding like a protective son. Let them think what they want. Any bit of information I can gather about these two could help us put the pieces together faster.

"Max," Taya says, and he moves in behind her, placing his hand on her shoulder.

"It's okay. I'll allow it. For now." He pauses lifting his dark gaze to me. "We are friends. We met through a mutual acquaintance."

"Are you in business together?"

Ash is likely too sly to admit anything, but it's worth a try. Any response he gives might be useful.

"Ah, I believe proper etiquette dictates it's my turn to ask a question." This asshole thinks this is a game and he's loving it.

Through a tight jaw, I nod. "Fine."

"What's going on with you and Thomasina?" He asks in such a way to suggest he already knows the answer.

I bristle at the familiarity in his tone, willing my body to relax. Ash is hyperaware and doesn't seem to miss a thing. He would take great pleasure in knowing he's gotten under my skin.

"We're friends." I want to say more. Declare she's mine and he's to stay the fuck away. But fortunately, it's like Van or Tommie are whispering in my ear to play it smart and keep my cool.

"Friends? With benefits?" Is he taunting me? I'm not taking the bait.

"I believe I get a question now." I flash a wry grin and go back to the question he dodged not too long ago. "Are you in business with my mother?"

He beams at my volley. "We could be."

His response is crafty, not giving anything away, yet Taya finds it displeasing. Her hard features sharpen and twist, and only confirm my suspicion. She has designs on this sick fuck and Ash isn't the least bit interested.

"Why are you asking about Tommie?" I slip in another question.

"Ah." His smile is huge as if he has me where he wants me, jabbing and provoking. "She hasn't told you."

His vile insinuation lingers between us and my gut turns to lead, expression hardening. The smug bastard likely thinks he's gotten one over me, but he'd be wrong. I know more than he thinks but his superior tone rubs my face in all the appalling and ugly shit he's done to Tommie.

And the worst part? I have to stand here and silently swallow that shit. Take it. I can't blow my cover and call him out, or better yet beat the crap out of him.

My anger fuels me. "Answer the question."

Ash is arrogant and resolute, never breaking eye contact, nor responding.

"Would the two of you stop talking about that woman?" Taya huffs, pushing her chair back to stand.

A phone buzzes and Ash pulls his from a jacket pocket. With a brief glance to the screen, his lips twitch in amusement and his dark eyes glitter as his gaze lands on me.

"It was nice to see you again, Max." He puts the phone away and buttons his suit jacket, nodding to my mother, and leaves.

I'm not ready for him to go. There's so much more I want to ask and I can't shake the feeling he's bested me. Taya and I walk away behind him and her reaction is curious, and something we'll have to leverage. As he exits the building, she scurries after him, paying me no mind. She does want more than business.

With them occupied, I slip out the door and pull my phone out, wanting to call Tommie, make sure she's okay. The thing buzzes in my hand and as if we're on the same wavelength, she's sent a text.

Tommie: Back at HC and going to sleep. I'm exhausted. See you tomorrow.

The second I read it, the tension seeps from my body like air releasing from a balloon. At least she's safe.

TOMMIE

Boom. Boom. Boom. My head throbs like a marching band. Something crawls up the back of my neck and my body trembles, the movement making my head hurt even more.

I try to brush whatever it is away, but my movements are sluggish, slow, as if I'm in quicksand. It's almost impossible to move. Am I dreaming? What's wrong with me?

The same tickling sensation tingles along the side of my arm and my slow, heavy movements only frustrate me more. Everything takes so much effort. The tickle now glides across my cheek, slithering down my jaw and neck. I tremble again. Irritated and confused.

With what feels like an impossible amount of effort, I blink and finally pry open my eyes. It's dark. Where am I? Oh my God, am I back in Ash's dungeon? No, it isn't that dark. Beams of hazy light filter in and I can make out a ceiling. Pre-dawn, maybe?

I can't focus. What is wrong with me? Panic smothers and unfurls in my chest and plants itself deep in my gut. I shift and the familiar feel of a mattress supports my body. A bed? I don't remember going to sleep.

Where am I? What's the last thing I remember? Coffee. My apartment. Everything upside down.

The mattress dips beside me. Someone is next to me. In bed with me. I try not to breathe, my will clawing at this oppressive force weighing down not only my muscles but also my mind. Icy tentacles of terror spread through my insides, my brain frantically searching for an explanation, some reason for any of this. *What the hell is going on?*

"Good morning. You still sleep like a beauty." His voice is an ice pick to my heart.

I freeze both thought and movement. I must be dreaming. No, a nightmare. This can't be real. Why does it sound like Ash is beside me?

Slowly, even more determined than ever, my body sluggishly turns in the direction of his voice. I want to scream. Ash is in bed with me, lying on his side with his head propped in his hand. His dark disturbing eyes drill into me and his wicked grin burns my insides.

A tornado of crushing thoughts and emotions flies at me. I thought I had time. I thought I could get in and out of my place without worrying about him. Stupid. Why did I underestimate him? Of all people, I know what he is capable of. Fuck!

A black feather is in his other hand, hovering in mid-air as he fans its wisps back and forth against the dark scruff of his neck. That was the tickling sensation.

"What are you doing here?" My mouth is drier than a desert and my words come out more like a croak.

Move.

Run.

These thoughts bombard my mind, but I've been drugged. It's the only logical reason why I feel the way I do. It's why I can't remember what happened before this or how he got into my home.

And as I lie in the bed, I'm suddenly and acutely aware that I'm naked under the covers. Oh my God. He undressed me and God knows what else. I fight the urge to throw up, my shame surging, bitter and fast, up my throat.

"I thought I'd pay you a visit. We didn't finish our talk. But truly, I owe you a lot more than talk. Or more accurately, you owe me."

"You drugged me." The urge to be sick is a fierce storm brewing in my belly.

His dark expression is blank and impenetrable. If I vomit on him, he won't get out of the bed. No, it'll enrage him and only make things worse. He'll hurt me. Punish me.

With a few slow and steady breaths, the brewing storm inside of me begins to settle, even if temporarily.

"The coffee. The older guy." Fragments of memories from the night before coming together.

A sly grin slithers across his full lips and it's as if I'm staring into the pit of hell. His gaze dances with devilish delight.

"Get out." My voice and body quiver with boiling rage.

I hate my fear.

Even worse, I hate the glint of smug satisfaction in his eyes. His triumph is a wrecking ball, shattering my composure into a million little pieces.

"Thomasina, need I remind you that you are mine? I could have taken you many times before now."

How did I let this happen? Van and his warning come to mind. I should have come to my place with him or someone else from HC. But surely, he knows something is wrong. I was supposed to text him. Maybe he's on his way right now.

"And before you think someone is coming to your rescue," he says, and I seethe with how easily he read my thoughts. "Zero has texted both Evan and Max. They think you're safe at HC."

My first instinct is to kick and scream—to fight—but I won't. My body is still sluggish from the drugs but I'm slowly growing more alert. I don't want him to know that.

"Did you forget Zero is the best? He'd be insulted. We've known where you were all these years."

I didn't forget Zero, his tech guy, or anything else from my time in captivity. But I refuse to answer him. While I rack my brain for ways to get out of here, I ask, "If you knew where I was, why didn't you come for me?"

The answer is written all over his face. He enjoys the anticipation. The game. The thrill of keeping me on edge, hanging, all these years.

He pushes to sit with his back against the headboard and casts the black feather aside. I want to stab the quill into his eye. Despite my therapy, conquering my past and surviving, he's still controlling me from afar. He has been all these years. The threat of when he would return.

"I'll admit, at first, it took some work to figure out who invaded François's home. But you know Zero, no challenge is too great for him. Soon enough, I knew everything there was to know about Evan Hart and exactly where you were in Manhattan."

He's talking about the mission Van carried out years ago when he found me in the basement of a house where I'd been banished for disobedience. I was left naked and chained to a wall.

The house was empty but for me, and that's the scariest revelation. When Van told me, I wondered if someone would have come back for me or did Ash leave me to die?

I've told myself, time and time again, he wasn't done with me. It was just another one of his ways to enforce his control over me. Punish me.

But even now, in some sick, twisted way, his intentions all those years ago matter. Did he send me to François's to die? I had already been alone for three days, I think, or maybe longer; I had no way of telling time or day from night.

If my death had been my punishment, then Van raiding François's mansion had saved me in more ways than one. And now, what did he want from me? To finish the job? Kill me? Or keep me captive again?

"Were you going to leave me?" I may be buying time with the question but I want to know the answer.

Despite all he had done to me, and even now with my life potentially on the line, I want to live. I want to know what his intentions are. It makes all the difference in how I play this.

He raises a brow. "At François's?"

"Yes. Were you done with me?"

He loves my question. His eyes gleam with an intense satisfaction and the corners of his mouth twitch upward. I want to punch him in the face. And I could.

The effects of the drug, whatever it is he gave me, are wearing off. Thank goodness, but I have to be careful not to let on, and I also can't rule out that he may already suspect I'm getting stronger by the minute. For now, I won't risk a hasty retaliation until I've figured out the best way to escape.

"No. Would you have liked me to be done with you?" His fingers pinch my chin, turning my face to look at him. "I will never be done with you, Thomasina. Even when I should be. I've been told to just cut my losses. End you. End this."

My heart jumps into my throat. I don't know how to feel about this. Surprise and alarm battle within me. I'd longed for him to leave me alone, even knowing that might mean death, and now I realize there is only one way for this to end. A strange, eerie calm plants itself in my soul and I stare at him as he waves his hand between us.

"Perhaps it's the smarter move to just kill you and be done. You are a lot of trouble. Always were. Even before you were a speck on my radar. Even when I took you, I knew I'd rue the day. But I will never be done with you."

I shudder at the sad, dark truth. The only end is for one of us to die.

"You disappoint me." He pushes off the bed, shaking his head reproachfully. His expensive black suit is still crisp, showing no telltale signs that he was just lying down.

Tall, feet shoulder-width apart, he flattens his black tie against his white shirt. "What are you doing with those men?"

"What?" Another reminder that he's never been too far away, even when on another continent.

He hovers over me, wipes at the wetness streaking down my cheeks. "Those men you have sex with. The countless men you have given yourself to over the years."

Dark clouds of rage shadow his face, tighten his jaw and spark his vitriol. "I am the only one who has ever seen you for what you are,

Thomasina. You belong with me. Those men don't see you. Not even Evan or Max."

He spits onto the floor as if their names leave a vile taste in his mouth. I stiffen when he leans in, fearful of what pain he is about to inflict. Instead, he cups my cheek, gentler than I anticipate. "None of them know your true worth."

If I could strike him dead with a mere look, he would be six feet under. "My true worth? You know nothing of my worth, let alone anything else."

"Ah, always so quick with that tongue. Lashing out to hurt." His thumb digs into the pressure point at the side of my jaw where, if he chose, he could pry open my mouth.

I want to shake him off and I could, but I don't. He can't know that I've regained the full use of my body. All my nerve-endings tickle, sparking with the desperate need to flee.

"One of these days you may lose it." He sinks his thumb further into my flesh.

Frantic, my pulse picks up speed and I clench my jaw tighter in case he decides to follow through and rip out my tongue. No threat is idle, no deed too messy or impossible where Ash is concerned.

And this particular threat isn't new. Once, years ago, he did torture my tongue. I flinch, remembering the day my mouth was forced open, tongue clamped while cut many times with the jagged edge of some kind of blade.

The pain was endless, lasting well past the torture. I could barely eat or drink for days. Years later, with time, distance and therapy, I discovered the technique was a form of torture used by medieval inquisitors. Tears prick at the back of my eyes when he finally releases my jaw.

"You're a brilliant mind. A genius. And your beauty. So much more than skin deep. I alone value your worth."

I convulse, rage like an earthquake thundering through my body. He speaks as if ours was some great love. There was no love. Only hate, power and pain.

"Get out." My scream is met with his laughter.

He takes several steps from the bed, pointing to the front door, taunting. The door is only a few feet away but it might as well be in another country. As if I could get up and leave if I wanted.

Even naked, which wouldn't stop me from running for help, I wouldn't get too far. He enjoys the chase, but he wouldn't let me make it to the door.

The bathroom. It's closer. I've got a gun hidden under the lid of the toilet. Unless he's already found it and taken it. The path to the only room in this place is clear with him standing to the side. I may be able to get there before he catches me.

With my gaze fixed on the door, I bound from the bed, legs wobbly and each stride frenzied and unsure. I stumble across the wooden floor, careening into the bathroom as Ash's movements are quick and loud behind me.

His dark, stormy gaze locks with mine as I slam the door and for a second, I wonder if he let me get away? My still-numb fingers fumble with the lock, knowing full well that if he wants in here, there's nothing I can do to stop him.

Edging away from the door, I crouch so my bottom hits the floor, eyes fixed on the door as my back rests against the bathtub. With my legs outstretched, the room is small enough that both feet press into the wooden door.

I tremble, arms around my middle to keep from falling apart. Look at me, I'm a blubbering mess on my bathroom floor. The monster is only feet away and if he tries to bust through the door… I need my gun.

Now on my knees, I quietly lift the lid off the toilet and sweet relief devours my terror. My Beretta M9 is where I left it, duct-taped to the underside of the porcelain.

Stilling, I listen for signs of Ash but there's only silence. What the hell is he doing? In one swift move, I rip the gun from its hiding spot, replace the lid and get back into position. Now, my hand wraps around the grip, arms outstretched and pistol aimed at the door, ready should he come crashing in.

Seconds tick by like hours. Finally the front door shuts and the faint vibration of the lock clicking into place carries through the thin walls. My limbs tremble, still rigid in their position, and I stay seated for a while longer, both scared and wired. I don't want to jump the gun and find Ash waiting for me or to wait too long and have him come back.

I'm hyperaware and tense. This could be a ploy to lull me into a false sense of security while he waits to pounce. He loves his games, but I've got a gun now and I'm more than ready to play.

I'll be in here all day if I don't do something. I snatch my silk robe from the hook on the back of the door and carefully, oh so quietly, open it. Nothing happens. Excitement prickles up my spine.

Stepping into the room, I search my apartment, starting with the rows upon rows, three deep, of clothes racks lining one wall, across the bed and into the kitchen. Nothing. I am alone.

Shaking, my body feels like it's encased in Jell-O, coming down from the high, as useless tears leak from the corners of my eyes. Everything is blurry thanks to the uncontrollable waterworks; I search for my phone as I recall what Ash said about Van not coming to look for me. I grab the device off the bedside table, angrily swiping at my wet cheeks.

Shit, texts were sent to Van, Max and Anna last night, letting them all know I was back at HC and going to bed.

Zero. Fuck!

Just then, there's a sudden banging on the front door and I scream, nearly jumping out of my skin.

Max calls my name at the same time Van's gruff voice reverberates through the wood, impatient and angry. "Tommie, open up or I'm coming in."

My knees buckle and I grab onto the wall for support, now more relieved than ever that they are here. Another fist to the door and I quickly throw it open.

Max grabs me in his arms. "Are you okay?"

Evan barrels into my studio, gun out. Tall, broad and muscled, he eats up most of my apartment. "Was Ash here?"

I nod into Max's chest, unable to control my trembling, and he holds me. His scent. A ball of inhibited emotions courses through me and I cling to him.

"Tommie girl, you okay?" Van is now at my side, hand brushing away the hair from my face.

Lifting my head, Van's countenance suddenly softens as he takes the gun from my grip. Max's fingers slide under my chin to turn my gaze to him.

The unabashed look in his sea green eyes is raw and honest. Compassion and concern and maybe even something more. "Thank God you're all right. You are, aren't you?"

"What the fuck happened?" Van rests his gun next to mine on the table.

I cave like a ragdoll, bursting like a dam into uncontrolled sobs. Relief floods my body, untangling my tight, at-the-ready muscles.

"Ash…" I cover my hand with my mouth, trying to hold back my distress and anger.

Max rubs my back soothingly and Van clutches my hand, reassuring both of us that I'm here and it's okay. When I finally rid myself of most of my pent-up emotions, I dry my eyes and straighten to my full height. Max reluctantly releases me, staying at my side.

I glance down at myself and shake my head, wondering what they must see. A robe haphazardly covering my body, hair in disarray and tears staining my cheeks. We move to the couch. Van sits next to me and Max on the coffee table in front of me.

I don't hold back and tell them everything. The little I remember from the coffee shop, coming home, passing out and waking up beside Ash. I also mention the texts they received from me and how they must have been sent by Zero.

The chattering of my teeth is relentless and the trembling of my body incessant. No matter what I do, reliving it sends chills through me and I'm unable to get warm.

A cold has seeped far and wide into my skin and bones, settling into my soul. Max wraps me in a blanket and scoops me onto his lap. Van fishes the coffee cup from my garbage. He'll get it tested along with my blood to find out what drug I was given.

"He's made two moves now. Fuck, the next one..." Van rakes his hand through his hair and crouches in front of me. "I'm putting someone on you at all times."

His expression brooks no chance of rebuttal or refusal. And I'm not about to argue.

"Why didn't he take you?" Max tightens his hold and I'm comforted by his protective move.

"I think he will eventually, but..." I bite my bottom lip, fighting any lingering fear.

"But what?" Van scowls, his frustration not directed at me but the situation.

"He's fucking with me. He wants me to know that he can, and he will get to me at any time. But I'm not going to let that happen."

MAX

"This looks amazing. I still can't believe you cooked all this." I carry the aromatic chicken tagine to the table in the HC dining room and set it next to the bowl of couscous.

Tommie follows, placing a Moroccan carrot dish with the rest of the meal. "I should be insulted that you're having a hard time believing I can cook."

Hands on her hips, she tries to pull off a glare but there isn't an ounce of offence to her countenance. I pull out a chair, motioning for her to sit, before taking the one next to her.

"I'm just in awe of your talents."

"This isn't difficult." She waves away the culinary masterpiece before us.

"I haven't had a home-cooked meal in I don't know how long." I spoon the fluffy orange-yellow couscous onto my plate and hope I can eat.

My appetite has all but disappeared today. After arriving at HC with breakfast burritos to see Tommie as promised, I nearly had a heart attack to discover she'd never showed up the night before.

I called in reinforcements and right away, Van checked the tracker on her phone—the little blinking dot said she was at her apartment, which made no sense. She'd texted me when she left her place last night.

Charged with fear and my heart in my throat, we broke every speed limit getting to Tommie. My mind was a mess with scenarios I would never hope for anyone, let alone the woman I love.

When she opened her front door, my relief was palpable, coursing through my veins like jet fuel. My heart nearly beat right out of my chest, and Tommie, shit, she was a wreck.

I almost threw up when she recounted what happened and how she woke up to Ash next to her. I was both incensed, wanting to kill him, and terrified. I'd never felt so helpless and scared in my life. I couldn't keep my hands to myself, clinging to her as I sank against the wall, no longer able to support my own weight.

Now it's early afternoon and we're at HC, where she'll be living for the foreseeable future. In addition to a toxicology test, which I've no doubt will prove the coffee was laced with something, we also reviewed the recording inside her apartment.

Thank fuck he didn't do anything more twisted than watch her sleep. Ash, the sick creeper, must have gone directly from the warehouse, where he'd been with Taya and me, to her apartment. The phone notification at the warehouse must have told him she was passed out.

If only I'd known...

After last night, with Taya holding Tate at gunpoint and threatening the baby, and Tommie being drugged by Ash, HC has closed ranks. Ry took Tate, his sons and his mother, as well as Van's wife and kids, to a safe house outside of the city. And tomorrow's farewell party for Anna and Coop—they leave for Italy in a day—has been cancelled.

Neither Taya nor Ash will get to us.

"Is that enough?" Tommie asks, dishing salad onto my plate.

Her question pulls me from the hell of the past day and I'm so relieved to be here with her. She insisted on cooking dinner, not only for us but those of the HC crew who are working tonight.

"Yeah, thanks."

"Good. I forgot how much I enjoy cooking. It's hard to make something like this for just one person."

"Where did you learn to cook?"

"My mom." Her tone is melancholy, as is her expression.

"Well, it looks like she was a good cook." I dig in.

"Yes, and a great teacher. We would spend hours in the kitchen together. I suppose that's another reason why I haven't cooked in forever. It makes me think of her."

"You must miss them. Your parents." I don't want to push too far, too fast, but I want all of her. Her past and her future.

She's been through a lot in the past day and while she seems to be dealing well with it, I'm not so sure.

"Yes." She plays with her food. "And with Ash coming back last night… my parents are on my mind more than ever."

"That's understandable." I take a mouthful of the rich chicken. "Mmm, this is amazing."

She returns the compliment with a genuine smile. "Thanks. I like cooking for you."

Gunnar whines from his position on the floor at our feet, begging for a morsel or two.

"Sorry, bud, there's nothing for you." Tommie also insisted on getting the dog on our way to HC and I was all too happy to oblige.

Squeezing her hand, I dip my chin to her full fork, and she gets my drift, bringing it to her mouth. I bet she doesn't have much of an appetite either, but she needs sustenance.

We attempt to eat at least half of what's on our plates and after dinner, I clean up while she checks out the other conference room, where the meal she prepared for her colleagues has been devoured. She returns beaming and we head to her room to grab Gunnar's leash for his walk. Her phone rings on our way out.

"It's Anna." She flips the screen to me and answers it. "Hey, you. How are you doing?"

It's a warm summer night and we interlace our fingers, my thumb drawing lazy circles on the inside of her wrist as we stroll the streets.

Even many hours later, I still find myself needing reassurance that she's okay.

She talks with Anna for a bit and her tone is wistful, almost melancholy. "Okay, yeah, I'll see you tomorrow. Say hi to Coop. Love you."

She shoves her phone into her pocket and I bring our joined hands to my lips, lightly kissing the top of her knuckles. "You okay?"

"Sure. She's going to come by HC tomorrow." She shrugs. "It just sucks that there's no party for them."

"And what about her leaving?"

"I always hoped she'd take this gig. It's a once-in-a-lifetime opportunity. I'm going to miss her, obviously, but I'll visit. And she's coming back."

"How about when this is all over we go to Italy together and visit them?"

She stops, glancing up at me, eyes wide and sparkling. "Really? I'd like that."

My chest warms at seeing her mood lifted, at giving her something to look forward to when this nightmare is behind us. "Good. It's a date then."

I open the glass door to the office building, and she leads the way to the bank of elevators.

"Are you going to come back up or head home?" Stepping into the car, she presses the button for her floor and then bends to nuzzle the dog's neck.

"I was hoping to stay a little longer." She lifts her head, and call it wishful thinking, but I swear there's a hopeful glint in her eye. "Maybe even stay the night? I could crash on the couch."

She's staying in the biggest of the rooms, with a double bed and pull-out loveseat, and while I would prefer sleeping next to her, I'm not going to be presumptuous.

"You'd stay?" Tommie exits, taking Gunnar with her.

"Yes. I wanted you to stay with me, but since Van won't agree to that and I can't say I disagree... Anyway."

I shake my head, trying to erase the dark thoughts whirring

through my mind. Her protection is real and top priority, and I want to do my part to ensure her safety, at all costs.

"I just want to hang out with you as long as I can."

I should be more careful with my words, more guarded so as not to spook her with the idea of us, but with last night's scare, I can't seem to hold back.

"Yes. I want that too."

Maybe she feels the same way? Forget dithering or wasting time, let's just be open and honest with each other about what we want. Life is too short and too precious.

"Good." I take her hand in mine and she punches in a code on the keypad above the door handle. "You up for a movie?"

"Always." Her smile is brilliant and my stomach flips.

"Great. That new action movie you wanted to watch is out. Do you have any snacks?" I suddenly have the munchies.

"We just ate." She lightly pats my abs before bending to remove the dog's leash. "But I've got popcorn."

"Sweet. Another reason we're good together."

Standing, she stills in the entrance, eyes darkening with yearning. Her hand sinks into my hair, fingers wrapping around the nape of my neck to pull me to her. I lick my lips, pressing them together, contemplating whether I should just devour her luscious mouth or start with soft, chaste kisses.

I want to kiss her. Taste her again. And maybe she wants it too but what if I'm reading the situation wrong, blinded by my own desire? What she may need right now is for us to go slow, or maybe even pause. Words are one thing, stating what you want or how you feel, but acting on them takes things to another level. I don't want to rush her.

Stopping myself from taking her mouth, my lips skate across her soft forehead and she digs her nails into my scalp with a groan.

"Max, don't treat me like I'll break." She pulls my face down toward hers.

"I'm not. But you've been through a lot and I'm good with slow. I want you in any way and at any pace you want."

An easy smile stretches across her face and my chest threatens to explode. The joy and tenderness in her features, not an inkling of darkness or doubt, settles all my worries before she even says a word.

"I've been through much worse than the past twenty-four hours, and believe me when I tell you, I'm okay. I promise if I wasn't, you'd know."

"Good, because you can tell me anything." This time I press my lips to hers and the kiss is long and lazy.

I want to do this for hours, for days, just kiss her, but I pull back before we get carried away. She may be all right despite everything, but I need to slow things down. My feelings for her are more than physical, more than sex and I need to show her that my need to be with her is about who she is and what we have. It's about our friendship.

"Where did you say those snacks are?"

She laughs into my chest, shaking her head. "Come on, I'll show you."

We make popcorn and settle on the bed, side by side, to watch a movie. Not too long into it, on the screen, a man springs from the dome of a cathedral, running down the arc of the building, only to come to a complete stop on a ledge.

"That's insane and completely unrealistic. That guy would be dead leaping from a building like that." My incredulous outburst isn't real, it's more for Tommie—she gets a good laugh out of it.

To add to my mock outrage, I toss a kernel or two into the air and Gunnar leaps from his resting position, all too eager to gobble up any bit of food before it hits the carpet.

"Hey, but it looks good." She laughs, raggedly running a hand through my already disheveled hair. "This isn't about facts and physics. It's a stylized action flick."

"Fine, I'll park my brain." I snuggle into the bed and draw her closer to me.

My body betrays me and my dick twitches, liking her soft curves against my hard frame. She seems to like it too as her face inches toward my mouth. Then she freezes and something flickers through her eyes. I stiffen, wondering what I did wrong.

"Hang on a sec." She bounds from the bed with the dog on her heels.

"What's wrong?" I hit pause on the movie.

She now stands at the door, pressing buttons on a keypad next to the light switch that I hadn't noticed before.

"Okay, that's better." She smiles, sauntering back to the bed. "Now, where were we?"

"What was that?"

She crawls up the mattress next to me. "I turned off the cameras to this room."

I glance around, looking to the ceiling for any signs of recording. I shouldn't be shocked that we were being watched. This is HC after all.

"Glad you remembered." I smile and she wriggles into my side, sliding her hand once more around my neck.

"Tommie, status?" a familiar voice says into the room.

"What the hell?" Tensing, I search our surroundings once more for any indication as to where the voice is coming from.

Tommie snickers. "Hey, Tango, all is good. I turned off the cameras. I'll switch them back on later."

"Oh, I see how it is." There's no missing the innuendo or smile in Tango's voice over the speaker system.

"Goodnight, Tango." She chuckles, shaking her head.

"You two enjoy yourselves." His voice is now extra deep and husky, followed by a sharp clip that I hope indicates the sound system is now off.

Her fingers weave through my hair and I don't have time to think about potential listeners or viewers or anything else when her lips crash onto mine, tongue stealing into my mouth. It's clear she's the one in charge and it's sexy as hell. Who am I to fight her lead? I give up the fight to go slow, hungry for more of her kisses, for more of her touch, for more of her.

I sweep my fingers along her jaw to her hairline, where my fingers tangle with the thickness of her hair. My hot mouth trails soft, wet kisses down her neck and across her collarbone and she emits a stuttering sigh.

Attached at our mouths, tongues exploring, she fumbles with the button on my pants and I pause, capturing her hands.

"Are you sure?" I search her deep, longing gaze for even a hint of hesitation.

"Yes. I've never wanted anyone the way I want you. Just thinking about you makes me wet." Her words come in a husky rush.

"Let's see."

TOMMIE

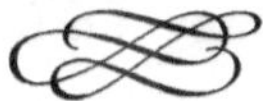

A wicked grin flashes across his face as his hand skates from my hip to slide under my dress. Quakes of pleasure shoot low into my belly and his strong fingers slide along my thigh, slipping into my panties. I jolt at his touch, firm and sure on my hot, aching core.

"Holy hell." His teeth sink into my neck. "You're so wet. So ready for me."

"Uh-huh," I whimper, wanting more of him as his warm lips cover mine in a languid, dizzying kiss that only intensifies when he slides a finger inside of me.

My thighs tremble, fingers digging into his shoulders as he pumps hard and fast, only stopping to add another finger. Sweet Jesus.

Sparks zip through my body and he swallows my moan. With his touch, my body burns, melting with Max all around me. In one fluid motion, my dress is over my head, then my bra and panties. I'm naked and he grinds against me, wearing way too many clothes.

Together, we work to remove his pants and then he does the rest as I push onto my elbows to watch. His body is incredibly defined. The corded muscles of his arms are firm and long, stretching across his broad shoulders down to his wide, solid chest.

His waist tapers into a V and those muscles are sexy, edible grooves on either side of his hips. My mouth feels dry and I swallow with difficulty as I stare at his beautifully honed body.

Max has always been attractive, sexy even, and I noticed from the day I met him, but now it's something altogether different. He's here in bed with me. Max.

My Max.

I get to have him, be with him and feel every glorious inch of him inside of me.

"Open for me. I want to see you." His voice is possessive, confident.

I widen my legs, baring myself as a slow burn simmers deep in my core. His smoldering green eyes dip between my legs and back to my face as he slides off his boxer briefs.

His throbbing shaft springs free, smacking against his hard abs, and moisture glistens on the tip. He takes his thick cock in his grip and pumps from base to crown while his gaze never strays from me.

My body burns, aches with my insatiable need for him and even more so as he moves off the bed, dropping to his knees, and yanks me by the ankles to the edge.

He flashes a crooked grin and kisses my inner thigh tenderly as the backs of his fingers caress my folds. I hiss at his touch and rock shamelessly against his face when he plants his mouth on me, his tongue doing wickedly magnificent things, licking and teasing.

Tension coils so deep, so tight within me and my fingers curl into his hair, holding his face to me as a sob escapes my lips. I squirm, moan, working myself against his mouth, almost there. One second I'm climbing, legs shaking, on the brink, and the next I'm soaring, crying out his name upon release.

As the body shocks ease and I catch my breath from the intensity of the pleasure, he pulls back, the pure lust in his gaze stealing the little breath I have left.

"Stay right there." His voice is rasped dominance and my insides quake in delicious anticipation. For more.

He grabs a condom from his discarded pants on the floor and climbs back onto the bed. The heat of his cock nudges at my leg and, unable to resist, my fingers curl around his hard steel. He jerks in my hand and I lick my lips, wanting to taste him.

"As much as I want your smart mouth around me, not now. I want to be inside you." He pushes back from my grip, putting on the condom.

He moves to fill his hands with my breasts, pinching my nipples, and I arch into his touch, his hot hands blistering every place they roam.

"Max, I want you now."

Holding my gaze, he moves to hover above me and slowly slides in, burying himself. I gasp at the feel of him. Fingers digging into his shoulder, I rapidly blink with sensations of him filling me and he stills.

I feel the change, the difference. This is Max. My best friend and now my lover. Feelings I've never experienced spring to life within me. My heart flips and twists, and the sensation is both magnificent and scary.

"Tommie."

My core pulses around him and he releases a whispered curse.

My hips buck, needing more of him. "Max, you gotta move. Please."

He nods, sweat beading along his hairline as he leans down to capture my mouth. He starts to thrust into me and I nip at his flesh, loving the way I cause him to hiss. His strokes match my moans as his cock fills me, my sensitive walls throbbing.

"Harder, faster," I beg.

Above me, he braces, pressing his hand into the wall over the bed, then picks up the pace. The sight of him, his body strong and lean, his breath hot and thrilling against my flesh, sends ripples of pleasure through me. I climax, strung tight at the same time every part of me scatters in the wind, and he follows, both of us screaming the other's name.

His hot body collapses on top of me and I love the way every inch of him touches me; his arms wrap around me, possessive and greedy.

Being this close to him doesn't feel like any of my concerns—going from friends to lovers—are founded. It doesn't feel like we ruined anything. I feel closer to him than I've ever been to anyone else.

And even if it's too soon to tell if any damage has been done, my stubborn heart already loves him and couldn't bear to lose him. After making love with Max, I'd sooner die than walk away from him.

"Why didn't we do this before?" His voice is low and rough, speaking into the crook of my neck.

"What? You mean sex?" My nails gently scrape down his back and he moans.

"Yeah." He pushes off me, rolling to my side. "But I mean you and me." He grins, squeezing my hip. "This. Us."

"It's a good question." I track his movements into the bathroom, likely to discard the condom, and when he returns, he gets back into bed, pulling the covers over us. "Did you ever think about me this way before now?"

"Hell yeah."

"Seriously?" I don't know why this surprises me. I thought of him this way.

"Yes." His lips hover over the shell of my ear and his warm breath warms me further. "Almost from the moment I met you, and my desire and attraction only grew as I got to know you."

His confession turns up the heat inside me and I feel his cock swelling against my thigh.

"What about you?" His teeth nip at my earlobe and tingles shoot up my spine.

"What about me?" I'm coy and he reaches to cup one of my breasts.

"Did you ever think about us like this?" He thumbs and pinches my nipple.

My chest heaves, pleasure sparking from where he is teasing me straight to my core, and I'm unable to think of a response. To comprehend what he's asking. I just want him. Again. I only want him and I tell him just that.

"All the time."

I move to straddle him, my bare chest pressing into his as my lips rain kisses, alternating between tender and urgent, all over his jawline, mouth and cheeks.

"We really were kinda foolish," I say between kisses as my hands roam of their own free will, memorizing and cherishing every hard plain and chiseled hollow of his body.

"Yes. We need to rectify that, stat."

"We most certainly do."

We kiss again and I feel that familiar tug of need, for him, low in my belly as he dips his head and takes my breast into his hot mouth, swirling his tongue around my hard bud.

Lifting his head, he looks at me like we belong together. Like we always have and none of that has changed, only become stronger. "I love you, Tommie."

I blink, my eyes wet, and beam. "Max, I love you too."

He grabs hold of my face, bringing his mouth to mine. He's gluttonous, ravishing my mouth, and I don't want him to stop. It's as if I've shattered his control and I feel the same way. I am lost and found in Max.

* * *

THE CALL COMES at five-thirty in the morning. Max fumbles in the dark for his phone, which is ringing on the bedside table.

Groggily, he answers, "Conrad."

He stiffens, rigid from head to toe as he sits up and swings his legs over the side of the bed. It has to be Taya.

"I'll be there in thirty." He hangs his head, legs open as he rests his forearms on his thighs.

"Your mother?" I rest my hand on his warm back, sliding the other arm around his waist and bringing my cheek to rest on the hard plane of his shoulder blade.

"Yes. I have to get going. Is someone around to wire me up?" He turns, taking my face in his hands, and plants a soft kiss on my lips.

"I'll do it." I run a hand through my mussed hair.

"No, sleep."

"I'm not going back to sleep knowing you're going to be with Taya." I throw back the covers. "I'll be in the surveillance room."

We dress, and while Max takes the dog for a quick walk, I set things up for when he gets back. We have to move quickly, knowing he's being watched, and Taya also has expectations on him showing up as soon as she calls.

I'm nervous for many reasons but most of all, this is the first time Max is wearing a wire. He isn't usually checked but there's always a first time.

"What if she pats you down?" I secure the last of his shirt buttons before taking a walk around him to make sure nothing is visible.

"She won't search me. She's never done it before."

"Yeah, but you said one time a new guy did. And you've never slept at HC before." I now face him again and swallow past the lump in my throat. This is serious. "What if she does this time? And don't forget about Ash. He doesn't trust anyone. He might demand that you're checked."

"If they search me then I'll use the code word." His chest rises on a deep intake of air before deflating with his exhale. "Isn't that what I'm supposed to do? And someone from HC will be close by."

"Yeah, I'll be there." Tango, the booming voice through the speaker last night, steps into the room. "And that's exactly what you do."

"I know but… just don't do anything risky."

Tango comes to stand next to me, placing a hand on my shoulder. "Don't stress. If anything starts to feel off, I'll get him out. Promise."

"I know." I don't sound convinced and I internally cringe.

Typically, I'd be okay with all of this. Our team has done this kind of thing more times than I can count and if the shit hits the fan, we get our man out. Always.

But this is Max.

And Ash knows what he means to me.

"Okay." Tango lifts his arm, glancing at his watch. "Clock's ticking, you better get a move on."

Max nods and, reading the room, Tango leaves the two of us alone.

"I'm going to be okay. Are you?" His hands cup my face and my fingers curl around his wrists, needing to hold onto him for a bit longer.

"Yeah. I'll be better once you're out of there." I try to keep any of the edge or anxiety I'm feeling from my voice.

"I've got to be at the hospital after, but I'll text you."

"You'll come by later?"

"Yeah. Is Gun okay to stay here? If not, I can get the dog walker to pick him up."

"No, he's fine."

"And I'll be fine too." His fingers tip my chin up and the tenderness in his tone matches his gaze.

Max pulls my head to his, bringing our bodies flush against each other. I wasn't aware I'd been holding my breath until he wraps his arm around me. He bends his head to mine and his lips destroy all thought or worry. I hold him close, arms sliding around his waist, needing all of him.

MAX

Removing the stethoscope from around my neck, I place it in the black bag on the concrete floor of the warehouse basement. I've examined nearly two dozen women this morning, although the term girls is more accurate. I'd wager the oldest is pushing twenty-one at the most.

And as if that isn't bad enough, more than a third weren't healthy. Some had walking pneumonia and one, I think, had syphilis. Taya isn't pleased with the news as she barks orders for the men to get rid of the girls.

There's a chorus of sobs, or more an outcry, across the basement as the men begin to gather up the women who are unfit for whatever is planned.

My fists curl, tightening by the second. "I'll take them to a local clinic. No one needs to know where they came from."

It's clear that some of these women were vulnerable before this, living in unsafe, maybe even just as dangerous situations. I want to stop the men from taking them away. Whatever their fate, it can't be good.

"No. That isn't your job. They're useless." Maybe sensing the tension building in me, my mother motions for one of her men to grab my arm.

Turning her back on the depravity she's the ringmaster of, she leads the way through the dark halls and up the stairs to the ground floor.

Because it's so dark, it's hard to grasp just how big the basement is or how many cells they have or most importantly, how many women. Since that night with the woman dying of a gunshot wound, I would guess that I've examined close to sixty women, with about thirty percent unwell.

While I didn't see it with my own eyes, I'm more than sure the sickly are no longer here. Bile rises in my throat, knowing the ill women are living on borrowed time and I'm helpless to stop it.

HC as well as the FBI and the NYPD have made it very clear that I'm to follow Taya's orders to the letter. I can't cause trouble or raise suspicion. They want to shut down the whole operation.

My mother leads me to her office and I shut the door, resolved to find out more, speed things up so law enforcement can do their jobs sooner.

"Why did you spend the night at Hart Corporation?"

She isn't even trying to hide the fact that she's having me followed. Does she suspect I've double-crossed her?

"Why are you having me watched?" My arms fold over my chest and I scowl, trying to act unfazed by this line of conversation.

"Answer the question." She matches my glare with her own.

"Tommie's staying there right now."

She taps her nails annoyingly on the desk. "What's going on with you two? You seem closer than usual."

I don't stop and think until the words are out of my mouth. "We're together."

Shit, Ash. If he's here or listening, he doesn't need to hear this. It'll only serve to enrage him.

"Together? You're an item?" Her lip curls as if she smells a skunk and with my nod, she snarls. "I don't have time for this. We're speeding things up. I'll need you twice a day over the next few days."

She isn't asking nor is she offering an explanation. She steels her spine, widening her shoulders as if anticipating my protest. I do have one rebuttal—well, many—but one for this purpose. The perfect segue to push for more details.

"You do realize I have a full practice, surgeries and community obligations. Getting away from the hospital is hard enough as it is. Now you're asking for more time?"

"Max." She curls her fingers into loose balls at her sides.

"No. Listen, Mother." I lean into her space. "How much longer?"

"Not much more." She surprises me with her response. I'd expected silence or worse, a dismissal.

"You mentioned a meeting or something you're working toward. When is it?"

Her glacial eyes skate over my face and the chill of her glare settles uncomfortably on my flesh. "A week from Friday."

Holy shit. It takes everything within me to keep my expression blank, uncaring at the news. We *finally* have a date.

"And what happens then? Am I expected to be there?"

Folding her bony arms over her chest, she makes a displeased sound in the back of her throat. "This isn't your concern. But yes, I might need you that evening."

Okay, another detail. It's at night. Nice. "And what exactly is taking place?"

"I can't tell you."

"Fine. If you don't tell me, I'm not showing up." I raise my finger to stop her response. "And don't start threatening Tate or my nephews. Or Tommie for that matter."

It's hard to keep the smugness out of my voice knowing Tate is out of town and Tommie is safe at HC. For far too long, this woman has had the upper hand.

Her hand lightly bangs on the desktop. "Why are you being so stubborn?"

"This isn't stubborn. I've been around long enough to know whatever it is you're working toward, it's something I want no part of."

"You'll do as I say." Dismissing me, she sits at her desk and opens her laptop.

I turn to leave and think better of it. I'm here, and this is an opportunity to find out more.

"Does Ash have anything to do with the upcoming auction?"

I've screwed up. Why am I asking for trouble? First, I admit I'm with Tommie and now, I've not only called this event an auction, I've also insinuated Ash is involved.

For a smart guy, I'm really bad at this covert stuff. I'm not used to analyzing and calculating everything I'm going to say or should say. Give me a broken heart or a blocked artery and I can do wonders.

It's a bold move, mentioning him and calling the event an auction, since I'm acting on what Tommie and the others at HC have shared.

But I'm hoping she thinks I've made this leap because Ash was at one of the warehouses and it doesn't take a genius to figure those women are being trafficked.

"What did you say?" Her tone is as sharp as a blade.

"You heard me."

It isn't clear if she's agitated by the suggestion that Ash is involved, or that I dared to label the event.

"We are done here. Be ready for your next call." She stares intently at the screen and I leave.

I check my messages and Edith has moved my day around, so I have time and decide to head to HC. I fire off a quick text to Tommie letting her know I'm on my way and her response is short and immediate.

Tommie: Good. We need to talk.

She's waiting for me at reception with our dog at her side. He bounces onto all paws, wagging his tail, happy to see me. Whereas her lips are pursed into a tight line, brows knitted.

"Let's talk in here." She turns and I follow her into a conference room.

"I know it's not breakfast but I brought burritos." I deliberately keep my tone light, even sensing she isn't pleased at something I did, and hold up the bag with the meal we never got to enjoy a couple of days ago.

"Thanks." She's single-minded, barely pausing to place the bag on the conference table without so much as a whiff. Usually, at the very least, she'd open the paper bag to smell the Mexican deliciousness.

"What's wrong?" I lean in to kiss her, needing to make this better and wanting to touch her, be near to her.

Our lips meet and she inches forward, laying a hand on my arm, fingers curling to tighten her grip. The kiss is quick, almost mechanical, and she's the first to pull away.

Her text said we needed to talk, and sure, while never a good sign, I figured it was to debrief about the warehouse. But this seems like more. She's definitely not happy about something.

"This morning was stupid." She examines me with a discerning frown.

"What was?" My nerves are sparking as I wait for her to unload whatever it is that's eating at her.

"Well, where should I start?" Her sarcastic tone causes me to tense. "You pushed Taya every chance you got. Coming right out and asking about Ash's involvement and telling her you know it's an auction. What were you thinking, Max?"

Despite her obvious agitation, she inches closer, grabbing my hand in what feels like frustration.

I've already berated myself for this fuck up, but we are also running out of time. I was trying to help.

"I was doing the job I was told to do. Get as much information as possible."

"Without raising suspicion," Van says from behind me. I turn on my heel only to be hit with his stern expression. "You were rattling her cage."

"I saw an opportunity and took it." There's a defensive grit to my tone I don't anticipate.

"She knew you stayed here last night." Displeasure clouds his voice.

"We knew she was watching me." This time I try to kill my bite but end up sounding more sarcastic.

Van doesn't miss my unintentional but demeaning insinuation and scowls, resting his hands on his hips, shoulders squared in a *let's not do this* posture.

Like a steamroller flattening the mounting tension, Tommie's injured tone hits me straight in the gut when she says, "And you told her about us."

"Yeah, I messed up. Okay. I'm not good at this." I angrily run my hand through my hair on a sharp exhale. "I shouldn't have said anything. I wasn't thinking about Ash."

My lips curve in a sorry excuse of a smile, more rueful than anything else. Even with the bold but no less stupid move I made, I'm not so sure I would change anything. We have more information than we did yesterday.

"Yes, there's Ash. But she's dangerous too." Her tone softens and she swings the hand she's holding between us. "Don't be naïve enough to think because she's your mother you're untouchable."

"You shouldn't be here. From now on, we debrief at the hospital. And you can no longer stay overnight." Van bends to rub Gun's coat once and stands, saying gruffly, "You guys should most probably cool things until this is done."

"What? I've been here before. Taya knows Tommie is staying here." I clench my jaw to stop more stupidity from spewing from my mouth. Of course he's right, even if I don't like it. Before I can say I agree, his sharp glare stabs me in the chest.

"Even more reason for her to be suspicious. And let's not forget about Ash. Or need I remind you Tommie was drugged?" He leans into my personal space and his waning patience is evident in his fiery eyes.

I'm trying not to take this personally. He's just doing his job and looking out for Tommie, and for me. I just really don't like how I feel like a useless idiot.

"Ash is going to make a move again and we might not be so lucky the next time. We don't need to be rubbing his nose in the two of you together right now. We have to be smart."

"I get it," I say through gritted teeth at the same time as Tommie releases my hand.

I glance to her and her expression is grim. Van nods, storming to the doorway, where he pauses to look at me over his shoulder.

"Max, good work today. We now have a date." He flashes a wicked grin and some of my ire disappears. "Tripp's waiting in conference room three to debrief. Don't leave him waiting too long."

Now it's just the two of us and I'm a ball of mixed emotions. Part pent-up frustration and part elated to get recognition for the new intel. I thought this morning had been a success and for the first time, I feel like I'm doing something to help those women. To stop my mother and Ash.

"Well, I'm glad to see someone is happy with the information I got out of Taya. We know more than we did yesterday."

I turn to face Tommie and she's petting Gunnar. Sensing my gaze, she stands and grabs a small bag at her feet to hand it to me. It contains the dog's things like his bowl and leash.

"Van's right. You should go."

"What? Aren't you going to come to the debrief? We could have a quick bite while I talk to Tripp."

"No, I think it's best if you go on your own." She hands me the food and I refuse to take it.

"You keep it." I don't like feeling this way.

She's already creating the distance Van ordered and I hate it. Hate the idea of being separated from her. We are stronger together.

"I'm not really hungry and if I put it in the fridge, someone will eat it before I can even say my name." Her levity falls flat like her smile. "Thanks, but please eat it. Tripp will go easy on you if you share."

Great, Tripp's going to pile onto what has already been an awesome visit to HC. I put down the bags and step in front of her. "Are we okay?"

"Of course." She rests her hands on my waist and the knot in my chest loosens a bit, taking her touch as a good sign that I haven't completely screwed this up.

"I don't like this at all. You're scared for me, I get that. And you don't like feeling like this. I get that too because my girl is never scared."

Now she smiles at the use of *my girl* and her eyes shine, making me feel ten times better than a moment ago.

"I just don't want you taking crazy risks. If anything were to happen to you…" Her voice wavers and water wells in her eyes.

"Nothing is going to happen to me. I promise I'll be more careful."

My mouth covers hers and her lips are soft and at first, slow and tentative. Her fingers sink into my waist and our mouths meld and meet, over and over again, more hungry and needy.

"Max, debrief, now." Van sticks his head into the room and I growl into her mouth, wanting to shut out everything but Tommie.

MAX

The sun is high in the sky and the day is hot but at least there's a warm breeze. Outside my building, Gunnar is at my side, tongue wagging and eager for his walk.

I miss Tommie.

The past couple of days have been exhausting, between work and the twice-daily calls from Taya. Half the time, I don't know if I'm coming or going, and Tommie... we haven't seen each other since Van told us to stay apart.

I want to see her. Be with her.

I'm frustrated, so a run seems like a good way to burn off some of this tension and clear my mind. I've got a few hours until I'm back at the hospital and I'm sure Mother will call again. The sooner we shut down Taya and Ash, the sooner I can be with Tommie again.

"Max," a woman calls from behind me.

Mid-stride, I pause and turn. My mother's driver is on the curb in front of her car. Taya peers out at me from the back-passenger window.

"Get in," she orders, and her visage gradually disappears behind the tinted car window rolling up.

What the hell? She is the last person I want to see or talk to. I'm already in a foul mood, things will only get worse. But ignoring her isn't an option and this doesn't feel like a summons to a warehouse. She usually calls.

The driver holds the car door open and my dog hops in first.

"He stays outside. Tie him to a post or something." She doesn't bother to hide her disgust for my four-legged companion and for the first time all day, I smile.

"No. He comes with me or we walk."

She glowers but keeps her lips sealed as we climb into the roomy sedan. Gunnar sits at my feet.

"What did you want?"

"How are things with Tommie?"

I narrow my gaze, what is she up to? "Please tell me you didn't come all the way uptown to chat about my girlfriend. What is it?"

A sharp glint flashes in her eyes before she dons a token smile. "If you're together, why haven't you seen her in a few days?

"What do you want?" I'm getting tired of her little digs and reminders that she's my shadow. Once again, she's fully aware that I haven't seen Tommie in a couple days.

"Did she tell you about Ash?"

Fire burns in my belly. I'm not talking to her about this. "Last time or I'm leaving."

I pick up the leash resting on my thigh and wrap the strap around the palm of my hand. "Why did you call me over?"

"I don't want to see you hurt." She sniffs and juts out her chin.

Oh please. She reeks of an agenda.

"Well, that's kind of you." My dry tone causes her to tighten her jaw. "But it still doesn't explain why you're here."

"Can you trust her? Ash and Tommie have a past and I wouldn't be surprised if she's sleeping with him."

"What?"

Her accusation is absurd. Is she really clueless as to their past? Or is she prodding to see what I know? And if so, why? What is she up to?

"Do you know where she is right now?" It's clear in her tone she does.

"Taya," I grit out, exasperated.

I've no idea where she is, and this little pop-up meeting feels like a set-up. Taya is about to drop some kind of bomb.

"Get to the fucking point. Do you actually have something of use to tell me? If not, we're done here." With leash in hand, I go for the door handle.

"Max, put aside your distrust of me for just one second and hear me out." She tugs at my arm and it takes all my restraint not to pull away from her touch.

"I'm listening." *Barely.*

"Tommie is with Ash right now." The knot grows in the pit of my stomach. What? That can't be. Van would never allow it unless it's some kind of planned operation. But would Van risk her life? Take that chance? I don't think so.

Taya is bluffing. Is she suspicious of my now-intimate relationship with Tommie and my more frequent visits to HC? Right now, she's examining my reaction with keen interest. That has to be it.

"Where is she?" I lean into her, placing my hand on her upper arm and getting into her face.

She points in the direction of my window. "Look over there."

Out the tinted window across a busy Fifth Avenue, by an entrance to Central Park, Tommie is there, in a striking summer dress and high heels. She's standing not even an inch from Ash.

Every nerve in my body fires with a burning need to be at her side. Ash towers over her seductive five-foot nine frame, looking at her as if he owns her. She's clearly upset and something inside me snaps. I open the car door, already feeling like I've failed her. I need to get to her.

Taya grabs at my arm. "Ash is obsessed with her."

Like a tightly wound spring let loose, I lash out at her. "Yes, he is."

I lean forward and my hand flies to her face, fingers gripping her jaw in place while the other secures both her wrists. "And he wants to hurt her. Take her with him when he leaves New York City."

Taya's eyes widen. She's surprised by my words. She doesn't know a thing about their past. Is she really that oblivious to who, or what, Ash is?

Out of the corner of my eye, there's a flash of movement and the slam of a car door. The next thing I know, her driver grabs the back of my collar and arm. Gunnar is pushing to stand, a low snarl rolling through his throat.

"Get the fuck off her," he says, trying to haul me from the car.

"It's all right," Taya says to him at the same time Gunnar barks in the car. We both wince at the piercing sensation in our ears and I release my hold on my mother. No longer fighting, the brute removes me from the car, and I try to reassure my dog that the man at my back isn't a threat. That's easier said than done.

Gunnar's ready to attack and as soon as I'm free from the vehicle, no longer touching Taya, the driver steps back. Eyes nailed to the animal, his hands move out to his sides, in plain sight, making it clear that he isn't going to harm me.

"Back off and he won't go any further," I say to the driver, pulling on Gunnar's leash, and the man slips into the front of the car.

"Stay the fuck away from Tommie." I bend to look into the car, and glare at my mother before slamming the door.

High-strung and volatile, I bound across the street. Ash is manhandling Tommie and their backs are to me as they walk into the park. Although it appears as if she isn't willing. She struggles to fight him off but it's subtle. You'd have to be watching to catch it. Is she hesitant to cause a scene? Fuck that.

They are too far away for me to do anything of significance and I can't seem to move fast enough. It's as if I'm moving in quicksand and for every step I take, I sink further into the abyss. Further away from Tommie.

His hands on her provokes a rage in the deepest and darkest parts of me that I never knew was possible. My body is wound tight and loaded, just itching to bring down that disgusting excuse for a human being.

"Get your hands off her." I'm practically yelling, not yet close enough to rip his hands off her myself, and that's infuriating.

Some of the people nearby stop what they're doing to stare at me and then the couple I seem to be focused on. But none of them matter. We might as well be the only three people on the planet.

At the sound of my voice, Ash stalls and looks back in my direction, as does Tommie. I can't look at her, make eye contact, or else I might lose it. I've got eyes for only Ash and the feeling is mutual.

His glare is priceless, and his calm confident presence slips for one split second. And then I see it.

The monster that he truly is makes an appearance.

Intense, fierce, and wholly evil.

Instead of shunning the danger, like many would, seeing him for what he is only serves to intensify my need to do something, to get to her. To make sure he pays for all his atrocities.

TOMMIE

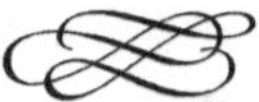

The yellow traffic light blinks to red, and I slow my pace, stopping at the edge of the sidewalk. Guilt eats at me for successfully escaping my protection. Since being drugged, I haven't been anywhere without a tail, and now I'm across the street from Max's building, waiting for the light to turn green.

Meanwhile, Tango, my colleague and agreed-upon bodyguard, is sitting in his car about a block away from the gym in Brooklyn where he thinks I'm working out. He'll be pissed and embarrassed, and Van will be furious, when they discover I left a clone of my phone at the gym. I'm using a cloaking device on my real phone so I could leave undetected.

It's been two days since I last saw Max, and true to her word, Taya has ordered him to a few locations twice a day. He's exhausted, and while we text daily, and have spoken once, it isn't the same. And even more importantly, there's still a lingering tension between us from the last time we saw each other.

That's my fault.

I was harsh, needing him to realize the stakes are high. His mother may be dangerous, but next to Ash, she's a puppy. And while he knows what Ash did to me and what we suspect he's done to countless other people, knowing it and actually living it are two different things.

And finally, Max likely suspects why Ash came to New York and he's most probably guessed that it's my greatest fear. But until today, I haven't dared say it out loud, not even to myself.

Today, everything changes.

I didn't endure unspeakable torture at the hands of Ash, time in a psychiatric hospital, and a decade of intensive therapy, to silence my power and courage or, worse yet, hand over everything to Ash.

He came here for me. To lock me away, and this time, I may never see the light of day. I have to explain this to Max. I have to tell him for his sake and mine what I am most afraid of. That's why I'd been harsh with him. When he pushed his mother, in turn, he was pushing Ash.

And on top of fearing my captivity or death, I have one fear that's far greater. I fear Max's death.

A shadow casts a dark looming figure over me, and it's the only indication that something is about to snuff out the dim light of hope with a cruel gust of reality.

"Thomasina." His thick, predatory tone is a hot iron to my senses.

A frisson of heat bubbles through me and I hiss at my arrogance. When will I learn?

I fucked up. Again.

No matter how vigilant I was to make sure I wasn't being followed, he still managed to sneak up on me.

Tall and imposing, Ash grips my elbow, turning us away from the street.

Away from my destination.

Away from Max.

We push through the small crowds of people everywhere toward the park and I'm grateful we aren't alone. At least, I have a chance of escaping, or at least causing a scene. Yet even knowing that, my insides twist and fear burns through me.

I could run or scream. But it may take someone too long to realize something is wrong. Ash is fast and has too many years of experience with capturing people in broad daylight.

And most importantly, these strangers likely won't see danger when they look at us. We're two people, some might even think a couple with his hand on me, strolling through the park. A confident, handsome man with a woman at his side. An expensive dress and high heels.

At first blush, some may even say we're married or in love. The thought sickens me. He inches closer, fingers like a sphincter on my arm to assert his control.

Shoulders squared, I equal him with my boldness. "What the fuck are you doing here?"

Black pools for eyes widen and nostrils flare as a hand flies toward my face, fingers latching onto my jaw. My spine stiffens, preparing for his blow.

"You have a dirty mouth." He digs further into my flesh. "Such a shame. This mouth used to be so sweet and innocent. So pure. I should wash the filth right out of you."

"Fuck you." My words bathe him in contempt.

"We can do this the hard way." He leans into me, one hand now at my waist and the other still clamped around my now-aching jaw. "I'd prefer that, but I was trying a different approach. And so far, it's done me no favors."

"What do you want?"

"I enjoyed watching you set up your life. Your illusion of freedom. I found it quite amusing. Although not your dalliances." His dark, menacing gaze feels like an invasion —his black soul infecting me.

"Many a time I was tempted to teach you a lesson. You so easily threw open your legs for men. Stupid, useless men. How you gave of yourself so easily. It disgusted me. Disappointed me."

He pauses and I want to punch him in the face and run.

"Why? Because you weren't getting your cut?" My chest heaves and his fingers sink further into my flesh as I release a long hiss of pain.

A strange, twisted satisfaction washes over me. I shouldn't be surprised he knows about my reckless days. The random guys, the public sex. That would have driven him mad, just another reason why I did it.

His cutting voice slices through my thoughts as if reading my mind. "Promiscuity doesn't become you."

"Neither does slavery." I practically spit the last word and his posture stiffens.

"Little One, don't tempt me. Not now. Not here." The knuckles of his free hand skate along my cheek and I bow my head, trembling.

Revulsion churns in my gut. I never wanted to hear those words again so long as I lived. His name for me, *'Little One,'* demands my obedience, and once upon a time that's what it would have granted him.

No longer.

Never again.

"Why are you in business with Taya?" At this point in time, it shouldn't be important but I want to understand their relationship, see if there's anything I can use.

His predatory gaze liquefies and a wicked grin springs to his mouth. "That's business. And that's all I'll say."

"Then I have nothing to say to you." I attempt to pull from his grasp but it's futile.

"We are not done, Little One." He releases my jaw, but swiftly yanks me to his side, hooking the hand at my hip around my waist. "We're going home."

My insides lock and heart-stopping fear floods my veins. "I'm not going anywhere with you."

I fight his desire to move, stiffening my limbs and turning my body into deadweight. He bends, every muscle in his hard frame strung tight like a garrote.

"You've more than tested my patience. I didn't care how or when I snatched you. If there were casualties, all the better, but Zero convinced me to keep it clean and simple. This was between you and me. Take only you. Harm no one."

Hot breath, as if from the flames of hell, singes my ear, and the hand at my waist slithers, lightning fast, to my nape, where it grips me like a choker.

"But Little One, you are making this difficult. Every time you fight me, I'm tempted to change my mind. Kill Evan, his wife and their children..." Every word is measured, designed to mutilate.

Like a shard of glass, my jagged breath lances my throat and I tilt my head to look up at him, no longer caring if he sees my anguish. "Please, no."

"Maybe even let you watch." His laughter is low and brittle. "You see, I want nothing more than to kill him. And kill Max." Laced with acid, everything from his mouth burns.

"Ash—"

"And every time you fight me, make this hard or messy, it only serves to remind me how you must be punished. And how men who take what's mine must pay." His fingers spear the skin along the column of my neck, such a tight grip that it feels as if he could snap my head right off if he wanted.

A child's delightful squeal rings through the air as the toddler is spun around several times by a man, perhaps her father. They are only feet away and we're still surrounded by many more people. I could make a scene, beg for help, yell fire.

As if reading my thoughts, he tightens his hold. "If you scream, Max's death won't be swift or merciless. I will make him suffer."

His threat breaches my chest and grabs at my heart, squeezing painfully. So much pain that I expect my ribs to crack and the organ to explode.

"Fine. Let's go," I say through clenched teeth, knees weak as my body aches with fear.

He's won. And once again, my stupidity handed him the opportunity to take me. I would have Tango at the ready or better yet, an entire HC squad, if only I'd listened to Van. How could I think I was smarter than Ash or Zero? They've always been one step, or more, ahead of me.

"Start walking."

"Get your hands off her." Max's commanding voice comes from behind and a few heads turn in his direction.

Judging from the sound, he isn't close but close enough that Ash stiffens beside me before catching himself. He loosens his limbs and casually peers over his shoulder, as do I.

Despite the aloof demeanor, his expression morphs into that of controlled rage as Max confidently eats the pavement toward us, the dog at his side.

I want to be happy to see him. Blond hair like a golden crown, piercing green eyes and a determined expression that bolsters my courage.

The possibility of escape is even greater now, but all I can think about is Ash's threat.

He will kill Max.

I can't let that happen.

Max won't leave without me and who knows if Ash will walk away. The only thing possibly in our favor is that there are witnesses. Someone could film this. Someone could call the police.

Ash wouldn't hesitate to hurt or kill anyone, but he doesn't want to be captured. He wouldn't want evidence that could be used against him at any time. His freedom is his most valued possession. Isn't that ironic?

"Leave now." I wrestle to break free of the hand still at the back of my neck. "People are watching. Someone could livestream this. Police could come."

I plant the notion in his head, prying open the door to the possibility of him simply walking away. His fingers pulse at my nape but he doesn't move.

Desperate to get him to leave, to save Max from any kind of physical altercation with him, I steel my spine, preparing to rip my heart out.

"I'll cut ties with Max, Van, all of them at HC. I promise. Just leave them alone and go now." My words are whispered and rushed, not wanting an approaching Max to overhear. "You and I both know we'll see each other again."

My heart breaks at the thought, but it isn't a lie. This isn't over. If he walks away, it only delays our inevitable showdown.

"Let her go, now. I've called the cops." Max flashes his phone and Gunnar bares his teeth, emitting a low growl at Ash.

"This is between Thomasina and me. Walk away, Max." His demand has no teeth and his hold on me is somewhat weaker. I sense he's considering what I've said and maybe he's trying to see if Max will back down.

"You've got it all wrong. You're going to walk away right now." Steadfast green eyes fix on me and I can't deny I'm comforted to see him. "Tommie, come to me."

I turn my head to Ash in an unspoken appeal for release. He loosens his hold and says menacingly, low enough so only I can hear, "Remember your promise. I will hold you to it."

His hand drops from my neck and I bolt toward Max, sparing a glance behind me. Ash's back is to us as he heads down the park path.

"Are you okay?" Max's hand cradles my jaw and I nod, relief rolling over me in waves.

"Yes. Let's get out of here." Grabbing his arm, I hurriedly lead the way to the street. Forget the lights or crosswalk, neither cautious or caring about the moving vehicles or my killer heels that may send me careening to the ground.

"Hey, slow down." His voice is soothing as he tightens his grip on me and we run to the other side of the street.

Once more, I glance back to where we were moments ago and Ash stands at the passenger door of a dark car, staring intently at us. He doesn't need to be near me, or even use words; I don't have a lot of time to follow through with my promise before he follows through on his threats.

TOMMIE

"Ms. Carrington, Mr. Conrad, good afternoon." The doorman's cheery greeting is a sharp contrast to the dark and troubling thoughts swirling around in my mind.

Max ushers me ahead of him into the building and I nod to Gerald, forcing a smile because I don't trust my voice at the moment. I'm too focused on what I'm about to do. What I must do for Max's safety. For the sake of all their lives.

I suppose I always knew it would come to this. Where Ash is concerned, I never really had any other choice. I'd only hoped we'd be able to find another way. But now it's clear there is only one thing for me to do.

"Good afternoon, Gerald," Max says, pulling myself and Gunnar with him into the elevator.

As happy as I am to see and feel him beside me, I can't indulge in this. And it is an indulgence. If I go up to his apartment, I will never leave. His place is like a home to me, maybe even *our* home.

This man is my home and I can't put him in any more jeopardy than he already is.

Wiping my tears, I steel my spine and press the red stop button on the elevator wall. The metal car comes to a grinding halt, an alarm sounds and Max grabs onto the brass hand railing. Gunnar springs to his feet, barking.

"What the—" Max reaches toward the rectangular panel by the door and then stops, snapping his head in my direction.

Confusion clouds his expression as his gaze falls upon me, where I'm crouched down to calm the dog.

"Tommie, what are you doing?"

I whisper soft soothing words into Gunnar's neck and he finally settles, sitting at my side but still alert.

"This is building security, are you okay?" A male voice crackles through the speaker on the elevator panel.

"Yes, we're fine." Max's aggravated tone is hard to miss. "Could you please get us out of here?"

"Yes, sir. Just give us a minute. We'll get the elevator going."

I stand and the sight of his prominent, handsome features, rigid jaw and gleaming eyes aimed at me pierce right through any of my real or metaphorical armor.

"Thank you for cutting in back there at the park." My arms fold over my middle, needing to keep my hands to myself.

"You don't need to thank me." He steps closer, intent on building a bridge to me. "Tell me what's going on."

"You're my best friend. One of the best people to ever come into my life, and I'm filled with gratitude to have had this time with you."

"What? You're not making any sense." His hand lands on my hip, and I pull back out of self-preservation. I can't handle his touch right now.

He stills at what looks like rejection and his gaze sharpens on my face. And then choosing not to read my body language, or more likely, dispensing his own rejection—he isn't going to let me shut him out—he pulls one arm from my body and takes my hands in his.

We're now standing only a foot apart and my world shrinks to this little space; all that matters to me is Max and our dog. And I want to cry. Escaping Ash all those years ago wasn't enough. It wasn't the end. Will there ever be an end?

And at what cost? What more do I have to give up? To lose? What more do I have to do to be finally and forever rid of that monster?

"Why does this feel like goodbye?" His tone is solemn, as is his expression, and he takes my other hand in his.

I swallow back the mounting regret and force my voice to the forefront. I have no choice. Yes, I'm acting out of fear. I promised Ash and need to follow through. It is the smartest thing I can do.

"I can't be in your life anymore. I can't be your friend. I can't be your lover."

"What are you talking about?" His fingers clamp around mine and my heart cracks. "Don't let him win. Don't do this."

His imploring tone batters at my resolve but I know what is at stake. I would rather die than risk Max's life.

"Don't you get it? I'm not letting him win. I need to protect those I love. And Max, I love you." I pull and he releases my hands.

I brush past him to stand by the still firmly closed door. "I would never forgive myself if you… if you suffered a similar fate to my parents." My voice cracks and I press my lips together, pushing back the tears. "We need to be apart."

Shaking his head violently, he gets into my space again, trying to take my hands, but I clasp them firmly behind my back.

He scowls, features taut and strained. "You can't do this to us."

"I'm doing this *for* us. For you. We need to get rid of Ash and right now... Right now, together we are a threat to Taya and Ash. They are concerned about us. Maybe even afraid."

"Did he say that? Did he threaten you?" His eyes gain a clarity I'm used to seeing when he's talking about his work, his patients. He's putting it all together. "No, he threatened me."

"Max, listen. Together we're in more danger than apart. They most probably think we've teamed up. If we're going to take them down, we have to split up. Ash has to think that he's won. He has to think that I'm actually doing what I told him I would do."

"What you told him you would do?" His brows knit and he cocks his head to one side, waiting expectantly.

"Yes. I told him I would end things with you. That I would walk away from you. From Van. All of you. I need to know that you are safe. You are my weakness and he knows that. I am leaving and you need to continue your work with Van and HC to bring them down."

"What? You're leaving? What the hell does that mean?" Frustrated and maybe even feeling powerless, his hand cuts a jagged path through his mussed hair.

"I'll be safe. He needs to think he's in control." The elevator jumps, surging back to life, and we're on the move.

"You'll never lose me. Never. I swear on my life. I love you." My hand rests flat on his chest, right where his heart is. "I'll always be here, but I have to go. It's best."

My hand drops to my side, still tingling from the heat of him and I spin to face the door, hitting a button for a floor well before his. I'll get off before it's too late. Before I change my mind and give in to my selfish need. I won't allow it. I can't have Max. Not now anyway.

"Fuck… how will I contact you? Know you are okay? And what about Van? Is he on board with this?"

He tugs at my elbow and a tear slips onto my cheek. The elevator stops, doors beginning to slide open on the floor I'd chosen.

"Goodbye, Max. Please don't fight this. Don't follow me." I hate how erratic my pulse is, threatening to explode.

"How can you ask that of me? I love you." The pain in his voice slices through me.

"If you love me, let me go." I exit, not looking back, and start to jog toward the stairwell at the end of the hall.

Hopefully our separation is temporary but nevertheless, it's breaking my heart. Ash is a formidable force. I've underestimated him before and while I won't this time, the future is unknown. Until all is said and done, anything is possible.

And even now, walking away from Max, Van and the others doesn't guarantee they're out of danger. Ash knows how much I care about him, all of them. They are my family. But at least this gives Max and the others a fighting chance.

Now I must sever ties with Van. I don't stand a chance if I go back to HC and do this face to face, so I go back to my place. It's a risk but I don't plan on staying there, just long enough to grab a few things, and I'm relieved to find the place empty. But I won't kid myself into thinking it isn't being watched.

I throw a few things, more electronics than anything else, into a backpack. I don't bother with my fancier clothing and opt for simple jeans and leggings. I'm going to be living on the street and need to dress the part.

My cell buzzes on the couch and I snatch it up, fearing I've run out of time but not knowing if it's Van or Ash.

Unknown: Boo

Unknown: Found you

My body clenches. *Shit.* I type out a reply.

Me: Zero or Ash?

Unknown: Guess?

Me: You're not very original. And you're slacking. It took you long enough to find me

I hit send and cringe, curling my fingers into a fist of regret. Why am I taunting him?

Because this is how we used to be together. Like it or not. At the time, I considered Zero to be my only friend. It didn't matter that he was just as deranged as Ash. It didn't matter that he could have helped me escape and didn't.

No matter how odd and twisted our friendship was, he kept me sane and helped me grow my computer skills. That in itself gave me a sense of strength. Control.

Unknown: I was waiting. I thought you'd look for me. Kinda hurt you didn't

Me: Still full of yourself, I see

Unknown: Did you miss me?

Me: What do you want Zero?

Unknown: I missed you and I'm excited to see you.

An icy chill prickles down my spine and I shiver, rubbing my hands along my arms. I shouldn't be surprised. Of course he's expecting to see me. He works with Ash, knows his plan. Ash would need his help to capture me.

Palms covering my face, I slump onto the couch and my phone buzzes again.

Unknown: Don't cry

My head snaps up, highly alert and concerned. Springing to my feet, I whirl around my home in a circle, several times, as if expecting him to be physically in my home. He's watching me. Where's the camera?

Running around the room, I pull back cushions and my fingers dance along the edges of surfaces looking for any signs of a listening device or camera. My phone continues to vibrate with incoming texts. Buzz. Buzz. Buzz.

Eventually it rings and I freeze, in the middle of examining one of the few paintings I have of Anna's. The frame and canvas are clean, no bugs. Carefully placing the art back on the wall, I grab my phone and answer.

"Fucker. Where is it?" Holding up my middle finger, I twirl around the room, making sure he sees I'm giving him the universal offensive salute.

I need to get out of here. Ash could be outside my door. I can't stay here any longer contemplating what I might need.

"Calm the fuck down," he says dryly, and I'm hit with a wave of nausea and bend over. His voice brings all of it back as if it were now.

Being watched.

Afraid.

Wave after wave of dark memories assault me.

So cold. Shivering.

Chains. My shoulder blades burn and wrists ache, bleeding.

The dank smell of mold and the endless black.

Trapped.

Breathe. I make myself stand tall, forcing air into my lungs, bringing calm to my mind.

It isn't working.

Short bursts pump through my lungs. Jagged in my chest.

My mind struggles to make the distinction. I'm… I'm not back there. I'm okay. I need to run. Get out of here.

Zero's voice, concern lacing his words, finally begins to register and make sense. I'm enraged. I have no room for anything else.

"Fuck you. Where's the camera?" I spin around the room.

"Thomasina, are you okay?" He may mean to be caring but I reject it.

"Fuck you." I end the call and toss the phone on the sofa, no longer willing to waste more time.

For all I know, he is supposed to be stalling me so Ash can get here. I don't care where the camera is. I am out of here. The ringing starts again.

Frustrated and crazed, I run my fingers through my hair and take one last look at my place before leaving. I'm sure to leave the cell phone behind.

At the corner bodega, I purchase a burner phone. Before heading out onto the street, I glance around, making sure no one is watching or following me. It's fruitless.

The city may be teeming with people, making getting lost rather easy, but I can't move freely. Ash's people likely know a lot about me. Zero would have made sure all of them would know what I look like, my hangouts, and while I've stayed clear of most of those places, they still have the advantage.

I don't know who his people are, and unlike some, he's an equal-opportunity employer. Both men and women work for him, and his people aren't the stereotypical thug nor do they fit into any other kind of box.

At the corner, I wait for the streetlight to change and the old lady shuffling down the sidewalk with a cane catches my eye. She could very well be one of Ash's. Or the teenage boy loitering by the subway entrance, he could also be one of his.

His people are not bound by age, gender, race or religion, and their responsibilities are just as varied. They all work the streets and communities, looking for the next victim. Trafficking exploits human beings and sadly, it is a low-risk, profitable crime. Awareness and prosecution are growing, but far too slowly for my liking.

I push in the numbers I know by heart and put the phone to my ear.

"Hello." Van's voice is wary, and he should be, as he doesn't know who is calling.

"It's me. Tommie."

"Fuck. You okay? Is Tripp with you?"

"What? No. Why?"

"Max called. He told me how you ended things and took off. Not cool." He isn't impressed. "Tripp is on his way to your place. He was closest when we picked up your phone signal."

I'm glad I ditched my phone. This is why.

"I'm not with Tripp and I'm going off the grid. Leaving you guys." The words sting leaving my mouth.

"Fuck, no. Tommie girl, listen to me, we can beat that piece of shit together. If you go it alone, he has a better chance of getting to you."

I hate it but I hear the fear in his tone and I'm not going to add to it by telling him about Zero's texts and phone call. The camera in my apartment.

"I know what I'm doing. You and I both know I'm right."

"Bullshit." His voice is like controlled thunder. "Tell me where you are. I can meet you. Or come to HC, the bar or our place. That's where I am right now."

"Van." His name slips out like a muffled sob. I clear my throat and inhale, burying my tears. "I can't. Ash knows how to get to me. Through you. Through Max. I can't have your death, your blood, on my hands too. I just couldn't bear it."

"Tommie, fuck, no. You're making it easier for him like this. Don't you see that?" His voice is deep and rough like gravel.

I can just imagine his hard glare and tight features, not liking or accepting what I'm saying. To make sure he is really hearing me, understanding fully why I must do what I'm doing, I deliver the hardest truth of all.

"Van, he's threatened Carys and the kids. He won't hesitate to kill them. Any of you. I can't let you put all that's important to you at risk for me. I won't. I love you. Bye."

I end the call, anger and melancholy clogging my throat, and dump the phone in the nearest trash can. With another glance over my shoulder, spotting no familiar faces, I pick up the pace to an easy jog despite there being nothing easy or simple about fleeing my life and friends.

MAX

No one has seen or heard from Tommie in the past seventy-two hours. I'd hoped calling Van the second she stepped off that elevator would have changed things, but she managed to slip past him too.

Her place is like it always is, empty. Her clothes are still there but that means nothing, she'd want to travel light. Van is beside himself and I'm not much better. I miss her. I'm worried sick and wonder if Ash has her.

From what I've been able to get from Taya, nothing is different. Even with our run-in, she doesn't know the truth about Ash and Tommie. She thinks they had a love affair, and even if she had illusions of more with Ash, it appears to be only business now. I don't tell her we can't find Tommie, although she likely knows Tommie hasn't been around in days.

Van was the last one to speak to her and he thinks she's going to do something on her own. We're desperate to find her. The auction is tonight, only hours away, and I don't like doing this without her.

Tripp strolls into the kitchen having just completed his third sweep of my apartment in as many hours. He snuck into the building early this morning, unnoticed, or at least that's what he says.

"You okay?"

I nod, turning to do another lap around the room. Ry wanted me in a bulletproof vest but both Van and Tripp shut it down. There's no way I'd get into the auction with that thing on.

At most, I'll have an undetectable tracker on me and that's it. No wire because even if I am Taya Conrad's son, I will be checked before entry.

The auction location is unknown but all three of the guys—Ry, Van and Tripp—guarantee it won't be any location I've been to before. There are a couple of options based on the surveillance of Taya's men and the rare sightings of some of Ash's men. Even still they haven't been able to infiltrate any of those locations.

Damn, I wish Tommie were here. She would know how to calm my nerves. She'd say just the right thing in her way to put me at ease. And most importantly, she'd be safe.

"Remember, keep a low profile. Only speak when someone talks to you." He gets directly in my path and I stare into his determined gaze.

"Yes, understood." I inhale deeply, trying to lessen the pressure bearing down on my chest.

"Be cool and don't take any risks. You just being there is enough."

I nod, swallowing with difficulty thanks to my suddenly dry throat. What if the tracking device is found on me?

Shit, I'm a dead man.

"I'll be close by. We've got Tommie's team... fuck." He clamps his mouth shut, his jaw tensing at the mention of our missing friend.

No matter what Tripp says about pulling me out if things go sideways, he won't get to me in time. We all know it. Tonight could be a suicide mission. But if I bring down Ash and Taya. Stop them and save those women. Grant Tommie her freedom forever, then my death will not be in vain.

"I get it. The guys will be tracking me from HC and you'll be on my tail. Right?"

Now it's his turn to nod curtly, a shaky hand raking through his already unruly hair. "Fuck. Why'd she have to pull this shit now? She better not go all vigilante or superhero on us."

I chuckle, and briefly, the pinch lessens in my chest. "She's smarter than that."

He cocks his head to the side, staring at me with a curious gaze. "Yeah, she is."

The truth is we don't know what she's up to. But whatever it is, she wouldn't set out to hurt or mess up our operation. I only wish she knew what we have planned. Unknowingly, she could hijack the entire thing.

He shoves his hands into his pockets and starts pacing the room. I've got orders from Taya to wait for her text with the location. Fortunately, we don't have long to wait.

The address comes in fifteen minutes later and Tripp shares the location with the team and ends with, "Alpha team, the prince is on the move."

I bite back my grin—the prince, really?—and head for the elevator. Alpha team will follow me, as will Tripp, and there will also be a beta team close by.

TOMMIE

It's been three days since I left Max and I've spent this time lying low. It feels longer and lonelier than I thought it would be. I use the time to learn more about Ash and his plans, the old-fashioned way, without the use of computers and technology, and rely on my CIs.

A few of them are less than savory characters but they can dig for the dirt in places I can't. They are also my eyes and ears across the city since I can't be in many places at once.

I also check in on Max. Last night, I followed him when he exited his apartment with Gunnar on their way to the park. The urge to join them, and screw my conviction, was a greedy beast, hungering for them. Ravenous for Max.

But Ash's threat isn't idle or empty. Unless behind bars or better yet, gone for good, I'll never really be free of him and Max's life will be in danger.

Now, on the third day of my self-imposed exile, I go back to Max.

Let's face it, I'll always go back to Max.

The auction is tonight. Do or die. If we can't bring Ash to his knees, I might have to leave New York City. There's a lot riding on tonight and I so wish I could be a part of it, but I can't so I'll settle for second best.

I'm going to follow Max to the auction and to do so, I hide out in an alley down the street from his apartment building. It provides a good vantage point, although I'd prefer to be closer. I can't though, or else I risk being spotted. HC are all over the place and I'm fully aware of their positions. It's one of the benefits of being one of the crew.

The waiting is agonizing. It always is with adrenaline pumping through your veins and the desire to go, go, go constantly nipping at your heels. I feel like a sprinter, body poised to burst from the blocks when that starter gun goes off.

At dusk, Max exits his building and gets into an Uber idling at the entrance, which I'm sure is driven by one of our guys. I slink into the shadows of the alley as the car drives by so as not to be seen.

It's time to move but I'm heavy with melancholy. Let's face it, I wanted to help Max get ready for tonight. I wanted to make sure he understood what to look for, what not to do and most of all, when to bail, if needed.

The goal is Taya and Ash behind bars, but my greatest wish is for Max to get out alive. Even if it means we come home empty-handed.

I inch toward the edge of the wall for another peek, to make sure all is clear, before I grab a cab or Uber. Instead, a man stands at the opening to the alley. His posture is imposing, and his expression screams just how enraged he is.

"Fuck, I thought it was you." He marches toward me, invading my personal space. "What the fuck, Tommie?"

"Tripp." My back sags against the wall with my palm still flush against my chest. "You scared the shit out of me."

"You're pissing me off." Blue eyes narrow into shards of ice. "You've got Van and Max tied up in knots. And what for? You aren't stupid and you don't play games, so what the hell is going on?"

If I wasn't already torn up about leaving the guys in the lurch, his bitterness cuts into me. He isn't cruel, and we get along well, but he doesn't stand for bullshit. Even if I have my reasons, he only sees it one way.

"I'm sorry. I needed to take myself out of the equation." I'm appealing to his logic. Tripp doesn't let his emotions come into play when doing a job.

"How do you figure running does that? You *are* the equation. Shit, you're most probably even the answer." He exhales a harsh breath and rakes his fingers through his already tousled blond hair. "Fuck, why are we talking about math?"

His lips twitch upward at the corners and I catch his almost smile before it's gone. He isn't upset with me, more concerned with what I've gotten myself into. I've worried him, worried them all, and I might as well add that to my list of things I'm messing up.

I smile. "Because we're both good at mathematics?"

"A word of advice." His glare pins me in place, all joking aside. "Don't fuck with tonight's operation. You chose to leave. I don't want to see you anywhere near the auction."

Ouch. I can't fault him for the truth or for looking out for all of us.

"Well, I don't know where it is, so you won't." I sound like a brat and he smirks despite himself.

Besides, he's stalled me long enough that I now have no chance of following Max. Plan B is now in play.

"I never underestimate you, so don't insult me. Get lost. And in return, I'll never speak of seeing you to my brothers."

He is nothing if not loyal. For him to make that kind of promise, to withhold information from his childhood friends, Van and Ry—and his word extends to Max, too, I'm sure—is huge.

"Thank you."

He turns on his heel, waving off my gratitude like a pestering fly. At the edge, where the alleyway and sidewalk meet, he stops, peering over his shoulder at me. "And Tommie?"

"Yeah?" I whisper, uncertain I want to hear what he has to say.

"We're going to get him. Stay out of this and be safe. You need anything, call me."

He waits for my nod, likely thinking I'm consenting to his wishes but it's more in understanding, before he leaves the way he came. I have immense respect for Tripp, and it just grew tenfold in the past few minutes.

I blink back my silly tears, again reminded of all the things, no, the *people* I'm trying to save, and that I'd be giving up if we fail tonight. If I have to leave this city.

As promised, I lie low, spending the night at a hostel, and stay out of the way. I don't sleep a wink, too wound up to relax and instead, I plot what comes next. If Ash isn't in jail tomorrow, I'm going to have to make my move.

MAX

The drive is interminable. I really don't know what to expect. Will the women be in cages? Tied up? It could be worse than I anticipate and through it all, I've got to keep my shit together. There's a lot riding on tonight and me keeping my cool.

The car stops in front of a men's clothing store and I double check the address. This isn't a warehouse and we're in a pretty decent part of the city. As I step out of the vehicle, I'm sickened to see average, everyday people going about their lives when behind a storefront some of the most unimaginable and inhumane acts are about to go down.

Tiny stands at the entrance and wordlessly ushers me inside. We walk to the back of the retailer where two large men stand on either side of a doorway. Just past the door is a staircase.

Beads of sweat pool around the nape of my neck and heat builds within me as the men pat me down. It could all be over right now if they find the tracking device.

It's only when my feet hit the staircase that my breath starts to move again. I follow Tiny up the stairs and down a long and narrow passageway, all the while, willing my body to relax.

There's no way this hall that appears to connect the buildings was part of the original blueprint. The walkway goes on for quite some time, at least three or four buildings over from where I entered at street level, before we finally come to the end.

I wonder if the team is still able to pick up my signal and even if they do, how long would it take them to figure out where the passage is?

We get into the elevator, going down three floors to a sub-basement level where we exit into a dark room. So dark it could be a dungeon.

Holy shit. I might as well be buried. When I had no clue what I was in for, I'd wondered if I'd get out alive. Now it feels like that's a distinct possibility, and all I can think about is how I will have failed if that happens.

None of those women in captivity will be saved, and Tommie? Fuck, what if Ash already has her? Why the hell did she run off? Why didn't I try to stop her?

Music plays softly and there is a low murmur from the crowd of mostly men, permeating the space. I've got to focus and keep all doubts or misgivings locked away.

If I didn't know better, I'd think it was a sex club. A kinky sex club. Women are barely clothed, many naked, all in cages. If tonight goes well, in a matter of hours, they'll be free.

Tiny orders me to stay in a corner and not to move unless someone comes for me. Neither Ash nor Taya are visible from my vantage point. I'm surprised not to see at least one of them.

Or maybe the risk is too high to be caught here? But if so, how the hell are we supposed to tie them to this fucking nightmare?

Finally, the music stops and a male voice booms over a speaker system. A number is called and on cue, a man in all black, including a hooded mask, parades a woman with a neck collar attached to a long rod, which he uses to guide her across the stage.

The bidding begins just like you'd see at any auction and my sickening repulsion mounts as the dollar figures climb. We're talking humans, not fucking art.

At first I count how many transactions, ten then twenty, at the same time looking around as much as possible without raising suspicion. Sadly, but not at all surprisingly, there are a few bigwigs in this crowd.

Powerful and noteworthy businessmen, for whose blood there would be an outcry if the public knew they were here, and in turn, what kind of horrific acts they were into.

There's no way Ash or Taya aren't here with this caliber of people and more importantly, their kind of money. But there's no sign of them.

Sweat clings to me and my hands are slick from nerves. Even hidden in the shadows that this corner of the room affords me, there's still a sense of heightened danger, tension, in the air.

Well past thirty transactions, I lose count when a woman, who was just on stage and sold to a Russian, refuses to go with her new master. He's a scary motherfucker, and furious, the asshole backhands her across the face, sending her to the floor.

Commotion ensues as men the size of bouncers circle the pair and a few others take it upon themselves to get involved. The Russian wants out of the deal. He wants a better slave, no longer willing to pay for what he calls damaged goods. Things look to be getting dicey.

My heartbeat kicks into high gear and I track the room, once again looking for any sign of Taya or Ash, when I notice one of her men headed toward me. Perhaps I'm going to be taken to her and I follow without question.

Two of the walls in this place are made of tinted floor-to-ceiling glass and as we pass by them, I get a better look. I'm pretty sure they are one-way mirrors. Ash and Taya might be behind one of those walls. What better way to watch over the debauchery without getting their hands dirty?

I'm sick to my stomach at being here. It's bad enough to see these people, mostly women, being sold like cattle, and what makes it worse is to think of Tommie in this world. What she endured.

I want to put an end to this, but I have to go along with it for now. Ry and Tripp made it clear that the plan is for the FBI to raid the auction, most probably any minute now.

My orders are to watch and share the details after the fact. I will be swept up with the rest of them when all hell breaks loose. If my mother and the asshole, Ash, are here, they need to believe I had nothing to do with it.

We stop just feet from the Russian and other men, arguing about the injured woman and getting another one. There's a man dressed in what looks to be an expensive suit and he's talking calmly, so quietly I can't make out a word, to the Russian. He looks to be running the show.

Taya's man points to a woman on the floor. The one who was hit, and I quickly remove her from the fray, into a corner where I can get a better look at the damage.

She's crying and cowering from me as if I'm going to hit her or hurt her. My chest tightens at how afraid she must be.

"It's okay." I brush back her dark bangs to get a better look at the gash. "I'm a doctor. I won't hurt you."

She trembles, shaking, but she doesn't fight me. Blood streams down her face, some of it getting into her eye. Head wounds always bleed like a son of a bitch.

From the way her skin split, she needs stitches. I grab a clean, unused napkin resting on a nearby table and bring it to the cut.

"Can you hold this?"

She nods, replacing my hand with hers, and at the same time, the double entry doors into this makeshift club are busted wide open.

The cavalry is here and relief surges through me.

One of the men leading the heavily-armed troops announces their arrival and identifies themselves as FBI, and any lingering fear evaporates.

It's short-lived when screams, yells and a few gunshots rip through the room. Even with the end in sight, I might not make it out alive.

The atmosphere is a powder keg. All it will take is a spark to set this place ablaze. The voice over the speaker stops talking and a sharp sound tears through the system, causing many to cringe and grab or cover their ears as a man mutters several expletives over the airwaves.

It's pandemonium for several minutes and I stay put, shielding the woman at my side as best as I can while she cries. People, men and captured women, are running in every direction.

An armed man in a flak suit, head gear and assault rifle—one of the good guys—descends upon us and while I should be relieved, I'm treated like all the other scum here.

I want to fight back and shout that I'm on their side but as another guy, also FBI, carefully takes care of the woman, I resist, glad to see she's going to be okay. I'm roughed up and thrown around as I'm hauled over to a group of men they have rounded up.

The exit from the building involves more hitting and shoving as I'm part of a line of men, shackled and led outside. Before being tossed into the back of a large van, I use the remaining seconds to scour the street and the small crowds of law enforcement and offenders.

I'm looking for either Taya or Ash. I wouldn't be surprised if Mother tries to play the victim, but still no sign of either of them.

A sinking feeling consumes me. Dark and oppressive as this muggy Manhattan night. What if all of this was for nothing and they got away? Or worse still, what if they were never here to begin with?

TOMMIE

From what I've been able to find out, Ash isn't behind bars. We failed. So plan B.

I'm the bait.

That's how this works.

If Ash knew how to find me, he would have by now. So I'm going to make it easy for him. I check out of the hostel and return to my apartment. I'm guessing the camera is still operational so Zero and Ash may already know where I am.

My phone is where I left it and I power it on. Bouncing on the balls of my feet, I release some of my anxiety. My plan isn't perfect, nothing ever is. The phone is a beacon. Soon HC will know where to find me and I'm sure—would bet my life on it—that Zero has piggybacked on the tracking system.

Within five minutes, I leave my apartment and head uptown to Central Park. Surprise, surprise, Ash is sitting on the park bench just like I expected him to be. *Good boy. Who's playing who now, asshole?*

I'm not sure if I should be glad that my plan worked and he's here. It only slaps me in the face once more with the reminder that last night's bust at the auction, or least that was the plan before I walked away, didn't go well. Ash is still free.

I had counted on Ash figuring out my destination once Zero had a lock on me. It was the last place we talked. And it's public.

For plan B—this meeting—to work, Max needed to be busy. The chance is slim that he'll see us but he did last time and I didn't want to run the risk of that happening again.

One of my informants is watching Max and I just got a text on my burner, confirming he's at HC. While I'm not sure why, my guess is to debrief about the auction—boy what I'd give to listen in on that, to know what happened last night.

Ash's dark gaze lands on me. "Well, Thomasina, you've outdone yourself this time."

"How so?" I'm somewhat comforted by a couple on the grass not too far from us. They may not be able to hear what we're saying but we aren't alone.

He pats the empty space beside him on the bench. I neither acknowledge nor decline his unwanted invitation. Last time he got too close, he nearly didn't let me go. I'll stand, thank you very much.

"Disappearing like you did. You left Zero in a dither." The monster smiles and I can't help but think of a shark's jagged, razor-sharp teeth. "He was really quite surprised and then angry that you got the better of him."

I press my lips together to suppress a grin to match my mounting pride. "What can I say, he taught me well."

What sounds like a compliment is more of a calculated concession. Ash pliant and amenable is my goal, and in truth, my cyber prowess in subterfuge and all things underhanded is all thanks to Ash, indirectly. He was the one to give me time with the computer wizard when in captivity. He was the one who allowed me to watch and learn from Zero.

What's even more present, as we warily stare at each other, is the game we've begun. He wants me back in captivity and I want him behind bars. Both our traps are set, and what's at the crux of this meeting is who will make checkmate first?

"Yes, he did indeed." His tone is dry, almost bored as he picks at a loose thread on the leg of his expensive dress pants. "Where have you been?"

"Let's play a game." A warm breeze thrusts a few strands of hair into my face and I brush them away as I did with his question.

"A game?" He cocks his head to the side, unamused with me but not annoyed.

"Yes. One of our old games. Quid pro quo." A tremor courses through my veins, not at the mention of our past but at the way in which I make it sound nostalgic rather than a horrific nightmare.

His lips quirk as he waits, prompting me to continue. "I ask a question. When you answer, I'll return the favor."

It's the game he played with Max. Ash enjoys this kind of recreation. He believes the banter and questions reveal so much about the other person. And in this case, he's right. I will be tipping my hand with my interrogation, but I'm hoping he does the same.

"Very well then." He straightens and uncrosses his legs, staring unscrupulously. "Sit down first."

"Is that a dealbreaker?" I take a small, subtle step backward. If I don't have to get within touching distance, all the better.

"Yes." Both his large, manicured hands now cup his knees and his gaze is intense.

It's as if he's daring me to disobey. Perhaps even daring me to run. My arm presses against the crossover purse resting at my waist, in front of me. It's empty save for two cellphones and a gun.

Fortified with that knowledge, I push past every nerve ending ablaze in warning and grant his wish. Sitting gives him the upper hand as I'm quicker on my feet, and I only hope he doesn't have a syringe. He's drugged me before.

Reluctantly, I squeeze my body onto one end of the bench, as far away from him as possible, which isn't much.

"I get to go first." I beam at him, hiding my aversion to our proximity.

My therapist would be proud. I'm presenting well—so well put together—but it's all surface. Inside, I'm breaking apart, struggling to keep myself in one piece, and judging from his expression, I'm succeeding. I doubt he's aware of my inner turmoil.

"Why would you think you go first?" His dark brow arches.

"I just gave you something you wanted." I pat the space between us reminding him I'm where he wanted me. "It seems only fair that you now return the favor."

He smiles. A bright smile for him, but no less bone-chilling to me. "Fine."

"You never answered my question from the other day about Taya. Why did you get into business with her?"

"That's your question?" A wicked grin slithers across his face like a venomous serpent. "I'm disappointed, Thomasina. You already know why, but I'll entertain your silly question. There are several reasons. Firstly, her business is appealing because of her network. Secondly, she interested me because of the connection to you through Max."

He stops, letting his implication sink in. I shouldn't be all that surprised but I still have to fight the urge to flee. Fidgeting in the seat, I battle internally to stop my body's betrayal.

"And finally, Taya Conrad is an easy mark." He licks his lips and I avert my gaze, my stomach somersaulting at an alarming, nauseous speed.

"What do you mean?" My eyes are on the couple lying on a blanket, making out. As the tumultuous wave in my belly calms, my chest spasms at the brief, forbidden thought of Max.

"Nice try. My turn."

"All right. Ask away." I turn to face him. The brief thought of my lover reminds me I risked this meeting. I can't help but look for another way to bring Ash down.

"Are you done with Max? Are you done with Evan? Are you prepared to come back to me? Or are you going to force me to take what is mine?"

I try once, twice, to swallow past the inevitable lump in my throat. I try again, almost choking on my fears. "That's more than one question. But I'll answer."

I'm much bolder than I would have been years ago. The girl he kidnapped may be a part of me but I'm no longer her. I love and cherish so much about her, but I will never be her again. And even if he scares me—he always will—I won't let him see or smell my fear. Never.

"I've left my friends. You know that since you've been watching these past few days. I haven't gone near any one of them and I won't. I promise."

"And?"

"And what?"

"Are you ready to come home to me?"

"Maybe. I don't know yet." It's a lie, I'll never go back to him, but I'm stalling.

He tilts his head back and barks out a laugh as if I'm the funniest person in the world. I frown at how hilarious he finds my freedom. I'm not joking.

"You're quite amusing, my dear. I'd forgotten how much so."

I dip my chin and steel my spine, ready with my question, not willing to waste another second on his question. His desire.

"You said Taya was an easy mark—how so?"

"She's of no consequence to me. She's a lonely woman. I'll take all that I deem useful or valuable from her, and I won't ask permission." His obsidian gaze threatens to eat me alive. "As for Taya, I couldn't care less what happens to her. She's vapid and boring."

I bite the inside of my cheek, fighting to school my features. He's basically indicated that he intends on taking her for all she's worth—her contacts, or network as he called it. Oh, and taking me as well. As for the rest, he wants nothing to do with it. The question is, how does he plan on getting rid of her?

Murder springs to mind. That's usually how he solves his problems.

"Now back to my question, which you averted with your lies. How do you expect me to believe you've left Max and Van, your *friends* as you called them, when you had a hand in last night's mess?"

"I don't know what you're talking about." *Last night's mess?*

A tremor prickles down my spine. He's likely talking about the auction. Obviously, he got away, and Max is at HC so he isn't hurt or worse. What happened? He isn't happy about it.

"Really?" He leans in close, and I spring to my feet before he can grab me.

A low rumble erupts from deep within him as he tightens his jaw. "Why are you so jittery, Thomasina? Is it because you've been a naughty girl? Don't play games with me. You know the FBI raided the auction last night and rounded up almost everyone there, including your dear Max."

Anxiety spikes my blood pressure. Max's arrest was always part of the plan, this doesn't surprise me, but Ash might think this meeting is a trap, so why is he here?

"I knew nothing about last night. I told you, I've cut ties with Max and Evan."

"Don't. I'm no fool. You expect me to believe you didn't have a hand in it?" He now stands tall, only a foot or two from me.

"I didn't, and I don't expect you to believe me but it's the truth. What do you want?" I whisper, now desperate to get away from him. To be alone with my thoughts.

"You know what I want. Don't be coy with me." With his one step forward, I take one back. "The fiasco last night… You cost me more than you can ever repay."

"I think you have that wrong." I stiffen my spine and nail him with a glare, my hand now clutching at the opening to the purse.

"How so?"

"I don't owe you. You owe me. And no matter what you do, you'll never be able to make it up to me."

I turn on my heel, briskly striding toward the street. I didn't gain any more information or any clue as to how to get to him and I'm angry with myself. The meeting was a risk and I had such high hopes for some kind of indication as to what my next move might be, but instead, Ash is ready to pounce. He may even have people ready to whisk me away. I can't stay here any longer. I need to get away.

He keeps pace with me, but fortunately he doesn't touch me.

"Remember what I do to people who cross me? You of all know best. You run from me and you'll regret it."

Run is exactly what I do. I run to a cab, ordering him to drive. Shaking in the backseat, I toss the HC cell phone out the window and next the burner phone, not willing to risk any kind of tracker.

We drive out to Long Island and then back to Manhattan, sitting in traffic for what feels like hours as I play over and over again my conversation with Ash. My plan had been to dig for more about his relationship with Taya. I can't shake the feeling she could be useful, that there may be something there.

And there are two goals here. Get rid of Ash. Get rid of Taya. But I come up empty. Until I don't. As the cabbie heads south downtown, I'm hit with what Ash meant when he said, "Remember what I do to people who cross me? You of all know best. You run from me and you'll regret it."

My parents.

He always believed I'd acted on my father's wishes to move his money despite my insistence that I had done the deed of my own accord. And even though I returned his funds, every single penny, he said it was a betrayal. Not my betrayal.

My father betrayed him. And in return, as punishment, he set my family home on fire. He killed both my parents.

Now, Max, Van and everyone at HC… they're my family. *Shit,* and last night's raid was another betrayal.

I jump out of the cab still a block away from the building that houses the HC offices. Fire trucks, police cars and an ambulance are scattered across what is usually a busy street. It's utter bedlam with police diverting traffic, people on the sidewalks and hoses of water spraying up into the air.

Water wells up in my eyes, spilling onto my cheeks as I run toward the burning building, yelling at the top of my lungs. Ash set my world on fire. Oh my God, who was in there when the place went up in flames?

MAX

I yawn, lying back on the hospital bed, and the second my head hits the pillow, my name booms over the intercom system. The female voice requests that I report to the nurses' station.

I'm not even supposed to be here and if I was at home, I'd most probably be sleeping right now. But my apartment was the last place I wanted to be. I couldn't bear the thought of my empty apartment without Tommie.

Yet I feel like shit for leaving Gunnar alone for another night. I'm grateful the dog walker has fed and walked him today.

Last night wasn't planned. I spent it in a jail cell with scumbags and sick motherfuckers. I'll make it up to him tomorrow with an extra-long run.

Leaving the unoccupied room that I just scouted this entire wing for is depressing. Who knows if it'll be empty when I get back? There was another doctor searching for a place to grab a few hours of sleep.

Down the hall is the front desk, where a woman with her head hung low, shoulders hunched, looms over the nurses' station. My heart kicks into overdrive. Her long black hair curtains her face but her tall, curvy frame is one I'd peg anywhere. Tommie.

A horrible knot of apprehension blooms within me. She looks

different, out of place with the jeans and hoodie… is that my hoodie? She turns to face me, and my chest seizes, hurting like hell to know she's alive but also torn up by the anguish written across her tear-stained face.

We run toward each other and she lunges into my open arms. "What happened? Are you all right?"

Through tears, she struggles to catch her breath and speak. "Max, thank God, you're okay." Tenderly, her fingers wander over my features.

It's her reverence that causes me to think that touching me helps her believe I'm okay.

"I'm fine." My hands cup her face, thumbs wiping at her cheeks. "Tell me what's wrong?"

My first thought is Ash and my anger wakes up, thirsty to hurt that man. Not only for all he's done to this woman I love, but to the countless others, like those women at the auction last night and in the warehouses leading up to the big night. He's a vile human being.

"Fire. Van and... I don't know and then I thought you and..." Her voice breaks and her eyes shut for a moment.

Eyes as dark as midnight but as turbulent as the sea wash over me. "Max, I thought I'd lost you. I can't lose you."

She clings to me and her distress cracks me wide open.

"Dr. Conrad, do you need some help?" a nurse says from behind the desk.

"No, it's okay. Thanks."

I draw her close to my side and guide us away from prying eyes. She's a mess and shouldn't be entertainment for the people who have nothing better to do but wait. We end up in the room I'd abandoned moments before.

"Okay, take a deep breath and tell me what's wrong? Start from the beginning."

"Ash threatened you, Van and HC. You're my family." She thumps her balled fist, white knuckles and all, against one of her thighs, frustrated. "I took too long to figure out what he meant. I was too late."

"Shhh, it's okay." I'm still not fully comprehending what happened and why she's so upset.

She pushes up against the side of my body, clutching my hand in hers as if I'm a life preserver.

"Tommie, you've got to give me more. I'm not following."

Her exhale is jagged, and she swipes aggressively at her tears. "Ash set HC on fire. I got there too late. The firefighters were trying to stop the blaze."

"Was anyone inside? Did anyone get hurt?"

I was there hours ago and the place was filled with the HC team, everyone debriefing about their role in the auction raid. Fuck. Ry, Van, Tripp… A profound pain sucks the air from my lungs. Are they dead?

She's nodding, a sheen of tears in her eyes and I want to vomit. My heartrate picks up. "Who? Are you sure it was Ash?"

"I don't know." Her voice rises. "My parents died in a fire. He told me without telling me he was going to do the same."

My phone rings and I don't even bother to look. "What do you mean you don't know?"

The phone rings again and I pull it from my pocket, ready to hit ignore when I see it's Tate. "Bear, is Ry okay?"

"Max, thank God I got you. I think Ry's fine but I heard some of them were taken to the hospital. I don't know all the details and they won't let us come home." Frustration and concern blankets her voice.

Tate, Carys and their kids are safely tucked away from Ash, out of the city, and it needs to stay that way. "Okay. Have you spoken to anyone?"

"No. Shadow is with us. He got a call about a fire but not much more than that. Carys and I are going crazy and just want to come home. I need to hear Ry's voice. To see him." A lump forms in my throat at my sister's soft cry.

"Hey, it's going to be okay." I hope what I'm saying isn't a lie because right now, I don't know anything and shouldn't be making any promises. "I'm with Tommie, we're going to find out more. And I'll get Ry and Van to call you. Do you know which hospital?"

"Tommie? She's with you? Last I heard, she was staying at HC. Oh thank God, she's okay."

"Tate, listen to me." My voice is steady and calm, nothing like the storm brewing within me. "Let me speak to Shadow. He must know where they were taken."

"Okay. Okay. Max," she pauses, sniffing and inhaling a jagged breath, "I love you."

"Love you too, Bear." Concern tints my words and I hold my breath waiting for Shadow.

Everyone has to be okay. There isn't any other option and even as I think it, it's absurd. Bad shit happens to good people all the time. I live it every day and yet as I listen to Shadow tell me which hospital and the little he knows, I will everything to be all right.

When we arrive at the hospital not too far from where I work, the emergency room is packed. Most faces we don't recognize but in the corner is a group from HC.

"Thank goodness, you're okay." Tommie runs at Ry, throwing her arms around him. "Where's Van?"

He's unkempt and exhausted, with smudges of soot on his cheek and arm. They stay connected for quite some time. When she tries to push away, he holds on and I think he's more shaken up than we can imagine. *What the hell happened?*

Finally breaking apart, he tucks her into his side and stares down at her. "It's good to have you back. I was worried you were next."

"I'm okay. Where's Van? Tripp?" She scans the waiting area and I follow suit but they aren't here. Dread coils around my gut.

"Van will be okay. He had a lot of smoke inhalation and so did Tripp." Ry's voice is calm, almost flat, but it isn't because he's hiding anything, or at least, I don't think so.

He's tired with dark circles under his eyes and tension lines not only his features but the way he holds himself.

"The doctor was running some tests and she wants to keep them overnight. But you know them, especially Tripp, he's giving the doctor and nurses a hard time." He attempts a wry grin but it's barely a twitch of the lips.

"Was anyone else hurt?" I shove my hands in my pockets, unable to keep them still.

"We fucking got lucky." The words are a sharp rumble, laced with agonizing relief.

Tommie releases some of the burden of guilt she's been carrying, sinking into me on a sob. "Fuck, yes. Thank goodness. Can I see them?"

"Maybe. Soon." Clearing his throat, Ry hangs his head and grips the back of his neck.

Swiftly, he turns on his heel, his back to us, and it looks like tonight is just now hitting him for the first time. Tommie slides her arms around his middle, hugging him from behind, and I rest a hand on his shoulder, offering support.

He takes a beat or two to pull himself together before turning to face us. His expression is composed and stoic.

"How did the fire start?" Her chin wobbles but she doesn't give way to her tears.

"It was a fucking nightmare. I don't know what exactly started it. There were about twenty of us in the building when there was a big-ass explosion. The walls shook, and within what felt like seconds, there were flames and smoke. It was fucking chaos." Shaking his head, he exhales, frowning. "The Feds and NYPD are all over this and I told them we suspect Ash is behind it."

She nods. "Yes. I know it. He killed my parents in a fire and threatened all of you tonight."

"What? You fucking saw him tonight?" Ry is now incensed, wearing an awfully familiar scowl.

A doctor swings through a door, calling out Van's name, and we rush to her. She'll allow one visitor and only for a minute. Then Van needs his rest.

Tommie takes a step in the direction of the doctor and then falters, glancing over at Ry. He's all gentleman, his hand out in deferral to her, but she likely sees what I do.

Ry is shaken to the core. Evan and Tripp are like his brothers, and he could have lost one or both tonight. And let's not forget, everyone in that building tonight from HC is like family, and he could have lost any one of them.

"You go." Her words are a shaky whisper and she pulls him in for a hug. "Tell him I love him, and I'll be back to ride his sorry ass tomorrow."

She forces a watery smile and he offers an uncharacteristic snort. "You got it, and I'm sure he'll have some smart-ass comment for you too. But hearing you're back will help ease some of the pain from tonight. He's been worried sick about you."

"I'm sorry. I'm sorry about everything."

"None of this is your fault." I'm fierce in my assertion. She isn't to blame.

She presses her lips tight but offers no agreement. Tripp saunters out, bedraggled and exhausted. His once blond head of hair is ashen.

"What the fuck?" Ry narrows his gaze on his friend. "Why are you out of bed?"

Tommie lunges at him, wrapping her arms around his neck, and he stumbles back, releasing a raspy laugh. "Hey, I'm fine. Good to see you got smart and came back to your family."

"I'm so glad you're okay." Her voice is muffled as she talks into his chest.

They stay like that for a few seconds and she starts to shake. Tripp tightens his hold around her crying form and kisses the top of her head.

"Hey, I'm fine. It's gonna take a lot more than a kickass explosion to bring me down." His tone is light, but his gaze is intense.

Silent but deadly is how I think of Tripp's many looks, and that's what comes to mind right now. I get the sense he's imploring me to stay alert. We all know Ash is a dangerous asshole and tonight's fire isn't the end of him.

"Answer me." Ry steps even closer, tightly wound.

"Easy. I'm fine. They wanted to keep me overnight but thank fuck I don't have a girlfriend or wife to gang up on me with the doctors." His tone is light but forced. There's no mirth in his gaze and he releases her hold, stepping back.

"Or are you gonna be my nag?" Tripp's challenge is aimed at Ry.

"This isn't funny."

"Never said it was. The doc said I need rest. I'm not gonna get a wink of sleep here. I will at home."

"You should stay the night." Tommie rests her hands on her hips and some of her spunk seeps into her stance.

Her strength and bravado are back in full force and it puts a smile on my face. Ry and I nod in agreement while Tripp shakes his head.

"Nice try but not gonna happen." His tone brooks no compromise.

Ry growls, turning his attention to me. "You have a tail from the Feds, for your protection." He motions to a small group of suits at the entrance. "And tomorrow, we need to talk."

Now his gaze bounces from me to Tommie. We both nod and then she looks to me, relief and fatigue mingled in her coffee bean eyes.

"Good." Ry then glares at Tripp, but there isn't any real anger to it and mutters something under his breath.

He then pulls his best friend into him, slapping him hard on the back and squeezing him tight before he slips out of the room to see Van.

MAX

Instead of trying to coax Tripp to stay, we get him to agree to us seeing him home. At least this way, I can give him a quick once-over to put Tommie's mind at ease, and he allows it—he's going to be okay. Once we're both satisfied he'll stay put and call if he needs anything, we head back to my place.

Hand in hand, we take Gunnar for a quick walk around the block, and I'm the first one to break our silence.

"You scared the hell out of me."

"Pardon?" She glances up at me, clearly lost in thought.

"When I saw you at the hospital. I was relieved to see you but also knew something was wrong. I'm just so glad you're okay."

"Me too, that you're safe and everyone else at HC. I don't know what I'd have done if someone had… if we'd lost…" Her lips mash together, and she blinks rapidly.

"Hey, everyone is okay." I stop us feet from my building, sliding my hands around her waist and bringing her into me. "Tell me what happened when you walked out the other day. What have you been doing? How did you end up talking to Ash again?"

It's tough keeping any kind of outrage from creeping into my concerned tone. She was with Ash, again. The thought rattles me. He could have taken her.

Poof and we'd never see her again. If nothing else, the man knows how to disappear without a trace.

On the way up to the apartment, she fills me in on her investigative attempts to find out more about Ash's plans, and no surprise, she comes up empty. When she recounts her conversation with the sick bastard in the park, I turn to stone, tension biting painfully into every muscle, tendon, and bone in my body. It takes everything in me not to lose my shit.

She then pushes for details about the auction and what happened. I fill her in as we lock up and head to the bedroom. We're both tired and want to crash, but we agree to a shower first.

In the bathroom, Tommie starts the shower and begins to shed her clothes. I love the way she looks at me with heat flaring in her deep dark gaze, so much heat, as if I am everything she needs.

My thoughts are unruly and jumbled, enthralled by how fucking edible she is in her birthday suit, so unassuming and comfortable with me. And I'm also confused—last thing I knew, she said we were over.

"I'm not surprised Ash got away from the auction. And it may be stupid, me being here." She gathers her long hair into a messy knot and secures it on top of her head.

My fingers clutch at her hips; her skin is soft and warm, and I bring her close. Her eyes grow heavy and dazed. I won't let her walk away again. Not a chance.

"You're not going anywhere."

A humorless laugh tumbles from her soft lips. "I'm not. I'm here to stay even if the smartest thing to do is leave. Danger still exists. Ash wants to kill you." Her gaze swims with unshed tears. "I can't stay away from you. I need you, Max."

"I don't want you anywhere but here." I drop my pants, then just as quickly latch my hands back onto her body.

"Ash needs to be stopped. Your mother needs to be stopped. But we're stronger together. It may be selfish but I realized that today. My biggest regret and perhaps my biggest misstep was in not telling my parents what I'd done. Maybe if my father had known, we could have gotten to Ash first, prevented the fire. I don't know."

She hangs her head, shaking it back and forth, and I slide two fingers under her chin, tilting her head to look at me. "Don't do that to yourself. You'll never know if you could have changed the outcome. And you're not to blame for what happened to your parents, or tonight's fire. That's all on Ash."

"I'm the reason for the fire. I betrayed him, or so he thinks. But when we're apart, we give him an advantage. And dammit, I'm not letting Ash ruin my life again, or hurt you. I won't."

"We'll do this together." I'm disarmed by her realization. We are stronger together.

Her fingers glide up my chest and over my shoulders. My cock is painfully hard and my body aches for her but this conversation is needed.

"We'll figure out a way to stop both Ash and Taya. And if that doesn't work, then we run."

She gasps, and blinks through the tears sticking to her lashes. "What?"

I'd never considered running until this very moment and I'm okay with it. If that's what it takes for us to be free of Ash and my mother, then I'd do it in a heartbeat.

"Before you, leaving Tate, my only family, wasn't an option. But she has Ry. He'd never let anything happen to her or their son." I brush a stray strand from her face. "And now, I have you. I can't imagine my life without you. Never."

"But—" she says, and I press a finger to her lips, guiding her into the hot shower.

Warm water sprays our bodies and I tip her head back to wet her long hair. A moan slips past her slightly parted lips as my fingers knead her scalp. I dip my head until my lips are a breath away from the shell of her ear. Her fingers grip my shoulders as her hard nipples press into my chest.

"It's you and me. Always. Don't ever run from me again." I draw her closer, bending to press my lips to her now-damp neck, water streaming down my back.

"I'm sorry I ran. I was—"

"I know why you ran. To protect me. But listen to me." My mouth dances across her collarbone, the fleeting trace of my lips making her quiver in my arms despite the hot water. "We stay together. We're stronger together."

I find her lips and kiss the breath out of her. Determined, passionate, my mouth devours hers as our tongues tangle. Gliding my finger along her throat, I feel her shaky swallow under my touch and she opens wider, my name escaping on a sigh.

Her hand wraps around my length and she strokes me as I bury my head in her neck, kissing the base of her throat before breathing in the familiar, heady scent of her.

She guides me to her entrance, and my desperate need to touch her, feel her, overrides all sense of control. I hoist her up against the wall and she latches on once more to my rapidly hardening shaft, guiding me to her entrance.

"Wait, condom," I grit out, my tip pressing into her wet heat. It's a herculean effort to stop.

"I'm clean and take the shot. We can go without it if you're okay."

"I'm clean. I get tested regularly. Are you sure?" My voice is a shaky rasp, finding it hard, in more ways than one, to stay as we are, the need to plunge into her irresistible.

"Max, I want you. Now, like this. It's ok—" Before she can complete the word, my tongue is in her mouth and her hands are tangled in my hair as I plunge into her.

Both greedy, we match each other thrust for thrust and she rides me hard, wild and crazed. She moans, twirling her hips, and I see stars. I've never been bare, without protection, with anyone and the sensation of her is fucking phenomenal.

"Tommie," I moan as she wraps her legs tightly around my waist.

My fingers dig hard into her ass and I drink in the rosy flush of her skin, hooded eyes and swollen lips. Blistering pleasure blazes through me, making me senseless with need. I stroke hard and fast and she returns the intensity with a cry of ecstasy.

"Max, we stay together," she says again, as if needing to reaffirm that she's doing the right thing.

She may think she's being selfish and putting me in danger by being with me, but without her is worse. And we're both in danger; neither of us is safe until we're rid of them.

She tips her head to one side, her walls clenching tighter around me, and I moan, the pleasure overwhelming.

"Love you so much." I thread my fingers in the mass of her wet hair, bringing her mouth to mine.

Fuck, I love this woman with an intensity that should but doesn't scare me.

TOMMIE

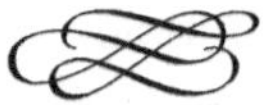

"You asleep?" His deep voice circles my body like a warm, seductive embrace.

"Hmmm." I snuggle closer, my ass pressing into his hard length.

He groans, kissing behind my ear. "Be careful. Don't start something you don't intend on finishing."

I slide my hand between us, down to his erection, and he sucks in air between his teeth as his cock twitches in my grasp. His already taut, hard stomach muscles turn to steel against my bare back.

"Who said I don't intend on following through?"

He thrusts upward into my grip and I lick my lips. "We've got work to do," he whispers in my ear, his lips tickling the soft, near-invisible hairs on my skin.

I want every part of him, now, even if we have work to do. I wish we could stay in bed forever. Just Max and me. His strong, fine hands ensnare my waist, rolling me over and causing me to loosen my hold on him. Now face to face, his hips grind into mine, no holding back as his hot, throbbing length slides through my slick folds.

"You don't play fair, Conrad." I pout, sliding into a gasp as his crown breaches my entrance before pulling out with a smug grin.

"Neither do you." He taps the tip of my nose, dives in for a quick kiss before sliding out of the bed.

"Grrr, I wish we could stay in bed all day," I groan, but then his firm ass cheeks and muscled thighs tease a wicked smile out of me.

As if sensing my salacious stare, he turns around fast, catching my gaze where his ass was just seconds ago. I don't blink or blush, or even drift my gaze upward to meet his because now I'm looking at his magnificent penis.

"You're just plain naughty." He tosses a pillow at me. "Get out of bed."

"I'm coming. Actually, I'm not coming and that's the problem," I grumble.

He laughs, pulling his boxers and then jeans on. "I'll go walk Gun and you make breakfast?"

He pauses to glance at his phone. "Make that lunch. I'll be back in fifteen."

"Mkay," I murmur, dropping my head back onto the pillow

A flash of Ash obliterates any bone-melting relaxation and I bolt upright in bed, running after him into the living room, buck naked.

"Max, be careful." I cringe at the panic circling each word.

The fierce desire in his gaze steals my breath as he takes me in. Then his features soften, morphing to concern as our eyes meet.

"I'll be alert and safe. Remember, I'm going to have Mister No-neck shadowing me."

"Okay." I smile, somewhat comforted by the reminder of the FBI agent standing guard outside of Max's place. Even still, Ash is the devil and one tricky bastard.

"Go put some clothes on or else I won't be going anywhere."

"Maybe that's my plan." I'm wicked and seductively thrust out my chest with a sway of my hips.

He brings his clenched fist to his mouth, biting on his knuckles. "Woman, you're going to pay for that. Now go. I don't want our friend outside to get a peek at your delectable body."

I turn on my heel and my cheeks heat at his appreciative growl that carries me into the bedroom. I tidy the room, make the bed, and then get dressed. Before starting breakfast, I call Ry, Van and Tripp to make sure they are all okay and confirm we're meeting them within the hour. We have a ton of work to do.

Between sex, some tears, and sleep, Max and I talked for several hours last night about how we could take another run at Ash and Taya. They are likely more of a threat than ever before and the problem is, we've got two targets and likely only one shot.

We played through several scenarios and sadly, the strongest option pits us against each other. Not literally, but in the sense that we couldn't both get what we want. Ash gone. Taya gone.

Or more specifically, none of our plans would get rid of them both and of course, Ash is the biggest and more immediate danger. It will be near impossible to get them both now that we've failed with the raid. They've likely gone to their respective corners, and who knew if their joint venture was even viable. I figured Ash would have at least one more move up his sleeve.

Besides, he wanted to grab me, and he still hasn't put that into play. But no matter, both would be waiting for us and so we have to make a play that they won't expect.

We finally came up with a plan and while it isn't the greatest, and not even that elaborate, it's our best shot. Ash admitting that Taya wasn't important to him was what gave me the idea. I only wish it didn't mean Taya would walk away free.

I crack a couple eggs and get working on brunch. I'm in the mood for an omelet. A smile crawls across my mouth at the thought of waking up in Max's arms. Paradise. It really was, especially because up until yesterday, I wasn't sure if I'd ever get to do that again.

The fire. My chest tightens as if an elephant is sitting on me. Someone could have died, but Ash messed up. Not only did everyone get out alive, his plan backfired in more ways than one. The fire was intended to make me pay when it only showed me how I should never have left my family. I should never have left Max.

After breakfast, we head to Ry's, where Tripp and Van are also waiting. I'm both nervous and excited to put things into motion, although Ash could mess up our plans at any moment.

He's out there and he's got to have another move.

When I walk into the kitchen, Van is the only person I see. He stands at the far end of the room, leaning against the island. He's in one piece, although showing signs of wear and tear. He sports a nasty bruise across one cheek and a white bandage covers a forearm.

Vivid hazel eyes hit me square in the chest and I'm running toward him, wordlessly throwing myself into the muscled arms he holds open for me.

"Van," I choke out. "You're safe."

He brings his lips down to my ear. "Yeah, I'm good. Better to know you're safe too. Missed you."

He nearly crushes me to him with the force of his hold, and I don't care. I'm more than happy to see him alive and well. Those many minutes after I'd realized Ash was going to torch HC but I didn't know if he'd succeeded were a living hell.

And even last night, when I knew Van was okay, it wasn't enough. I needed to see for myself. I needed this.

We break apart to all gazes on us. I glance up at him and he looks tired; fatigue lines his mouth and the corners of his eyes but his smile is bright and all I care is that he's breathing.

"So you said you've got a plan? Let's hear it." Ry is all business, taking a seat at the table and holding a chair out for me.

All of us sit and I straighten my spine, knowing this isn't going to be an easy conversation. Sacrifices will need to be made.

"With the increased FBI heat on Ash and Taya thanks to the raid, we've tipped our hand even if we have plausible deniability. There's nothing concrete linking HC to any of it but they aren't stupid." Max's grim features matches his tone.

"When I spoke to Ash yesterday, he told me that he has no interest in Taya. Or more specifically, that he was using her for her contacts." The guys nod; we'd suspected that was the case. "It's a safe bet that the auction attendees were her connections."

"Yeah, so far, from who the Feds rounded up, it looks to be," Ry adds.

"Ash pretty much said that he planned to build connections with her network based on her introduction and then dispose of whatever he felt was of no value."

Max shifts beside me. "We're thinking if we tell Taya what Ash's plan is—to double-cross her—and that she's likely in danger, she'll cooperate with us."

I inch closer to the edge of my seat, eager to put things in place but also not content with what we might have to give up. "Yeah, but the thing is, we're going to have to bargain with her."

Max and I fall silent, letting what that really means sink in. Understanding is quick to come, dawning on their faces almost immediately.

"Fuck no." Tripp points into the air like a switchblade, fast and sharp.

Pressure weighs on my chest. Taya isn't a good person and her organization has done a lot of damage to not only her children but also Ry, Van and Tripp. While it might not have been her directly, her husband and Tate's ex-husband ordered the death of Tripp's younger brother, Griffin.

"Ash is the imminent danger. He won't stop at just taking me." It's painful to have to reason with Tripp when he's already lost so much. "He has threatened to kill Van and Max. And last night's fire…"

"She's going to negotiate her freedom," he grits out and I nod, biting at my bottom lip.

"It's the only way," Max says, trying to keep any irritation out of his voice.

He's also losing something in this. He's giving up his desire to see his mother behind bars for me, and I get why he's doing it. He loves me.

"Is it?" Tripp's voice is a boom.

"Easy, bro." Van clamps a hand on his shoulder. "I don't like the idea of her walking any more than you do, but have you got a better one?"

There is another option, but I didn't mention it last night to Max. I knew full well he'd flat-out refuse. This could all go away if I go with

Ash. I could bargain with him, me for their lives. Their freedom at the price of mine.

How dare I ask any of them, most of all Tripp, to give up his retribution for mine? It's wrong. My problems shouldn't negate his.

Griffin was killed by the Conrad organization. We've all suffered, and my suffering isn't more important than his.

"I shouldn't be asking this of you. Of any of you. I'm sorry." I push from the table and all the guys stand.

"We don't have anything to use as a bargaining chip with Ash. And he can't be trusted anyway." Max's eyes fix on mine and I swear there is dread lurking in the depths of his green irises.

"There is one thing we can use." I'm queasy with what it means.

"No." All four of them are fierce and forceful, speaking at the same time, none of them skipping a beat in the implication of my comment.

"We're not putting your life on the line." Max comes to my side, his hands anchoring me to him.

"Not a fucking option." Tripp's voice is a heavy, unapologetic rasp.

"So now what?" A hint of a frown creases Van's forehead as his gaze lands on me.

Tripp paces the room, no one saying anything for several beats until Ry takes a step, exhaling, and says, "How do we draw her out? Has she contacted you?"

He motions to Max and he shakes his head no. "And we can't contact her how you would normally, anyway. Ash has to be watching her and his computer guy must have all her shit tracked."

Max pulls out his phone, holding it up. "I still keep in contact with a housekeeper that used to work for us. Taya still talks to her, too, but only because the woman's son is in her organization. She can get to Taya in person. No electronics."

"But can we trust her?" Tripp joins the conversation once more and I should feel relieved that he's warming to the idea, but I only feel sick with my selfishness.

And grateful.

Grateful to have a friend like him. One who is willing to put aside his wants for mine. I will make it up to him. I don't know how or when, but if I make it out of this alive, I will if it's the last thing I do.

"We'll make it worth her while. Her son may be in the life but he's a heartless bastard and doesn't take care of his mother." Max's hand tightens on my hip. "As for Taya, I'm sure she's furious with me. I'm sure she suspects I had something to do with the raid. She'll want to meet and then we'll go from there."

The meet with Taya has to be carefully planned, and we'll bring in both the FBI and NYPD because they need to be on board if we're going to get Ash. They have to agree not to touch Taya for her involvement in the auction. Thankfully, they do. Like us, Ash is their main target right now.

As we plan out the operation, the decision is unanimous—Max will meet with his mother. No one else. I hate it even if it makes the most sense. He could be hurt or killed.

Ash is out there, close by, I feel it in my bones, and if he even gets a whiff of this, or a chance to get Max, he won't hesitate. And what if his mother is so angry with him that she kills him?

They both have their backs against the wall and like cornered animals, fear permeates and clouds their judgement. They are unpredictable. At any moment in time, the tables could turn, and we'd lose the upper hand.

MAX

I meet with Taya outside Manhattan. Before my parents' empire took off, we lived in New Jersey. At the time, Tate and I were too young to remember the place, but I have the address.

The message to my mother is cryptic enough to not give anything away should Ash intercept its delivery, but there's enough detail so she'll understand both the need to meet and where. Her response is quick, and the meet set up within a day.

I'm both relieved that I don't have to work at getting her to meet with me, but also wary. What if it's a set-up? What if Ash got to her first and told her we'd tell lies about him? Anything is possible but it's our only move.

In preparation, I'm given a burner phone and all my clothes are triple-checked for any kind of bug or other device.

"I'm not sure what you guys are going to find?" I try to keep my tone neutral but feel like a fraud. It's a flimsy cover for the anxiousness brewing in my belly.

Van finishes patting down my leg and stands. He's the third one to do it today. Tripp tears his gaze from the street to glance at me. "What do you mean? We don't want anyone tracking you. If someone's onto you, you're a dead man."

"Tripp, not helping." Tommie tenses at my side despite her light tone.

"Hey, relax, it's going to be okay." I massage her tense shoulders and she slides an arm around my middle. "These guys are just being careful. Like they think Taya had my dry cleaner or someone stitch tracking devices into my clothing?"

Dark, warm eyes stare up at me solemnly. "No, but Ash would."

Head back, I glower at the ceiling and stifle a snarl. That man is a lunatic. Brilliant and lethal. Righting my head, one hand lets go of her to rub down my face. I've got to keep it together. Tommie doesn't need to witness my mini internal freak-out at how unpredictable all of this is.

Everything is going to go as planned.

It's my mantra for the day. It has to.

"Listen, it's going to be okay." I kiss her full lips, and she responds in kind.

"You two, focus. There'll be time for that later." Van wanders over to us with a black wire in one hand and tape in the other.

I know the drill by now. As he unwinds the long cord, she takes the surveillance equipment from him and sets about getting me ready. I love her hands on me, even if it's for something as clinical as taping wires to my chest. Her touch settles my restlessness.

Once ready, we say goodbye. It's deliberately brief. Neither of us will even consider any other outcome than success for today.

"Be careful. I love you and come back to me." She presses a kiss to the underside of my jaw and there's a stirring low in my belly.

This woman.

"Love you too." I crush her to me.

My hands slide up her back to tangle my fingers in her silky hair and press her head to my chest. The feel of her is all I need to focus. To get my head on straight.

I drive myself and several of the HC crew follow from a distance to the house in Jersey. Most are watching for any tails or surveillance, and if they come across one, they'll get rid of them.

I'm optimistic this will go well. I have to be. My mother is all about self-preservation and she's in a certain headspace right now. The whole thing about a woman scorned… She likes Ash, a lot, and most probably envisioned a future with him. When she learns of his intentions, his planned betrayal, she will want revenge.

There is only one other car parked in the driveway, as it should be. Taya's driver sits in the front seat and he doesn't even glance my way as I walk by the car. Her driver was our only concession, but I was warned to anticipate she'd have more men.

I walk down the side of the house to the backyard, where we agreed to meet, and I find Taya standing by the back door.

"Max, I didn't expect to hear from you." She taps one of her peep-toe Stuart Weitzmans on the cracked concrete slab just outside the door into the house.

It's an old tell of hers. She's eager to get this over with, annoyed, maybe nervous, or both. Her goons are likely on the other side, ready to whisk her away should there be any indication of danger.

"Mother. This was purely out of necessity. If I never have to see you again, that would be fine by me."

She chuckles, more a cackle than laugh, and sticks her nose in the air. "Before you get started, let me tell you, I'm only here out of curiosity, not because I care to hear your demands. We no longer have any business, son. I will exact my revenge for your betrayal."

Her eyes echo her threat and her mouth is an angry slash like the blade of a knife. Surprisingly, I'm not chilled nor do the hairs on the back of my neck rise. Her threats no longer have any hold over me. I can almost taste my freedom, and with it comes an unexpected arrogance.

"My betrayal?" I arch an eyebrow.

She steps closer. "You double crossed me with the raid. You don't think I know it was you? I watched you that night from behind the glass. You were nervous. Constantly scanning the room, looking for something or someone? Was it for me? Ash? Both of us?"

Ignoring her desire to rehash that night or my perceived betrayal, I push on. "I came here because of Ash. It isn't clear what your intentions were where he was concerned, but I've got news and I'm here to make a deal."

"A deal?" Her eyebrows rise as she scans the background, as if expecting people to just appear.

"Do you know where he is?"

She grins, folding her arms across her chest. "You expect me to tell you?"

"His plans never included you. I'm not sure what he promised you, or if you had illusions of a partnership or more, but I have it on good authority that he only used you for his own gain. He was going to take your contacts and leave you."

"Leave me?" A sinister smile crosses her heavily made-up face. "That's quite funny. I don't need a man and if he left me, as you say, I wouldn't be sad or destitute. Get to your point, Max. This is getting really tedious."

I'm used to her arrogance but she's bluffing. I saw how excited she was around him. The stars in her eyes and the blush on her cheeks whenever he was near. This news has got to hurt. We're banking on it.

"Ah, I suppose I shouldn't say he'd leave you. That's misleading. How about kill you? Does that make this more interesting or more serious a conversation for you?" She straightens, now keenly interested in what I have to say, and I continue, "I'd have thought that Ash taking your contacts right from under you might piss you off. So leaving you alive wouldn't be a smart move, and Ash is nothing if not smart. Mother dearest, you'd be a loose end."

Something dark, maybe even surprising, flickers through her icy blue eyes. I've hit a nerve and maybe, just maybe, Ash stealing her network *is* against whatever arrangement they had. We knew this information was a gamble, not so much in news to her, but in how big of a betrayal she would think it was.

"Go on. What's your deal?" Her posture softens a touch and I've got her.

"Work with us and we'll leave you alone. The authorities won't come after you for the raid." She opens her mouth to respond but I barrel past her.

"But there's a condition. We won't turn over what we have on you to the cops or the Feds—and we have a lot they'd be interested in—and in exchange, you work with us to bring down Ash, and afterward, you leave both myself and Tate alone. Forever."

Her lips twist into a snarl and her hands ball into fists at her side. But she remains silent as her cold, calculating eyes take me in. Because I know her so well, we have her where we want her.

She doesn't have to agree to our terms. We may have brought the FBI in on the auction, but HC didn't share everything they have on her. We're ready to turn all of it over to the FBI right now, if needed.

"I'm not a snitch. You of all people know, based on your time in this organization, that men have died for lesser crimes. I'm no rat."

She may be calling my bluff or stalling right now, but she will close the deal. I've no doubt. Straightening to my full height, I saunter toward her.

"Don't think of it as snitching. Think of it as survival. Isn't there something in your world about survival of the fittest? Or retaliation? Revenge? Call it what you want." I pause for effect.

"This isn't you ratting on a business partner, because I promise you, Ash will come after you. And my guess is, he's a patient man. You won't see him coming. He may even wait until you're so comfortable and so sure he's no longer a threat and then strike."

"And why would he come after me if I keep my mouth shut? I'm no threat to him."

I smirk, admiring her bluff. "Don't play games. I may have never wanted to be part of your world and hated every minute of it, but I learned a lot. He betrayed you and you know it. You won't let that go, just as he wouldn't. You'll want to kill each other. And I guess it comes down to which one of you is smarter?"

She taps her toe, pressing a finger to her red lips, and I wait her out. Finally, she agrees without much fanfare. Of course, she wants a signed agreement before she'll do anything, and luckily, we have the Feds nearby.

She gets her immunity for her crimes related to the auction, which burns when I think of all those women, but it's the price we pay for snagging the bigger culprit. Ash.

And now, the plan is in motion. She reaches out to Ash and we find another go-between in the city, one of Tommie's CIs. Taya will get word to us once a meeting is set up and the plan is for the authorities to make the arrest this time.

But even with NYPD, the FBI and Interpol backing this plan, catching Ash proves difficult. Nothing happens. Days pass, too many days to count, or at least that's how it feels. We thought it would be quick even with Ash wary; we figured he'd want the opportunity to face Taya. We were wrong.

It's almost as if he has either left New York City or he's on to us. He must figure Taya's attempts to contact him are a trap. Not once has he replied to her, and while it's only been three tries, we've been instructed to stand down.

My mother isn't to try again. If Ash isn't already suspicious, any more attempts and he'll smell our desperation.

TOMMIE

"There. It's done." I take one more look at my text to Zero.

"This is fucking crazy, I oughta have my head examined." Van curses under his breath, pacing once more back and forth in front of me.

I sigh, not sure I can reassure him again but willing to try. "Listen, we've been over this, it's the only way. Van, we've been at a standstill for weeks and no sign of Ash. This is the only way we bring him out of hiding."

He stops to stare at me, or maybe it's more a glare. He knows I'm right, but even still, I do feel a little guilty. I haven't played fair.

Ash didn't fall for Taya's call and as the days slid into weeks, all our leads dried up. The waiting is agony and both Ry and Van are still without their families. It's still too dangerous to bring them back to the city.

And Max and our life together is what propels me to face Ash head on. I can't wait for him to come. I won't let him destroy my life again. And this time, I'm not a helpless little girl. He doesn't know who he's dealing with, and most of all, that's what I'm banking on. I hope he underestimates me.

I have to put an end to this endless waiting. While we've waited for

Ash to surface, we've also been trying to rebuild what Ash destroyed. HC has relocated to an office building in Brooklyn and it looks like we are going to be there for a while. The damage to the building is extensive. But even with this momentum, we're on tenterhooks.

So I start with Van. Max isn't an option. There's no way he'd even entertain the idea of me putting myself at risk.

Van, on the other hand, is a professional. This kind of thing is his job. So I raised the idea, again, and started chipping away at all of his excuses or rebuttals.

I was relentless.

"I fucking hate this. I'll tell the guys and you're talking to Max tonight, right?"

"Yes." I stand with the apartment door open.

"And you remember our agreement. I call the shots." He buttons up his jacket.

"Yes. I promise."

"Be safe and I'll talk to you tonight." He kisses my forehead. "Let me know how Max takes it. The poor bastard isn't going to like it."

Shaking his head, he heads into the hallway as I say, "I will call you. Bye."

Max is at the hospital tonight, and while I always look forward to his return home, this evening, I feel shitty. I'm going to tell him the plan and he'll hate it. He'll also be upset with me because I've already set the ball in motion by contacting Zero.

He's the best one to get in touch with Ash. And I'm no fool. They're going to be mistrustful of me, thinking it's a set-up. They'd be crazy not to even consider it, but to lessen their suspicions, I'll give them the control. They get to determine where and when we meet.

Max comes home after midnight and finds me in the living room, waiting up, with Gunnar beside me.

"Hey. How'd it go tonight?" I swing my legs onto the floor so I'm sitting upright on the sofa.

"Fine." He leans down to kiss me.

I haven't let go of my apartment yet, but for all intents and purposes, we are living together. And I like coming home to him or vice versa. I never imagined domesticity being this awesome and I'm afraid to admit I'm hooked. It's all about Max, not the monotony of life that keeps me smiling and feeling as if I could conquer the world.

"Doesn't sound like it was fine." My fingers dance along his face and neck. "You look tired."

"Long night. Things didn't go so well with a surgery. It might be touch and go." He exhales harshly, running one hand through his hair as he stands. "I might have to go back tonight."

"I'm sorry." I'm only going to add to his bad night.

Shit, no, I'm putting all we have on the line and he's already dealing with life and death situations on a daily basis.

This is our only choice. I can only hope, with time, he sees it the way I do.

"Have you got a minute before you crash?"

"For you? Always." His voice lowers as he pulls me to my feet and into his warm embrace.

He lightly kisses the top of my head, leading us to our room while Gunnar walks beside us. Once the place is dark and quiet, we sit side by side on the edge of our bed.

Taking his hands in mine, I force my voice to sound clear. No doubt. No hesitation. I wouldn't do this if there was another way.

"You know how things have been tough with no word from Ash?"

He nods slowly as his eyes now narrow and he tilts his head to the side. Every part of his body has gone rigid. It's almost as if he knows what's coming.

"Van and I have been talking and we set plan B in motion."

"Plan B?" His voice is barely a whisper but it carries such weight that it might as well be thunder for how I feel it in my chest.

Now it's my turn to nod, swallowing with difficulty as the familiar feeling of dread and terror seeps into me. There's so much on the line.

"There was never a plan B. We said we both had to agree to the idea for it to even be considered. Tommie, we never came to an understanding. I never agreed. Tell me I'm jumping to the wrong conclusion."

My brain searches for the right words. I thought I had this all figured out. What I'd say, what he would say, and even how I'd respond to some of the trickier things he might say. But real life never goes as planned. I hear my breath, shallow and shaky, and he curses at my reticence.

"Why are you doing this? I won't let you do this." Fury blazes in his eyes.

I brace, anger stirring inside me. "You won't *let* me?"

"That's not what I mean." Now standing, he paces. "I'm not trying to control you. I'm worried. This is a stupid idea and if something goes wrong, what happens to you?"

My teeth tug at my bottom lip, needing the discomfort to somehow try and equal the pain and anguish I'm causing him. I feel my face fall and my eyes burn.

"It's all we have. It's our only play."

His laugh is hard and brittle as his expression turns granite. "It isn't a 'play,' it's fucking suicide."

"He's going to come after me either way, Max." I touch his hand and he pulls from my touch, skewering me with a hot disappointed glare. "I don't want to sit around, fretting about when he's going to show up. I'm not powerless. We can change the game and put us on the offense. Take our confrontation to him."

He stares into the distance, and it feels like he can't look at me; his jaw ticks, as does time as the silence swells between us.

"And this way we get him. We screwed up with Taya. We gave her a deal, and now we're stuck honoring it even though our plan was worthless."

All isn't lost there. We've talked as a group about the other information we have on Taya. She's a mob boss for fuck's sake and we've got more on her. She isn't completely out of our sights, but for now, she's clear. Ash is our target.

"What if he's left New York?" He's grasping at straws, trying to deter me as he runs a hand through his hair.

"He hasn't left. We both know it. His main purpose was me." Max looks at me like a little boy, lost and alone, and my heart hurts. "I reached out to Zero and it's only a matter of time before he replies."

I desperately want to close the space between us and touch him. Take away all his anger and concern. His wrath isn't enough to keep me away and I near him, my fingers barely grazing his stubbled jaw.

He twitches at my touch but stands still. He feels far away, closed off to me, not happy with my news. I get it. I would feel the same way if the roles were reversed. I'd be scared and absolutely against anything that put him in danger. It's how I felt when he met with his mother. But he did it and I supported him. I only hope he can do the same for me.

Finally, glittering sea green eyes fix on me and my insides clench and sing, happy he hasn't completely written me off.

"We're gonna get Ash." My expression is determined. "It'll be a bait and switch. He'll think he's meeting me, but Van and the FBI will be there."

"I don't like this." His arms slide around my body, crushing me to him as he buries his nose into my hair and whispers, "I can't lose you." There's a strange hitch to his voice as he pulls me in to his arms.

"You won't. I promise." A barbed sensation tightens in my chest.

TOMMIE

Within forty-eight hours, Zero contacts me. Ash has agreed to meet with me. Of course he has.

Trepidation and anticipation weigh me down, swamping my limbs. There is no turning back now. I don't know when the meet is, it's their terms.

So I make sure the drop phone, the one I'm using to talk with Zero, is on me at all times. I don't have to wait long for him to send me the details.

Only a day later, I get a call with an address in Brooklyn. The meet is within the hour. Thankfully, we are prepared and have been for the past three days.

In addition to the phone I use with Zero, which no doubt is being monitored, I have another burner to communicate with Van and the team.

We went over how today would go down at least a dozen times, and that doesn't include how many times we walked through the plan during the days before the meet was set. I'll go in alone, keep Ash occupied, and then reinforcements will swoop in and arrest his sorry ass.

Max's abhorrence for all of this has been evident in every look, word, or movement he has made in the past three days. But he no longer voices his opposition, understanding I need to do this and maybe secretly knowing it's our last option.

Lightning crackles across the heavy grey sky and the clouds teem and roil. A thunderstorm is coming fast and furious, and somehow, it's fitting for what's about to happen.

I'm alone in the car driving to meet Ash, and there are no signs of the FBI or police even though they are there, or on their way. Our HC team is also close by. Van went ahead the second I got the text and Max insisted on going with him even though he has no training.

It was my concession to Max, despite my concern, and I begged Van to agree to it, as well as promise to watch over Max. They are hiding in plain sight, close to the rendezvous.

Ash chose an abandoned warehouse and given he likely knows this meet is a trap, the location could be rigged with any number of things. It took him two days to respond to my request, so we have to assume he set up the location, giving him the best advantage.

I can't think about that now. All I can do is be alert, remember all of my training and hope for the fucking best.

Cratered asphalt runs the entire length of the dilapidated structure, and save for a black sedan with tinted windows parked at one end, the area is empty. I wonder if Ash is still in the car or inside?

I won't get in the car. No matter what. That was one of Van's orders and he's right. If I get in the car, I'm a goner. Even if I'm the one wired for audio and video. As for inside, I suppose if I have to go inside the warehouse, I will. Outside is best.

As I step from the car, a deafening crack rips through the gloomy afternoon sky. I shudder, slanting my head heavenward, expecting devastation. A fracture far and wide, breaking the sky in two. But there's no sign of damage; the atmosphere is still intact, fully charged as clouds gather and the wind howls.

I feel his eyes on me before I see him.

Movement many feet away causes me to hold my breath as the large rusted doors swing outward. My hand grips the side of my head, holding in place the hair whipping around my face. A man steps out. Ash.

He pauses, clothed in another one of his dark suits, hair slicked back though lifting at the ends with the force of the wind. As usual he looks unfazed.

Fat raindrops fall, splashing onto my eyelashes, and I blink away the wetness as more rain comes. I step toward him, partly wanting to go inside because of the storm but knowing outside is smarter.

The closer I get the wetter I become. Clothes now cling to my body and I worry about the equipment and wires. Will he see them through the now-soaking fabric? What if moisture damages the audio? *Fuck, it's too late to worry about this now.*

Ash doesn't move a muscle, as if oblivious to his surroundings or the weather. His jacket and pants now stick to his tall muscular frame, but his predatory gaze never strays from me.

I stop several feet away from him. This is close enough. I'm not going inside unless I absolutely have to but then it occurs to me. How can backup arrive if we're outside? There'll be no surprise. He will see them coming. Maybe that's the point and why he's out here in the pouring rain.

"Thomasina." He raises his voice above the whining wind. "Not long after you came to live with me, I realized you'd be the end of me."

He's told me this before and I wonder why he bothers if I'm such a threat? I force my feet to stay put even as my body wants to seek shelter or move closer to hear him better.

"I never intended to keep you." He wipes at the water gathering on his face.

He still doesn't move.

"What are you talking about?" My brusque tone signals my growing agitation.

I don't like how calm and in control he is. It's as if all of this is how he planned it. A brewing storm, lightning, thunder, rain. All of it. He's the one in control and I'm playing into his hand.

Am I?

"All those years ago… what did I want with a girl? I thought we'd have some fun and then I'd kill you just like your parents." One long stride and he's closer. Suddenly this large open space seems too small, too tight. "But you proved to be just what I needed. So smart and strong. Even at your age, you astonished me. You are really quite remarkable."

He's reverent as his dark, dark eyes drill into me and I fight the familiar feeling of filth. His touch, his gaze, his words used to fill me with shame.

"Why are we talking about this? I didn't come here to rehash the past. Or romanticize it like you have. I want your word that you'll leave me alone. I'm not yours. Never was, and I want you to forget you ever met me."

The wind picks up and so does the rain. I'm almost shouting to be heard over Mother Nature. A wicked grin carves its way across his sinister features.

"I'll be gone soon enough. The question is whether you're coming with me. We both know my preference."

I shake at how cold I am and fold my arms over my chest. No words easily spring to mind. The wet wire and tape scratch against my flesh.

"Even these years apart, it was so tempting to take you back, but I meant what I said—I enjoyed watching you live your ordinary life. It wasn't what I wanted for you, but it made you happy. Sort of."

His words strangle my insides. In his sick way, he thinks he cares for me. It angers me. "Stop playing games."

"You're the one playing games. You think you can be happy in that life? We are a lot alike. That life won't fulfill you. And your doctor friend won't make you happy."

Somehow during his bullshit speech, he has inched closer to me. I could reach out and touch him and my muscles tense.

"Stay where you are." Van's authoritative voice cuts through the wind and rain as if he's right beside us and confidence blooms within me.

I never saw any movement or indication he was here. Ash doesn't even bother to look in his direction, but I steal a peek. Beside him is Max, on the edge, figuratively. His expression is both hard and troubled, his mouth set in a thin line and a vein throbbing in his neck.

"Ah, your hero is here. What a surprise." He spares them a glance and a snarl takes shape, directed at Max, before coming back to me. "Is this what you really want? I can make this go away."

"What go away? You?"

He winces at my jab, placing his palm upon his chest. "You always know how to hurt me." A hand reaches for me but I'm quick, getting out of his grasp before it's too late. "You are the only one."

Like the crack of a whip or the flash of lightning, it happens so fast. I'm too dazed to see where he pulls the weapon from as dull metal glistens in the rain. Raising his arm, Ash points the barrel of the gun at my forehead, only inches away.

I'm still, statue-like, losing myself in the depths of his kettle black eyes. A sharp pop explodes into the air and Ash's head tips back as blood sprays, a red mist coating my face.

Warm and sticky.

My nostrils fill with the coppery scent and my stomach roils. Ash's blood.

His arm, the one holding the gun, veers upward when the bullet hits his skull, causing his finger to press the trigger. Another, louder, closer pop goes off. So close. My head feels like it's ripping apart, much like the thunder did to the sky.

My knees buckle and my hands cover my now-ringing ears. An arm snags my waist and I fight until his scent hits me. Max. He pulls me to him, one hand holding my head to his chest.

Thump. Thump. Thump.

I feel more than hear his heartbeat. It thunders in my ears and it's soothing, as is the scent and feel of him. From the corner of my eye, I watch Ry shouting something at Max as he slips a gun back into his waistband. His lips are moving, but I can't make out a word.

Sirens blare, or at least I think that's what the sound is, as Tripp and Van followed by several men and women covered in combat gear descend upon us.

Tripp kneels beside the body, pressing his fingers to the neck to check for a pulse.

Ash is dead.

The man who tortured, defiled and hunted me is gone.

I'm empty.

Numb and cold.

I shiver and Max squeezes me tighter to him and leads me toward the flashing lights. An ambulance is parked several feet away from the commotion. Once inside the vehicle, he crouches in front of me, gingerly patting down my arms and legs.

"You okay?" is what I think he says.

I think I say I'm fine. I'm wet and cold but I don't feel like I was shot or injured in any way. It's still hard to hear anything with the ringing, let alone my own voice, to be sure of my response. And as for feeling. There is none.

While the attendant checks my vitals and cleans my face, I wonder how he had planned to escape after killing me? Ry and Max would never have let him get away.

An obscure but insistent memory from years ago slithers to the forefront of my mind. It had been right after Ash came back from a trip. It was still in the early days of my captivity and I was too young to fully understand what was happening to me. I still didn't fully understand the kind of man he was, yet.

I was able to discern from his cryptic conversations with Zero that Ash had almost been caught. He'd slipped from the clutches of the law, but he raged about exacting revenge. And then coolly, almost too calm, he turned to me as I peered up at him, scared but trying so hard to hide my fear.

With that voice of his, the one that always demanded my obedience, he said, "They'll never take me alive. I'd sooner die than be locked up in a cage like some animal."

MAX

We've been in Florence for close to three weeks with Anna and Coop. These past few days, we ventured outside of Florence to the country home of the sculptor Anna works for. The man treats her like his daughter and she's thriving under his tutelage.

We have one more day here and then Tommie thinks we're heading home. But I've got a surprise for my girl. We aren't getting on a plane just yet. I extended our stay for a week, alone, in Capri, a small island off the Amalfi coast. I want her to myself for just a little while longer before we have to join the world.

After Ash's death, and what felt like endless briefings with the FBI and other law enforcement, Tommie was more than numb to her past. It got to the point that she could recount every sordid detail as if counting to one hundred. Something we all do by rote. I had to get her out of there.

In addition to helping the agents working on the Ash Naire case, she offered to go over all the information they'd gathered, verifying what they already knew or filling in the gaps or dispelling assumptions. And as if that wasn't enough, she also insisted on listening to every single audio tape we still had to examine from the many warehouses we'd wired while watching Taya.

She was manic, and while I understood her drive and obsession, first and foremost as a doctor, I also got it as someone who wanted justice for all my mother had done. But she needed a break or else *she* was going to break. When we left for Florence, she was dead on her feet.

Our vacation was just what we needed. Everything slowed. Time has become our friend here and every moment with her is golden and magical. Memories I'll cherish and moments I want to savour.

Tonight's our last night here and all is quiet, everyone asleep as we sneak out to go swimming. Earlier that day, on one of our many walks around the farm, we wandered across a small natural pool located below the ruined walls of what once was fortified Roman thermal baths.

Now giddy like teenagers, we cling to each other, laughing and whispering as we make our way to the spot.

"What ya think?" She pokes at my side as we undress.

"You need to get rid of your apartment when we get back. Make our living arrangement official. And permanent."

"Permanent? Why, whatever could you mean?"

"Okay, how about forever? I want us together for forever."

"I like the sound of that." She pushes onto her toes and kisses me.

Her plump lips open and her warm tongue slides into my mouth. I taste all of her and a hint of the Brunello we had with our antipasto. Candied cherry, leather and chocolate.

She's bold, threading her fingers into my hair, voraciously diving deeper into my mouth, and it goes straight to my heart, a flutter and a squeeze.

I could kiss her all day. All the time.

We break apart. "Let's get in."

I lead the way and we slip into the warm water underneath the stars, and it's magical. Tendrils of steam rise into the air, and together, naked in the moonlight, Tommie huskily whispers words as if she's afraid to say them out loud.

"I want a family. Children. With you." She slides further into the water, her chin dipping below the surface. "I feel selfish or undeserving just saying that."

"Why?" My fingers stroke her collarbone and she shimmies closer to me.

"Most of my adolescence was about survival. Maybe even most of my life. Living was my most audacious wish. I'd wanted it desperately. To make it to the other side of life without Ash. To live and no longer be afraid or haunted by those years," she says, her lower lip trembling.

Under the silvery moonlight, her tears fall silently. "And I got my wish. I'm one of the lucky ones. There are so many out there that never get away. Never get a chance at life. At freedom. To want more seems greedy. Almost ungrateful for what I have."

"No. It's not greed. It's hope. There's nothing wrong with hoping or striving for something else. And while you got your wish, it wasn't handed to you. It sure as hell wasn't easy. You're forgetting the most important part of all."

"What's that?"

"You played a huge part in making your wish come true. Van may have got you out of that place, but up until that moment and all that came after your rescue was because of you."

I move us to the edge of the pool, where there's a narrow shelf carved from the rock. Perching on the edge, I lift her by the waist and deposit her so she straddles me. Her firm, toned thighs rest on either side of my legs.

"You could have easily given up. Succumbed to the horrors done to you and that would have been it. You had years of ongoing therapy. Don't diminish all of that. The work *you* did."

She nods. "It just feels like, how dare I think I can have it all?"

"I'd be surprised, disappointed even, if you didn't dare to dream."

She grants me a lopsided grin. "I feel like I can do anything. Have anything, and it's because of you. I was strong before, but Max, with you… my greatest wish is us. I want you. I want to build a family with you. Start my day with you. Take Gunnar for walks. Do all the normal things together like grocery shopping, cleaning, cooking. Getting knocked up." I waggle my brows, squeezing her middle, and she laughs.

The vibration of her joy causes her to wiggle in my lap and I groan as my hardening erection jerks against her soft body. She doesn't seem to notice, or if she does, she doesn't let my arousal slow her down.

"The late-night breastfeeding, diapers, runny noses, and all. I want all of it." Her tongue darts out to lick her lip and she leans into me, her teeth snagging at my bottom lip. Her bite is followed by the lick of her tongue and then a suck, shifting into a kiss. We lose ourselves in each other.

Much like we are doing right now on our walk. Our lips break apart, both of us taking in a lungful of air, smiling at each other with our bodies still entwined.

"It's time we get started on that life of ours. The one you so beautifully described to me. I want that too. I want you and me, Gunnar and kids."

"Hey, slow down." Red lips curl into a smile. "You're talking like I'm already pregnant. I want some time for us first."

"Me too."

EPILOGUE

TOMMIE

I rub at my eyes and yawn, stealing a look at the time in the bottom right-hand corner of the computer screen. Max should be back any minute now; he just stepped out to talk to Tate, and I'm near done.

Unexpectedly, I ended up working late tonight, covering for one of my team who was out sick. I had promised to drop by the hospital with hot dogs for dinner as Max was working, but he got off early and surprised me.

Tonight, he came to HC with takeout from our favorite Thai restaurant and we'd dined in my office, gorging on green papaya salad and panang curry. I can still taste the rich savory broth of the red curry and coconut milk. When done with our meal, I still had to document the final minutes of a surveillance tape.

"Hey, you done?" Max stares at me, eyes shimmering, as he walks to my side and bends to lightly kiss the curve of my neck.

I brighten, the corners of my mouth lifting at the sight and scent of him. "Yup. I just need two more minutes. Do you mind sticking this in the fridge?"

He takes the box of spring rolls. I'd been too full to eat mine and while we could take them home, HC is a twenty-four/seven shop, and someone is always hungry. I like to do my part in keeping our crew fed.

My phone pings on the desk beside me and I glance down at the screen.

Zero: Boo

Sighing, I pick up my device and tap out a response.

Me: What do you want?

Zero has taken to texting me randomly since Ash's death four months ago. Interpol, FBI, and who knows who else are still looking for the hacker extraordinaire. They'll never find him. And even though I don't owe him anything, I won't help the authorities catch him either.

He will always be Ash's guy, even after his death, but he also helped keep me sane all those years in captivity. And while we never spoke of it, I know he tried, in the ways that he could without suffering Ash's wrath, to limit my pain.

Zero: How are you doing

Me: Fine. You?

Zero: Okay. Are you going to give me more than that?

Me: Where are you?

I ask every time I get a text and it isn't because I'll turn him in. I've reassured him that I won't. It's more out of curiosity. I don't fully get why he maintains contact with me. Max would prefer I get another phone or ignore him.

If I'm being honest with myself, I stay in touch to keep an eye on him. I wonder if he'll come after me for the death of his master. He's a cocky bastard and we were never enemies, in fact the opposite, and while I don't know how he came to live with Ash, the man was the only family Zero had. And now, thanks to me, he's dead.

He could hurt me without ever leaving whatever hole he's hiding in.

Zero: That's not a question I'll answer. Try again.

Me: What do you want? I can't help you.

Zero: This is the last time we'll text. Promise.

Me: Then what?

Zero: Then nothing. I'll leave you alone. I believe you.

Me: What are you talking about?

Zero: I believe you aren't going to turn me in. You haven't mentioned our contact to anyone but Max.

His knowledge isn't surprising, but it chills me nonetheless. He will always be able to get to me. If he so chooses.

Me: Told you I wouldn't and so long as you don't give me a reason to, I won't.

Zero: I'm busting a gut over here. you're adorable and gotta give you props. This is goodbye Tommie. As a parting gift, I thought you might enjoy this.

I wait for his response and it takes longer than normal. Seconds later, he drops an MP3 file.

Me: What is this?

Zero: Have a listen

Me: I'm not doing your dirty work so don't even ask.

Zero: Just listen.

Me: What am I supposed to do with this?

I'm filled with apprehension. There has to be something of meaning to it.

"You ready now, babe?" Max stands at the door and my phone pings again.

Zero: You'll know what to do.

"Um, I just need to have a listen to something."

"What's wrong?" He comes into the office, concern now creeping across his brow.

"Nothing, I think. Just give me a sec."

I download the forty-five second clip and pop in my earbuds. I could just hit play with Max in the room, because I will share it with him. I just… I just need to know what it is first. Because it could be a recording of so many things. Ash was my captor for five long years. It could be so many ugly, vile things that I never want Max to have to hear.

"Okay." He nods, eyebrows still pinched as he kisses me one more time.

He plants himself on the edge of the desk and leans down to give my thigh a reassuring squeeze. I don't have to tell him I'm troubled, he just knows.

Hitting play, I listen, and at first, my heart violently jerks at the sound of Ash's voice. It's eerie and unnerving to have his deep, commanding voice in my head again.

I don't think I'll ever forget his face or his voice, and I've come to terms with that. Long before he came for me here in New York. But in this moment, with his voice in my ears, I wish I could.

The tape is a recording of Ash and Taya. From the sounds of it, it's recent, or at least in the past six or seven months, during the time he was here and in business with her.

The air is sucked from my lungs and Max straightens. "What is it? What are you listening to?" His hand now rests on my shoulder. "Are you okay?"

I nod, unable to break my concentration and I shift the mouse pointer to bring the recording back thirty seconds so I can listen again, unable to believe what I've just heard.

The second time is no less surprising.

"Holy shit." I yank out my earbuds with a shaky exhale.

"What's going on?"

"One sec."

I furiously text Zero, needing more answers.

Me: Is there more to this recording?

Me: When was this recorded?

Me: Tell me what you know.

Me: Zero answer me.

I wait for what feels like a long time, but nothing.

"We gotta talk to the guys." I pull the cord from the outlet and press play from the beginning.

Ash's and Taya's voices fill my office. Max frowns, stiffening as he gives all his attention to the recording. I watch his features morph from confusion to awareness to alarm with his realization.

"Shit. Where did you get this?"

"Zero." I needn't say more; we both know the recording is authentic.

"We gotta call the guys," he says, fishing out his phone as I press stop on my laptop. "You call Van and I'll call Ry."

He stops, lifting his head from his phone screen, and we share a look as we say, gravely, at the same time, "Someone has to tell Tripp."

If you need help:
Canada: Ending Violence Canada
UK: National Domestic Abuse Helpline
US: National Domestic Violence
1-800-799-SAFE (7233)

THANK you for reading Relentless Night. To read the epic conclusion to the New York Knights, grab Tripp's story in Broken Night! Available at all major retailers and www.smwestauthor.com.

THANK you for reading and please leave a review on your favorite book site, including tell a friend. Reviews help readers find books!

FOR EXCLUSIVE CONTENT, a free book and to find out when I have new releases, please sign up for my newsletter at www.smwestauthor.com.

OTHER BOOKS BY S.M. WEST

WWW.SMWESTAUTHOR.COM

New York Knights Series

Reckless Night

Fallen Night

Captive Night

Relentless Night

Broken Night

Scarred Hearts Series

All can be read as standalones

Prophet

Kit

Nomad

Griffin

Zero

6ix Loves Series

All can be read as standalones

Trusting the Ex

Scoring the Player

Promising the Billionaire

Stealing the Billionaire

Falling for the Charmer

Winslow Grove Series

All can be read as standalones

Close to You

All of You

Here with You

Canyon Spring Series

A collaboration with Kimberly Quinn

The Cowboy Bargain

The Cowboy Hitch

Trojan Series

All can be read as standalones

Clutch

Reverb

Smash

Rush

Standalones

Made to Love

Resisting the Best Friend's Sister

ABOUT THE AUTHOR

USA TODAY bestselling and award winning author, S.M. West writes sexy, angsty stories about brave hearts and wild love, including, more times than not, heart-pumping twists and turns.

Apart from her infinite love of books, she's a self-professed wine, chocolate, and travel junkie. When not writing or hanging with her family, she's usually talking to her characters (in her head) or planning her next adventure.

www.smwestauthor.com

Pinnacle Book Achievement Award

Griffin - Best Thriller

Smash - Best Romance

Global eBook Awards

Griffin - Gold, Suspense

Scoring the Player - Silver, Romance

Global Book Award

Griffin - Silver, Romantic Suspense

Independent Press Award

Griffin - Distinguished Favorite, Audiobook, Fiction

Griffin - Distinguished Favorite, Romantic Suspense

NYC Big Book Award

Reverb - Distinguished Favorite, Romance

Finalist National Indie Excellence Awards

Griffin

For new releases, exclusive excerpts, giveaways and more, sign up for her newsletter.

www.ingramcontent.com/pod-product-compliance
Lightning Source LLC
LaVergne TN
LVHW091128080826
845145LV00008B/2086